⚡ **RIDE THE LIGHTNING** ⚡

RIDE THE LIGHTNING

A CRIME NOVEL

DIETRICH KALTEIS

ECW PRESS

Published by ECW Press
2120 Queen Street East, Suite 200,
Toronto, Ontario, Canada M4E 1E2
416-694-3348 / info@ecwpress.com

LIBRARY AND ARCHIVES CANADA
CATALOGUING IN PUBLICATION

Kalteis, Dietrich, author
Ride the lightning : a crime novel / Dietrich Kalteis.

ISBN 978-1-77041-150-0 (bound);
978-1-77041-211-8 (pbk)
Also issued as: 978-1-77090-506-1 (pdf);
978-1-77090-507-8 (epub)

I. Title.

PS8621.A474R53 2014   C813'.6
C2013-908022-8   C2013-908023-6

Cover design: David Gee
Printing: Friesens 5 4 3 2 1

The publication of *Ride the Lightning* has been generously supported by the Canada Council for the Arts which last year invested $157 million to bring the arts to Canadians throughout the country, and by the Ontario Arts Council (OAC), an agency of the Government of Ontario, which last year funded 1,681 individual artists and 1,125 organizations in 216 communities across Ontario for a total of $52.8 million. We also acknowledge the financial support of the Government of Canada through the Canada Book Fund for our publishing activities, and the contribution of the Government of Ontario through the Ontario Book Publishing Tax Credit and the Ontario Media Development Corporation.

PRINTED AND BOUND IN CANADA

For Andie

A scrawny guy in his mid-
thirties with a weasel face, Miro
Knotts took his eyes off the
road, flicking the Newport butt

Straight From The Hip

out the window. Fumbling around, he relit the pipe, holding
the smoke until the floaters came back, melting into the seat,
laying down the accelerator, calling up the two hundred and
ninety horses.

A truck whooshed in the opposite direction, stacked with
lumber, the two-lane becoming his own. White lines and
pines blurred by, Miro in the radar-red Challenger, pushing
ninety-five, toking his way through God's country.

He let the MyGIG do its thing, the seek button landing
on some Tom Jones number, not the "What's New Pussycat?"
crap but one from *Praise & Blame*, Tom Jones belting it out
about heaven and hell. Drumming his fingers, Miro bopped
in his seat till his bladder reminded him he hadn't pissed since
the McDonald's in Spokane. The supersized drink. No way
he'd make it across the top of Idaho without a pit stop.

Pulling off the interstate at the Farmingdale exit, he rode the back road a half mile and stopped by a stand of cedar. Throwing the door open, he stood in the cool air, getting relief, writing his name in the gravel.

Filling the pipe with the last of the honey oil, he looked around, everything so green. Lighting up again, breathing the smoke into his lungs, he lay across the hood, looking up at the boughs and rolling clouds, dozing off.

Waking, he reached for a Newport, catching movement through the trees. Three hundred yards off, a bighorn sheep stood munching grass. Heart leaping, Miro made out the trophy rack and slid off the hood. Easing the door open, he reached under the seat for his Vaquero and was moving easy, careful not to snap twigs. He stepped his way around moss-covered trees, making it to the edge of the clearing. A few more bighorns grazed in the distance.

Before the big boy could catch his scent, Miro took his stance and brought up the revolver, sighting down the barrel. On a breath, he picked his moment and squeezed, the .357 bucking in his hand.

The ram froze, then dropped where it stood, the other sheep scattering at a run. Miro paced off ninety strides, thinking Bob Munden couldn't have made a shot like that; neither could Todd Jarret who once shot a thousand rounds in about ten minutes.

Not exactly dressed for hunting in his Polo and Tony Lamas, he pulled out his iPhone, snapped a few shots of his kill, then held it arm's length and got in the portrait.

Grabbing the horns, he tried dragging the two-hundred-pound ram to the car, thinking to call the Guinness people, guessing he had a record shot on his hands. He got about ten feet, slipping in the grass, blood on his pants. Wiping his hands on the grass, he thought better of it, snapping a few more shots before giving up and walking back to his car.

Back in Belltown, Miro wouldn't shut up about it, sitting on the stool at Monty's doing shooters with a school-aged Lolita

SALT IN THE WOUND

named Anita. He let her smoke his Newports, bragging about the shot he made.

Monty, on the other side of the bar, didn't like this guy pawing the girl, felt sure she was underage, but who could get a word in to ask for ID. Miro was showing the pics of himself with the dead bighorn, telling how he counted off ninety strides. Anita, on her third Irish Car Bomb, seemed intrigued and didn't mind his hand on her leg, asked him if he ever shot anybody, Monty saying yeah, somebody that wasn't a sheep.

Explaining how dangerous a ram could be, Miro got set to tell her about a guy he shot when the kid came in wearing the kind of jacket football jocks wore around high school, hair up in spikes. One look at Miro with his hand on the girl's knee and he came over, yanking the hand away.

3

"Fuck are you?" Miro said, looking surprised, then pissed, his other hand wrapping around his glass.

"You screwed my kid brother out of a vial of oil yesterday, remember?"

"Like fuck I did. Don't know any kid brother."

"See if I can jog your memory." The jock caught a handful of shirt and lifted Miro off the stool. "You give me back Jimmy's C-note, and maybe I'll let you get back to your faggy drink." He turned to Anita, half this creep's age, asking if she was blind.

Miro threw his Car Bomb in his face, the jock sputtering, hands going to his eyes. Miro shook loose, landing a head butt, sending him to the floor.

Monty wasn't having any of this shit in his place, yelling, "Hey asshole, knock it off!" Reaching under the bar, he slapped his blackjack on the wood top, glaring at Miro, making his point.

If Miro had let it go at that, the shit that followed might never have happened. But Miro was putting on a show for the girl. "You heard the man, kid." He sent the toe of his Tony Lama into his crotch. Then he dragged the howling kid to the door, tossing him out on the pavement. For a topper, he unzipped his fly and marked his territory, telling him to try some of his faggy drink.

≈

The Seattle narcs that paid him a visit the next morning were Holsten and Quinn, two GIU officers, said they were acting on a tip.

"Got a warrant, boys?" Miro blocked the door with his foot, standing in just his briefs, with Anita behind him, a Seahawks jersey fitting her like a nightgown.

Quinn pulled a baggie of pills from his own pocket. "Got probable cause right here."

Miro put on the grin, saying, "I know my—"

Holsten straight-armed the door, shoved Miro against the wall, telling him if he didn't shut up, he'd get more rights than he could handle.

Miro stood with Anita and watched them toss the place, turning up nothing but a dirty pipe, some butane and PVC. Not enough to bring him in.

"Happy?" he said, shivering from the cold.

On their way out, Quinn pocketed his baggie, picked up the framed photo of Miro's kill from the coffee table, asking, "You do sheep?"

"For your info, it's a bighorn."

"Yeah?" Quinn studied the photo, listening to Miro brag about his record shot from ninety paces, Miro forgetting he was half-dressed and cold. Quinn held up the photo to his partner, asking what he thought.

"Looks like a sheep to me," Holsten said, adding that nobody could make a shot like that, not from ninety paces.

"Not the first time you boys been wrong today, huh?" Miro said.

At the door, Quinn looked at this bone-rack in his dingy briefs and told him this wasn't over, then told Anita to give her head a shake. Then they were gone.

The next morning Miro stood under the shower, the water never hot, the pressure so weak he could keep his cigarette from getting wet just by tipping his head back.

True to his word, Quinn came back, Anita answering the knock at the door, and being on a first-name basis now, she let him walk in with the two guys he introduced as Pierce and Newcombe from Fish and Wildlife.

"What the fuck is this?" Miro came into the hall dripping, a towel around his waist.

Quinn picked the photo off the coffee table, handed it to Pierce, Pierce asking Miro to explain this. Wrapped in his towel, Miro found himself charged with felony and misdemeanor poaching, staring ninety days in the face, along with restitution for the domestic Merino ram that had spent its days chomping grass on the Chugwater Ranch of Montana. Pierce and Newcombe let him get dressed, then led Miro out in cuffs, Quinn hanging back, doing his best to convince Anita to call her folks and get as far from this guy as possible. She guessed he was right, looking to his holstered sidearm then back to his eyes, and asked if he ever shot anybody.

Wally Levitt scratched under the black do-rag, telling Mitch Reno how he got chummy with Sunny, the waitress down

GETTING IN TIGHT

at Chickie's Diner. She'd been supplying them with names for the past six months, fat-cat customers with nice places to break into. And he'd been paying her fifty a pop, Wally not mentioning he laid another hundred down each time he climbed into her bed.

"We just kind of hit it off, you know." He put on his shit-eating grin, took a toke and turned his head, hearing a thump from the garage. "You hear that?"

"What?"

Just his imagination. A couple more tokes and he'd be Gumby with no feeling below the knees.

Mitch waved off the joint, the smoke making his bowels churn—high time to ease up on it, the Thunder Chicken, too, the name Tolley had for Wild Turkey back in the Hat. Trade it for some Sunny D.

"What I'm saying is we make what," Wally said, "a hundred bucks to run this shit, fifty each?"

"Yeah, so?" Better than nothing, waiting for Sunny to come up with someplace worth hitting.

Wally puffed smoke at the ceiling, looking down the hall of the grow house, making sure Jeffery was still in the can, keeping his voice low. "So, why not grow our own—make some real dough?"

"What the hell we know about it?"

"Half the people in B.C. grow the shit."

"Going against these guys . . ." Mitch shook his head, but then pictured getting Ginny a stove with all the burners working and slapping new shingles on her roof.

Holding the smoke in his lungs was like trying to hold a beach ball under water. Letting it out slow, Wally drew forward, the sofa springs digging into his ass. "This shit goes for what—two Gs a pound?"

Mitch shrugged. It wasn't time for math.

"Thirty plants to a pound. We bagged what, a thousand or so last night?"

Mitch cleared his throat, a signal that Jeffery was coming out of the can, the old man flushing, hacking like he was passing a furball, tugging his jeans over his paunch, snugging the chromed Python into his belt. Jeffery called it the king of handguns, the thing sticking out from his pants like a big dick.

"What're you girls jawing about?" Jeffery put on the hard-ass, flexing his knees and zipping up, no use for either of these assholes, two-bit punks Stax sent over, mules making the drop to JayMan at the docks, something he'd done solo going on a dozen years. Suddenly Artie was letting Stax run things, making Jeffery feel too long in the tooth to take care of simple shit. It pissed him off, thinking he deserved better after taking care of the Asian guy who owed Artie ten grand six months ago. No questions asked, Jeffery got it done, catching the guy in his garage, knocking him down, setting a Lawn-Boy over the black-haired dude's face, giving him a choice, pay or get his face mowed.

Jeffery reached for the joint, Wally letting go of it, thinking no way he wanted it back after this guy put his scurvy lips on it, lips the color of earthworms. Reek rose off Jeffery like smog, his leather neck disappearing under the dingy wife-beater, his yellow eyes with the white shit in the corners, hair tipped with grey, looking like it was greased with Valvoline.

"One of you girls out in the garage just now?" Jeffery asked, nodding toward the side door, trying to remember if he had locked it.

Wally shook his head.

"So what you hanging around for?" Jeffery wanted to get back to his April issue of *Barely Legal*.

Wally and Mitch started to get up when the side door flew in, kicked off its hinges. The crack felt like an electric charge. Wally and Mitch dove for the floor, Jeffery yanking the Python from his belt, running into the kitchen and ducking behind the counter. "Come on, girls, let's get dangerous."

The blast of the hand cannon got them crawling for the front door, four sets of fingers scrabbling for the doorknob.

The intruder fired, the shotgun blast tearing a six-inch hole in the kitchen ceiling. Another bark from the Python, Jeffery fired through the wall, guessing where the guy with the shotgun was. It sent the intruder running out the side door and around the front of the house. Jeffery headed him off, shoving Mitch aside, ripping the front door open.

The guy with the shotgun outfoxed him, standing poised, the Slugster barrel up as Jeffery opened the door. The blast knocked him back, tore him out of his sneakers and punched him down. A grunt came from his throat, Jeffery's doll's eyes looking up at the Florida light.

Mitch and Wally were both down on the floor, looking up. A second guy in a white van, pointing a shotgun out the window, peeled down the driveway, screeching rubber. The gunman ran and dove into the open back of it, yelling, "Go, go, go."

The van hopped the curb, wobbled on jelly springs, the driver bouncing like a bobblehead. Swiping the neighbor's mailbox, the bumper torn off, the van ripped through a bed of marigolds before getting back on the road, racing to the intersection, making a hard right and was gone.

Mitch got to his feet, watching the getaway, Wally crawling to Jeffery, the king of handguns slipping from the old man's fingers, a wet sucking sound coming from his throat.

Jeffery stared up, blood bubbling from his mouth, finding it hard to speak. "One of you dickheads give me a hand."

Wally knelt next to him, caught the foul breath and the sucking sound, blood pooling under him, Jeffery's chest looking like bloody hamburger. Wally picked up the Python, saw himself in the chrome, spinning its cylinder, saying, "Think you're done being dangerous, huh, Jeff?"

The distant sound of sirens got them moving, Wally tucking the Python in his belt. He ran across the street to the knocked-over mailbox, getting out his all-in-one, thinking he'd look up the guys in the van, give them first bid for the license plate, pretty sure he'd seen the one driving someplace before. The second bid would go to Stax, the guy who hired him and Mitch to transport the weed. With a few twists, he had the plate from the bumper and chased after Mitch, going through the backyards, the pickup he stole waiting on the next street.

Marty Schmidt was doing it again, that infectious laugh getting everybody going in the Global Trace office. Great

TAKING THE MICKEY

sense of humor for a bunch of bounty hunters, all of them in shirtsleeves, handguns in shoulder rigs. Karl Morgen crossed the room, tossing back what passed as coffee, crumpling the takeout cup and scoring a basket in Marty's trash.

Marty showed him the pickup order Albert the manager had left on his desk, pointing with his finger. "Get a load of this one. Guy skips on a five-K bond, charged with gunning down a sheep."

"A what?"

"Thing that goes *baah*."

"Yeah."

"The asshole likely sampled more Special K than he should've, drove all the way to Montana and shot this thing standing in a field minding its own. Thing is, the asshole did it with a handgun."

"Yeah?"

"Farmhand witnessed it, a single shot from near three hundred feet. One of them cowboy guns."

"Guess he got lucky," Karl said, guessing Marty was getting stranger by the day.

Marty didn't buy it. "Guy's too high to tell a bighorn from something you make sweaters out of, but he hits it with a single shot from a handgun, and from distance."

Karl looked over the paperwork, saw that Miro Knotts' grandmother put up the bail, guessing they had a real sweetheart on their hands, asking, "Where you want to start?"

Marty checked the clock next to the photo of the pair of them, same photo used in the *Seattle Times'* story about their exploits. The sign underneath repeated a quote from the article: "If your man's breathing, we'll find him; if he's not, we'll point out where he's buried."

On a twenty-dollar tip from a hooker out front of the Jack in the Box, they tracked Miro to an all-night rave in Belltown. Sipping Cokes and stuffing down cold Jumbo Jacks and fries, they waited in Marty's Cooper, listening to the thump of techno coming from the house.

Around two, most of the partiers had gone home and things quieted down. Karl and Marty went in like they owned the place, checking the faces of the zombies left doing their rave dance moves, found a few more lying around like refugees. Miro Knotts was in the basement, out cold and bare-assed on a sofa, arms and legs spidered around a skinny girl with red hair and a black eye.

"You Miro Knotts?" Karl asked, nudging him, knowing he was from the photo in the file, the oldest guy there by a mile.

Miro popped an eye open and made a move for the

Vaquero under the sofa, yelping when Karl pinned his fingers under his shoe, empty wine and beer bottles rolling around on the floor, a water pipe tipping on the table.

"Fuck are you?" Miro cried out, guessing it was a cop shoe standing on his fingers, and this was another bust.

Yanking him up by the hair, Karl cuffed his hands behind his back, telling him who they were.

The girl looked like she didn't know Monday from Sunday, her eye nearly swollen shut.

"Got two questions for you," Marty said to her, holding up a pair of fingers, checking her eye.

She nodded when he asked if this guy gave her the eye and told him fifteen when he asked how many birthdays she'd seen.

"Told me eighteen, lying bitch," Miro said, catching Karl's elbow. When he got his breath back, he said, "You here for me skipping, right—like that Dog asshole on TV?"

The next shot left Miro sucking air, trying not to puke on himself. Marty took a closer look at the girl's eye, finding out her name was Alice.

Five diehards with pool cues came down the stairs, the fat one saying this was his place, asking what the fuck was going on.

"This guy's in custody," Karl said. "Have to ask you to stand back."

"Soon as we see some shields," the fat guy said, the five guys fanning out.

"This do?" Karl lifted his windbreaker, showing his Smith, watching them turn and file back to their techno and lights, the fat guy asking them to close the door on their way out.

Marty and Karl made it policy to let any skip come in easy, no guns, no cuffs, skip's choice—but not this time. Dragging Miro out in his briefs, hands cuffed behind him, Karl stuffed him into the back of the Cooper. Waiting at the top of the stairs till Alice got dressed, Marty escorted her out, trying to talk some sense to her, asking where her parents lived, staying with her until the cab showed up.

At the West Precinct, they caught a hard time from Pender, the desk sergeant who didn't like the condition of their prisoner, Miro shivering in his underpants, ugly welts on his midsection. Karl told the sarge they found him getting beat up by some teenaged girl, no other clothes in sight, Karl and Marty just doing the cuffing and stuffing. Miro was screaming about getting even when they walked out of the station, the two of them happy to call it a night.

"So this Artie guy's been growing dope for a while?" Dom LeGuille asked, wondering what the loot would do

Every Bush A Thief

if he stuck his Oxford up on his desk. Likely blow a gasket, those veins going at his temples.

"Thirty grow houses up and down the Lower Mainland as far as we know, runs them like a Swiss watch," Lieutenant Frederick said. He had twenty years and fifty pounds on either of the detectives sitting across the desk. "Took the tax boys a couple of months to do what we couldn't do in over twenty years." He remembered Artie Poppa's name from his rookie days. Nobody able to take him down in all that time. "Turned up some income he's having trouble explaining. But it won't be enough to bury him."

"Those guys sniff money like dope dogs," Luca Botzo said. "I remember when my wife's uncle was late filing—"

The lieutenant's stare stopped him. "What we need is to link him to one of these places." Picking up a file, he read from it, "Bought his first place in West Lynn for eighty Gs back before Expo, had it titled to a brother-in-law in Gyeongju. Guy's name's Choi Sung-Kuk."

"That's a name?" Dom asked.

Loot looked at him, waited, then went on. "Place sold last year for ten times that. The next one went in his mother-in-law's name. Third one to a cousin, then an uncle—no shortage of relatives. A dozen places sold off in the last six months."

"The Sung-Kuk's doing alright," Luca said.

Pulling some black and whites from a file folder, shots of Artie Poppa taken on stakeout, the long lens capturing Artie sitting on a nude beach, Frederick kept talking. "The wife, Ho Sook, goes by Sookie, got a gift for fudging the books, running their interests through a puppet property-management company called East West Holdings, leasing the houses via a bunch of fake names. Way the tax boys see it, profits get filtered through different accounts, ending in a bank in Gyeongju. Bank's owned by an uncle. Twenty years of shitting on us, the Poppas pocket something like twenty-four million in real estate holdings alone, looking at early retirement, less we come up with something."

Luca and Dom were looking at the photo, Poppa not a big man, trim goatee, dark eyes, heavy brows.

"Word is the Poppas got a sixteen-room place being built on the East Sea."

"That in Korea?"

Frederick said yeah. "Sookie oversees construction while Artie hangs back wrapping things up. Meaning we haven't got much time."

"We're on it," Luca said.

"Start with the place that got hit, one with the dead guy." Meaning the grow house, Jeffery Potts lying dead in the kitchen, the shotgun slug blowing him right out of his sneakers.

"That one of Artie's?"

"Far as we know." The lieutenant nodded. "Dead guy's one Jeffery Potts, a known dirtbag, worked for Artie since way back." He laid down another photo, saying, "Artie's number two is Danny Arlis, goes by Stax. He handles the rough stuff. He'll likely be looking for whoever made the hit."

"He know his boss is ducking town?" Dom asked.

"Why don't you go ask him?"

Dom looked down at his Oxfords.

"Our people tried to work a deal with Poppa. He gives up some names, we go light," Frederick said. "He told us what we could do with our witness protection plan. Laughed at us. My guess, his suitcase is stuffed, and he's set to split town. Bouncing grandkids on his knee's better than looking over his shoulder in the prison showers. Till he makes his move, he'll stop at every red light and let Stax dirty his hands. So, find out who put one in Potts, and look for a connection." He folded his hands and looked at the two of them. "You waiting for me to write it down?"

Deep in the Pudding

"You're one dumb fuck, you know that?" Stax said, looking past Wolf Klinger at the construction site, the building a skeleton of girders on a muddy patch of ground, the sun beaming through the clouds, lighting Indian Arm and Balcara on the opposite shore. About a dozen guys were on the job, welding in lift buckets, guiding beams with ropes, nobody walking the girders like they did back in his old man's day. Beyond the crane, a dump truck was on the rise, backing up with a load of gravel, its reverse alarm going.

"The fuck could I know the bumper came off? I mean we were flying out of there—had my shotgun out the window, covering Vince." Wolf stood taller, but not as wide as this no-neck with his massive torso set over legs too short for his body, making Stax appear apelike, tats of serpents running up both arms.

"All you had to do was drive," Stax said, getting in Wolf's face. "And you fucked that up."

Wolf turned to see where his foreman was, the guy nowhere in sight. "Look, we got the stuff, every fucking ounce, right? Put a hole in your guy, right? So chill."

"Chill when I find out what happened to the plate."

Wolf felt the sweat under his arms. "What's it matter, the van was hot anyway?"

"Problem, brainiac, is you stole it from here."

Wolf wiped his hands on his pants, taking a new tack. "Okay, I didn't want to set you off, figured I'd take care of it myself."

"What are you talking about?"

"This guy called me . . ."

"What guy?"

"Guy that picked up the plate—one of your two mules."

"Told you to make sure Jeffery was alone," Stax said.

"Thought he was. Guess they were inside. Anyway, guy calls up, doesn't give me his name, just says he was there and wants five bills for it. Cash."

"How'd he know who to call, the van was hot?"

Wolf shrugged. "Said he'd seen me around."

"So he made you?" Stax had to laugh. One of his mules was turning entrepreneur, selling the license plate back. "And you didn't think to tell me?"

"Telling you now. Said I'll take care of it."

"That's all you got to say, you'll take care of it?

"What do you want me to say, it won't happen again?" Wolf stood his ground, going eye to eye.

First thing you got right, Stax thought, turning and walking up the incline toward the Mustang hidden behind the gravel truck. Wolf watched until Stax got to the top, then he stepped through the muck to the Port-O-Potty, thinking next time Stax had a job, he could go fuck himself.

THIRD PARTY

The lieutenant had handed them the grow house hit this morning, wanting them to connect Artie Poppa to it, making like it was some big break. Now, Dom stood with clay sticking to his new Oxfords, scratching his head. The sheet on the first dead guy, one Jeffery Potts, read he'd been busted twice for firearms, once for drug trafficking and assault, did time at Ferndale and Mission and was released six months early for good behavior from Matsqui.

Dom wasn't convinced this one was related, wasn't even sure if it was a crime scene or one for WorkSafeBC. Him and Luca were looking at the overturned truck, gravel spilled all over the place, burying both Port-O-Pottys. A couple of bricklayers said they saw Wolf Klinger talking to a big guy minutes before stepping into the one on the right, just before the truck on the hill backed and tipped its load. Neither of them got a good look. The driver said he went on his lunch break with the foreman, the two of them having bologna sandwiches his wife made, swearing he pulled the brake before he got out. Finishing their interviews, Dom and Luca wanted to get away from the stink of shit and chemicals.

Luca made the call to the lieutenant, touching base, while Dom checked his chicken-scratch notes, witness statements not worth a damn. None of these construction guys saw a thing. Typical. He slapped the notebook closed. Half a dozen guys working overhead on the beams, each with a different story, the foreman and driver eating bologna when it happened. Aside from the two bricklayers who saw Wolf step into the shitter, nobody got a good look at the guy he'd been talking to.

Only thing for sure, eight tons of gravel flattened both Port-O-Pottys, and Wolf Klinger picked a bad time for a crap. The two paramedics on the scene guessed death was instant, standing around waiting for the firefighters and the guys with shovels to clear the gravel away.

Dom was thinking, what do you put on the guy's head-stone? Making a doodle in his notebook.

Luca clicked off his cell phone. "Gonna be hours before they get this cleaned up."

"What did the loot say?"

"Scrape our shoes before we come back."

"Nice. Wonder which one of us pissed him off?"

Luca shrugged, saying it never took much, checking his watch, thinking he could use a coffee. "There's a Tim's down on Main. What say?"

Luca hailed the rookie standing over by his unit, telling him they were done here, wagging his notebook. The young cop said he was sticking around, told to call the ME once the firefighters and work crew got done shoveling, said he'd call them when they got to the body, Dom wondering what the rookie did to deserve this duty.

They got into the Chevy minivan and drove off, clay splashing up at the fenders.

"How about we take a spin by the grow house, take another poke around, knock on a few more doors?" Dom asked.

"Why not?"

"Pull in at Park Royal, we'll grab coffee there."

"Starbucks or the other one?"

"The Bean, they got better muffins."

Back in Seattle. First smart
thing Miro Knotts did was find
the junk shop with the photo
booth in the back, a dump of a

TIT FOR TAT

place down on Aurora. The sign on the booth read four shots
for a buck. Miro took a fistful of change and got behind the
curtain, stripped down to his skivvies and stuck in his quarters, showing the lens his bruises, the shutter clicking.

Next thing, he walked into the Salvation Army store up
the block, flipped through a rack of sour-smelling clothes and
picked out a navy jacket. He found a pair of pants that more
or less fit, and a shirt and tie, and haggled the price down
from sixty to forty bucks for the works.

Standing next to his appointed lawyer in his mix of short
sleeves and long cuffs, Miro listened while his lawyer addressed
the judge, trying to get the charges dropped, pointing out
the lack of a warrant by the GIU cops who showed up at his
door in the first place, then pointing out the subsequent mis-
handling by the bounty hunters who had dragged his client

to the station, saying with the right amount of outrage how his client was apprehended in just his briefs. Miro played the model citizen with his hair in place, keeping his mouth shut. Tired of the legal showboating, the judge pounded his gavel and handed down ninety days, ordering Miro to pay a two-thousand-dollar restitution for the farm animal he had gunned down.

Muttering "fuck me" got him a two-year suspended DOC commitment, the judge explaining next time Miro ended up with a conviction, he'd get an automatic two years tacked on. Miro fired his lawyer on the spot, the lawyer saying not to do him any favors, grinning as the bailiff led his former client from the courtroom.

After serving the ninety at Coyote Ridge, Miro handed in the orange jumpsuit and was released with his new prison tat. Worst ninety days of his life he told his grandmother. He put on his Sally Ann outfit once more and headed straight to the Department of Licensing with the shots he took back in the photo booth on Aurora. Demanding to see the director got him a smile, the clerk handing him the appropriate service complaint form, telling him to tick off where it said the complaint was against a bail bond agent, told him to print neatly and paper-clip the photos to the form when he was done. Asking how long the process could take got Miro another smile.

Vince Vetri wiped his hands on the striped apron, getting his attitude right, toughening the look that said no way. He was **FORTE** looking at the deadbeat who lived under the Capilano bridge. A couple of regulars had talked about the guy yesterday over mocha cappuccinos, couldn't get over a deadbeat drinking four-buck coffee and living under a bridge. Deadbeat left his shopping cart, plastic bags full of returns hanging from the sides, and walked across from outside the insurance office. Vince blocked the door, telling him no way, didn't want bums smelling up the place. The only other customer looked up from his newspaper, flipped a page and went back to it.

"But I can pay." Deadbeat showed a palmful of change.

"Heard what I said."

"Takeout, then. Just something hot."

"Take a hike." Vince pointed down the avenue, folding his arms the way his wife used to when she was through talking. He was still pissed at the way Stax had talked to him on the phone. He'd put a slug in Potts, and they got the kilos. Now Stax had a bee up his butt on account of a stupid license plate.

Deadbeat shoved his coins back in his pocket, Vince watching him shuffle back to his cart, sitting next to it on the curb. Vince went behind the counter and got the French roast going, playing the grow house scene through his head: snapping the lock on the garage, going around the far side of the house with the Mossberg, leaving Wolf to load the bags of weed from the garage into the van. Kicking in the side door and firing a round into the house, he'd hurried around to the front, waiting with the barrel pointed, nailing Potts coming through the front door, the king of handguns no match for the Mossberg.

The black Shelby GT pulled up out front, the throaty rumble of the V8. Vince figured it for a shadow of the 428s Carrol Shelby was putting out in the late sixties; only thing, this Shelby belonging to Stax Arlis. Patting the pit bull sitting in the passenger seat, Stax got out and said something to the bum on the curb, pulled his ball cap down and headed for the door.

The clock told Vince the West Van squad should be coming in for free coffee, cheap fuckers talking about their wives and kids and cases they were working on. Occasionally, Vince picked up a tidbit Stax found useful. He wished he had one now.

"What's with him?" Stax asked, coming to the counter, looking out the window.

"Tossed him out." Vince shrugged. "Soon as the cops come around," he looked at the clock again, "they'll drive his ass across the bridge."

"Yeah."

"Don't need them around here."

"The cops?"

"The bums."

Stax eyed the menu board, tapping his Ford fob on the melamine. "Give me a large black."

"Forte," Vince said.

Stax put his eyes on Vince.

"That's what they want us calling large, *forte*," Vince said, pointing to the menu board showing the sizes: pico, fisso and forte.

"You a corporate boy now, Vince?"

"You know me." Vince smiled and got to work, this guy unraveling his nerves. He drew the Italian roast he had on the go, slapping on a lid and a sleeve, setting the cup down. "On the house."

Stax glanced at the guy reading the paper, asking in a low voice, "Want to tell me what happened?"

Vince leaned close. "Did like you said, took out Jeffery, picked up the pot. What you wanted."

"Then how come I hear one of my mules is auctioning the plate off your van. Wants five hundred for it."

"You kidding?"

"I look like I kid?"

"Talk to Wolf. Dumb shit panics and hits a mailbox."

"Dumb shit you brought along," Stax said, keeping his voice down.

"Heard sirens, you know . . . anyway, the van was stolen, right?"

"Except you bozos stole it from his work."

"Talk to Wolf, man."

"Already did. Now I'm talking to you."

Vince put up his hands like what could he do. He felt them shake.

"Those new?" Stax finally asked, looking at the pastry case.

"Yeah, streusel-tops and fruit fritters came in fresh this morning." Vince got his tongs and plucked a few into a bag, put it on the counter. Vince wishing Stax would just pay him for the hit and get out of here.

Stax looked at him a moment, then said, "Fill another one."

"What?"

"Fritters and a forte—stick them in a bag."

Vince got to work, thinking Stax was going to feed fruit fritters to his psycho dog.

"Now take it out to that guy."

Vince looked at the bum out the window, hesitated. "How's he want it—the forte?"

"Why don't you go fucking ask him?"

Vince got a handful of creamers and sugar packets from the island and walked them out to the guy. Handing the bag to the bum, he said if he ever came back he'd kick his ass; that's when Vince saw the minivan pull up, letting out a sigh as Dom and Luca stepped out.

"You're turning into a regular Saint Francis, Vince," Dom called to him. The two cops walked to the door, Dom holding it for Stax as he left, Stax thanking him and wishing them a good day. Nudging his partner, Dom watched Stax get in his car and drive off.

The photos Miro took of him-self in the photo booth did the trick with the Department of Licensing. Really showed **SERVED UP HOT** the bruises. Several partygoers, the guys with the pool cues, swearing to his story. Karl and Marty found themselves sit-ting across from Benny the manager, hearing about the secu-rity bond Global Trace had to put up for each of their agents, how they were expected to behave. Throwing up his arms in surrender, Benny shoved the paperwork with the federal seal on top at them, saying it was out of his hands, nothing he could do. Karl had been suspended indefinitely for taking part in prohibited acts, Marty getting off with a thirty-day suspension, the director of licensing taking pity on a family man with a wife and kid and no priors.

Could appeal it, but Karl's days as a bounty hunter in Washington State were over, so were the days when anybody in Seattle was hiring. Jobs were scarce, the whole economy in the toilet. Marty steered Karl to Sea-to-Sky up in Vancouver.

Longtime friends Bob and Joyce Young were looking for a process server—summonses, writs, subpoenas—the job offering a third of the pay in a town that cost twice as much.

Trying to cheer his friend, Marty told him Bob Young once served a guy on a nude beach—walked up in the buff with the envelope tucked between his cheeks—surprised the hell out of the guy. Joyce, his wife, topped it by serving a gynecologist. Booking an appointment, she served the doc his divorce papers with her feet in his stirrups. Marty promised Karl these were his kind of people.

Karl took the job over the phone, talking to Bob Young for a half hour, went home and told Jerry the news. Jerry, his girlfriend of two years, asked if he was kidding, called him an asshole and told him they were done. She moved most of their stuff that afternoon while he went back to clear out his desk. Saying so long to Marty, Karl gave him his Smith, Canadian gun laws being what they were.

Packing what he could into the tiny trunk, he got into the replica Roadster and drove north on the I5, Chip, his black and white cat, on the passenger floor. Karl tossed his jacket over Chip's cage when he neared the Peace Arch, telling Chip to keep the meows down until they got by the border guards.

〽〽

Two months in and Karl was liking the new job, adjusting to a city where the locals settled arguments with middle fingers instead of firearms. Sleepless nights imagining sweet revenge on Miro Knotts gave way to sweet thoughts of PJ Addie, the legal assistant at Walt Wetzel's law office three floors up from Sea-to-Sky. Lunch at Joey Tomato's progressed to dinner at Umberto's, followed by the new Coen picture, to drinks after.

Now, here he was going once around the living room with the Swiffer. Karl tilted the only chair in the place, getting

Chip's fur from under the tabs with his sock. He unfolded his scribbled notes, the chicken tikka recipe he copied from the Jamie Oliver cookbook at Indigo, laying it in a wet spot on the counter, the naked guy's words turning Greek as the ink ran.

PJ loved curry. That's what she told him, the hotter the better. And hot it would be, the bird's-eye chilies blasting off the Scoville chart, the wet recipe looking like tie-dye.

With the pan on the stove, he tested the sharpness of the new German blade that set him back two hundred bucks. Good of Jerry not to leave anything sharp lying around after she left, in case feelings of ruin turned him suicidal.

By the time the aroma of curry overtook the sandalwood incense, Karl was setting out paper plates on the coffee table, leaving him scant time to shower. The phone rang and he answered thinking it was her, wanting him to explain the directions he gave her.

"Hey, man." It was Marty sitting back in his cubicle at Global Trace in Seattle, calling to catch up, getting past the small talk, then saying, "Wanted you to hear it from me."

"What's that?"

"Our old buddy Miro Knotts got picked up in a pot raid in Lynnwood."

"Yeah." No surprise there. Karl stirred the curry, turning down the heat to keep it from sticking to the pan.

"Asshole got released by the courts, something about pending review of federal and state charges."

"They released a known bail jumper?"

"Yeah, just another fucking glitch in the system, and guess what?"

"The asshole fled?"

"Yeah, but the good news is where he fled to," Marty said.

"Yeah?"

"Guy at the sheriff's department figures he went through the brambles along the border."

"So he's up here?"

"Canadian as a beaver, born in Chilliwack, wherever that is—used to run his shit down here from Vancouver."

"Yeah?"

"I'd love to see the look on his face when you serve him."

"Serve him what?"

"The copy of the bench warrant I'm sticking in the mail."

"This is Canada, amigo," Karl said. "They got sheriffs for the fun stuff."

"Yeah, what I'm sending's not official, just a copy, thought you might want to have your own fun, let the scumbag know the feds down here are waving extradition papers, looking for his provisional arrest."

Karl was liking it. "A friendly reminder from the guys that dragged his ass to jail."

"Downright righteous, you ask me."

"Could use some excitement. Speaking of which . . ." Karl checked the time, told Marty he had a date.

"Oh, yeah? Canadian chicks any good?"

"You kidding?"

"This one got a name?"

"PJ."

"Short for anything?"

"Nothing that I can tell."

"PJ, huh? Happy for you, bro. Things are looking up on all fronts."

"Listen, I got just enough time to roll on some Ban."

"Hey, don't let me stop you. Have fun, but, hey, I want details."

"Getting stranger by the minute, Marty."

"Didn't mean details with her. Meant with the douche bag."

Karl was laughing. "I'll keep you posted. And, Marty?"

"Yeah?"

"Give my love to Chris and the kids." With that Karl hung up and fished his cleanest Polo shirt from the laundry, feeling the adrenalin, thinking about getting a second shot at Miro Knotts. After the world's fastest shower, he finger-combed his hair and rolled on the Ban, looking in the mirror at the guy wrapped in the towel with more hair under his arms than on his head, getting a little soft around the middle, thinking Fitness World was only a block away.

BUMP IN THE ROAD

Chickie's neon sign flashed blue by the door. The diner was trying for a vintage railcar look, a stainless steel counter, swivel stools anchored to the floor, tables covered with red and white tablecloths. The kind of place where if you checked the washroom before sitting down, you'd go someplace else.

"So what the fuck I need you for?" Stax looked at him across the table, thinking he never liked Miro, even back when they both worked for Artie Poppa: Miro growing weed, making oil, Stax running the shit up and down the coast. Glancing up as the waitress approached, Stax read the name tag that said she was Sunny. Not bad for a scrawny blonde. He ordered coffee for both of them, watching her go.

"Who's going to make the oil, you?" Miro said, pulling a cigarette from his pack.

"Oil, huh?" Stax looked around Chickie's. "Lots of guys do oil." Knowing nobody did it better than Miro.

"Yeah, these guys ever work out strain hybridization, mix sativas and indicas, get the curing down right?"

Stax put up a hand for him to stop.

"And how many of these guys get six good crops a year? How many know dick about resin?"

"Okay, I get the point," Stax said, waiting as Sunny came with the coffee pot and a couple of mugs, watching her pour, telling her not yet when she asked if they were ready to order. When she left, Stax took a sip, the coffee hot and horrible.

Miro continued, "With Jeffery gone, thought you'd be open to something new."

"Came all the way up here thinking that, huh?"

"The old man's on his way out. You know it; I know it. Me, I figure you're looking after your own ass," Miro said, pretty sure Stax was behind hitting Artie's grow house.

"Yeah?"

"And I'm guessing you're as sick of working for him as I was."

No doubt Miro knew his way around cooking. The right product, the right channels, and a guy like Stax could do alright.

"Been working out the bumps," Miro said.

Stax guessed a guy as irritating as Miro could end up being one of them, just like Jeffery, but still . . .

LIKE A HOUSE ON FIRE

It was the smoke alarm's bleating that got Karl slapping the lid on the pan and dialing down the heat. The flatbread was black, but the curry survived. Marty's call got him thinking about bumping into Miro Knotts again, distracting him from cooking. Fanning a flyer at the shrieking ceiling contraption, Karl cursed whoever had installed it this close to the stove. He fanned until his arms were sore; still, it wouldn't quit. Then came the knock at the door.

"Hey, there she is," Karl said, pulling the door back, putting on a smile. He leaned in for a kiss, PJ looking good with her strawberry blonde waves, wearing a kind of Indian kurti with beadwork around the neck. She held out wrapped flowers and a bottle, looking at him like what's with the alarm? He hung her jacket over his, held the flowers and wine in one hand and jumped, yanking down the housing, sending sparks, crippling the circuit, the dead alarm hanging by a wire. The pounding from the bridge construction replaced the sound of the alarm, a giant crane-operated hammer driving in bridge supports half a block away, shaking the whole building.

"Next time try the reset button," she said.

He looked up at the housing, the mess of wires hanging down, pointing and asking, "That the one?"

"Uh huh."

"That could work," he said, wondering how he'd explain it to Anton the super.

Her heels made a hollow sound on the laminate floor as she walked by him. "Nice echo."

He checked her out as she passed him, caught her scent. "Just wait till I get it furnitured."

"Furnitured?"

"Yeah, I'm stumped by it, absolutely no sense for it."

She looked around, assessing, guessing a man put the fireplace on the only wall that would take a sofa.

"Maybe we could do IKEA sometime, you and me?" He came behind her, drawing her against him, the two of them getting into it until he remembered the pan on the stove. Taking her by the hand, he led her to the kitchen, telling her she didn't need to bring flowers and wine, wondering what he could use as a vase. The only thing he had that might pass for wineglasses used to hold Dijon.

"I know flowers aren't a guy thing," she said, "but more romantic than a six pack of Bud, don't you think?"

"You kidding, I love these." He put his nose against the petals.

"Yellow's for friendship," she said.

"That right?"

"One that's going places. At least that's what the florist told me."

"What's the wine do, help it get there?"

"The wine's my favorite: Beaujolais Cru."

Reaching a mixing bowl from the cupboard, he dubbed it a vase and took down the mustard glasses.

"Smells real yummy," she said, sneaking a peek under the lid, the aroma reminding her it had been hours since the energy bar and latte. "Sorry if I held things up." She looked around, the counter like a war zone of pots and dishes. "Had the worst case of Oompa Loompa hair, then got into it with Dara . . ."

He wondered what he could use as a corkscrew, trying to avoid a conversation about her daughter right now, knowing it would upset her, asking, "Oompa Loompa, that a native thing?"

"It's when no two strands get together, and the whole mess just clumps."

"Looks pretty amazing if you ask me," he said, getting close. "Smells good, too."

"That's the Giovanni, but you don't need to butter my toast, cowboy. A man that cooks gets you points where I come from." She watched him half-fill the mixing bowl with water and prop the roses against the backsplash, asking what she could do.

"Could play some tunes. Drown out that bridge noise." He motioned to the old Sony on the living-room floor, the one he found in the hall closet when he moved in, telling her to wiggle the aerial around. "Try for some FM. It's that or what's left of my collection."

She went and picked up the stack of CDs. "Dear God," she said, flipping through the Travers, Atkins, Wills, Orbison, Nelson and Cash, putting Karl somewhere between Hicksville and the sixties. "You from Mayberry, Karl?"

That got him laughing.

"No Smokey, no Aaron, no Aretha."

"Aretha Franklin? She still around?"

"You kidding? Love her honey voice, the way she hits those notes." She clicked on the Sony, saying, "Least there's no Stompin' Tom."

"A guy's got to draw the line."

She settled on Roy Orbison, humming along to *A Black and White Night*, getting comfy on the beanbag in the middle of the floor.

Impaling the cork with the Phillips, he forced it into the bottle. Fishing out bits of cork, he brought a glass over, told her dinner was minutes away and kissed the top of her head.

"Great, I'm starved." She sipped her wine.

"Hey, I'm serious about needing help decorating this place."

"I can see that." She picked cork off her tongue.

"IKEA—any day you say, and I'll throw lunch into the deal."

"Make it Antique Row and dinner at the Blue Water, and it's a date." She sipped, watching him dish curry onto the paper plates, her radar trying to pick up Jerry's ghost. She crossed her legs, sitting Japanese-style in front of the coffee table, letting Chip curl up in her lap.

Karl came with the plates and slid a packet of plastic utensils in front of her, apologizing for it, saying it was going to be a little like indoor camping.

She tore into the cellophane, her teeth fantastic. "So long as you don't make me sleep on the lumpy ground, cowboy."

THE MIDNIGHT OIL

It didn't look like much—just a storehouse with the windows all soaped; a chipped, painted concrete floor, old power tools left on a bench. The place held a funky smell like it was used to store seafood at one time. From the door, Miro could make out a barge out on the Fraser River, this part of Richmond all industrial, Chinese and Thai importers, one after another. Not a lot of road traffic, just the odd truck making a delivery.

Stax unloaded the last of the sealed garbage bags, the weed Wolf and Vince stole from Artie's, killing Jeffery in the process. Letting Ike the pit bull out of the car, he closed the Mustang's door with his foot, saying to Miro, "When you get done, got a couple of guys I want you to meet."

"What guys?" Miro said, holding the door to the warehouse, looking at the car, thinking about his Challenger back at his grandmother's in Seattle, one eye on the pit bull, the thing growling at him as it walked through the door, then sniffing that fishy smell in the place.

Stax got a kick out of seeing Miro afraid of the dog, saying, "Guys I been using as mules."

"What do we need with mules?"

"They're going to hit Artie again, another grow house." Stax told him about Wally calling Wolf up and offering to sell back the license plate.

"No shit," Miro said, grin going ear to ear.

"Got Jeffery's Python, too, chrome one with the big barrel." The way Stax told it, the cops had Artie Poppa under surveillance, looking to flip him or take him down. Artie was set to bolt with enough cash stashed in his safe to buy Malta. Aside from hitting the grow houses, the idea was to find his safe before he made his move.

"We keep our hands clean, make the two clowns kinda partners," Miro said, getting the idea.

"Temporary partners."

"Temporary, huh?"

"Till Artie sends me to find out who did it."

Miro agreed on a lesser cut this time around since Stax was supplying the raw product, the weed Jeffery Potts was killed over. Next time it would be an even split. But he didn't care about that right then, spinning the idea of hitting Artie again in another direction, thinking back to the call he made in Belltown. The girl picking up the phone at Global Trace told him Karl Morgen no longer worked there, told him he quit the business and moved to Vancouver. Made his day. The photos Miro showed the director of licensing had done the trick, got one of the bounty hunter canned, the other one suspended. Point was, the asshole that had dragged him to jail was here in town, and here was his chance to square things once and for all with Karl Morgen, adding a few pieces to Stax's plan: the two clowns rob the grow house, Stax puts a bug in Artie's ear, and Artie hires Karl Morgen to find out who did it, the guy with the reputation Miro had heard of back in Belltown: if your man's breathing, Morgen will find him; if he's not breathing, Morgen points to the spot. Morgen being a hotshot, couldn't resist a guy like Artie asking him to find the guys that ripped him off. So, Morgen gives up the clowns for a cheap reward, Stax takes them out and Miro makes sure it looks like Morgen did it. Morgen burns for the double homicide.

Stax went out the door with Ike, left Miro daydreaming. Stax wasn't sure about this guy Miro wanted to set up, but at least the two of them were on the same page about hitting Artie.

Still juggling details, Miro locked the door and started stuffing the bud into glass jars, topping them with alcohol and swirling them around, straining them, picturing the look on Morgen's face when he found out Miro had set him up. He flipped the fan on high, blowing the smell out of the place through the open windows.

When the bud reduced to resin in the pans, he set them aside to cool. Taking it from under his jacket on the tool bench, he strapped on the holster rig with the hand-tooled floral design and worked his draw, pulling the new Vaquero with the pearl grip over and over, thinking he could use a mirror in this place.

The wooden floor was killing him, PJ's head on his arm.

THE THING WITH DARA

"A girl that sleeps on the ground gets you points where I come from," he told her, lifting up, wiggling his fingers, trying to get circulation back in the arm.

"Got crawly things on the ground where you come from?" She pinched a puff of Chip's fur off the floor and blew it at him.

"The odd Seattle sewer rat." He held his hands apart, showing the size. "Come right up your toilet."

"Lovely."

The curry had hit the spot while Roy sang about pretty women and Willy sang of Spanish angels, and the wine worked its magic. The talk was easy, PJ throwing decorating ideas around: cloud white for the walls and ceiling, a sisal rug under a bamboo coffee table, a pair of bookcases, a print of Paris by Doisneau over the gas fireplace. Karl tried to keep up, taking it all in, picturing a sofa facing the window, asking what a camelback was.

They got cozy on the floor like that, talking, looking at each other, then he got her to her feet, bopping to the music with the bridge construction crew working overtime into the night in the background.

"What are we doing, cowboy?" She moved her hips, playing along.

"Dancing." He tugged her gently down the hall toward the bedroom.

Easing onto the mattress next to Chip, she glanced at his bedside clock, wondering if Dara was home. She'd already decided to stay the night, guessing they were ready for it, just wanting to slow it down a bit, saying, "It wasn't just the Oompa Loompa hair that held me up today."

He pulled his shirt off, looking at her, wondering where that came from. "Yeah?"

"Came home hoping for a shower, pissed my AmEx got refused at the Sushi Mart, not looking forward to getting on the phone, straightening it out." She was looking at him with his shirt off, kept talking, stroking Chip. "I was tugging off my shoes when I saw it—shopping cart at the end of the hall, thing heaped with melting Popsicle boxes, a puddle under it."

"Yeah?" He eased onto the pillow, looking at her—hadn't guessed her for a talker.

"Stepped into the living room, dozens of the things leaking like a Vancouver condo all over everywhere. And guess who's sitting there?"

"Dara?"

"Her boyfriend, Cam the purple-haired groper."

"Huh."

"Been sneaking him into the suite with her. Anyway, there he was plopped on my sofa, *Jerry Springer* on the tube, my tube, assaulting the viewing world with what passed for entertainment. Peeling wrappers like a man possessed, tossing the goop in a Coleman, stacking the wrappers on my table. I come in 'what the frig,' and Cam says Popsicle Pete's giving him Air Miles."

"Who's Popsicle Pete?" He cozied up to her, Chip having to move, paws hitting the hardwood.

"That's what I said. Idiot picks up a dripping box and shows me Popsicle Pete's likeness, guy's a cartoon if you can believe it."

"What was he on?"

"God knows. Cam goes, if the labels are postmarked before the end of the month, Popsicle Pete'll double the Air Miles."

"These the Popsicles that break in half?"

"Yeah, used to love the banana."

He ran his mouth down her neck, hoping for an end to the story.

"So Cam's sitting in my trashed living room, saying he's taking the three of us to Venice."

"You, Cam and Popsicle Pete?"

"Think he meant Dara and me."

"Yeah."

"So, here's Cam buying all the Popsicles in the Lower Mainland when it hits me—my AmEx bouncing."

"He ran it up?"

"Must have got my account number off a statement. Threw him and his shopping cart of Popsicles out, neighbor looking at me like I was a crazy woman."

"And Dara?"

"She took off after him."

"She'll be back." He kissed her mouth, fumbling with her buttons. "You know the one thing I don't get?"

"What's that?"

"How *Jerry Springer*'s still on the air."

THE ONCE - OVER

"This thing's getting complicated," Dom said, dumping a packet of sugar into his coffee, not sure if that was two or three.

"Why they pay us the big bucks," Luca said, looking over, watching Vince stack packs of roasted beans behind the counter. Something about the guy told Luca he was up to more than grinding coffee beans, Luca's cop instinct telling him the something wasn't good.

"Loot called, told me the Drug Squad's working it, too."

"Our case?"

"Yeah, looks like everybody wants Artie Poppa—say they got somebody on the inside, but that's all they're giving up. Loot says we run everything by them, not wanting to put their guy in danger."

"Give and take, as in we give and they take."

"Beyond our pay-grade bullshit," Dom said.

"So what've we got on the dead guy in the john besides a name?"

Dom flipped open his notes and read, "Wolf Klinger. Guy was a welder going on two years with Millennium, ran with the Throttle Rockets in a younger day, same puppet gang Jeffery Potts ran with on the Island. Also an alumnus from Matsqui, served there the same time as Potts."

"Coincidence, huh? Ballistics turn anything up on Potts?"

"They dug out the slug that went through Potts. Shooter picked up his shell. No way to match the extractor marks on the brass base without it."

"Yeah, and Potts?"

"Residue on his fingers, but no sign of a piece. Crime scene dug a .357 slug from a neighbor's tree, but no gun, bumper off a pickup or van, but no license plate, and one crumpled mailbox."

"What else we got?"

"Potts had trafficking priors linking him to Poppa," Dom said. "That, and Artie's boy Stax Arlis, guy at the coffee shop, got spotted coming out of Chickie's diner with another known scumbag, Miro Knotts."

"What's the connection?"

"This guy Knotts got picked up in a raid in Abbotsford couple years back. Again, ties to Artie. Lately, he's been working south of the border."

"And?"

"Just fled back, ducking the feds looking for extradition."

"Dope charges?"

"Get this, the idiot shot a farm animal thinking it was big game—jumped bail, ducked restitution, got a two-year suspended DOC."

"Just what we need."

"Top it off, the family of some fifteen-year-old's looking to drag his ass into civil court."

"A real peach."

"Yeah."

BUM'S RUSH

If the scene was on a postcard, the caption would have read, "NASCAR's the sport, bingo's the pastime, and squirrel's the dish—welcome to Shitstain." That's what Mitch was thinking about the place, sitting in his lawn chair next to his car, the Camry dying of cancer.

Not much of an exchange between Miro and Mitch, the two of them sitting and waiting for Wally to show up. Miro chain-smoking his Newports—the reason why they were sitting out in the drizzle in the first place. No way Mitch was having his double-wide smelling like an ashtray, not with what was going on in his gut these days.

All Stax told him on the phone was he had something else for them, wanted him and Wally to have a sit-down with this guy Miro, said he was sending him over, Mitch hoping whatever it was, it worked out better than the last time. So far the only thing that passed for conversation between them was when Mitch asked about the clock without any hands. Miro lifted his sleeve, giving Mitch a better look at the prison tat on his forearm, Miro telling him it meant doing time. Mitch asked where he did it, Miro saying he didn't like talking about it, tugging the sleeve back down, sliding his duffel bag under the chair, trying to keep it dry. And that was that.

Puffing away, Miro sat scraping at his thumbnail, thinking it would be noon before the hangover faded. The chick named Bruna James worked at the topless shoeshine joint downstairs and two doors over. Miro had let her buff his Tony Lamas, the snakeskin ones that matched his shoulder holster, the boots reserved for clubbing, the heels giving him the right lift. Asking her up for a drink, they had drained the Southern Comfort, Miro having to take a rain check on getting to know her in the biblical sense. Maybe, when he got back, he'd give it another shot. Funny, he never had trouble getting it up back when he was with Pinkie Fox, drunk or sober, the only other older chick he'd ever been with, back before Pinkie dumped him for Loop, another loser who worked for Artie. Another score he needed to settle.

The drizzle picked up, angling between the low-rent rooftops, the houses little more than trailers with the wheels knocked off. Miro guessed what he smelled over the Newport was coming from the wastewater treatment plant, a half block away, a smell as foul as farts. A crippled Ford hung a foot over Mitch's parking pad, cinder blocks wedged behind the wheels, an old Lund tipped against it, a patch of grass as tall as prairie wheat.

The neighbor came out of his place, giving a wave and walking by soaked bedsheets on a line sagging to the ground, wicking up dirt. Angling his satellite dish that hung off his eavestrough, the guy hurried back inside, yelling for his wife to get her goddamned laundry in the house.

"So where the fuck's your guy?" Miro asked, looking at the girders of the Lions Gate Bridge looming above them, cars zipping to and from downtown.

Pulling out his cell, Mitch punched in a number, calling over to a bunch of boys while it rang, telling them to get their butts inside before they caught their deaths, the boys doing their own yelling, getting a tennis ball past their black Lab and raising hockey sticks in victory. Mitch telling Miro their old man was down in the Capilano fishing with his drinking buddies.

The crunching gravel got Mitch looking. A two-tone Blazer that was around back when Joe Clark took office, its left headlight out, rolled up, its rocker panel chewed by rust.

Mitch stopped dialing, sighing as he said, "Here he is."

Wally stepped out with that shit-eating grin and his do-rag, jeans stuffed into high-tops. He held up the license plate he'd taken from the grow house, then threw a thumb back at the truck as it death-rattled, like he was saying, "Get a load of this heap."

"This is him, huh?" Miro asked, sizing up Mitch's partner. "He the one that got Jeffery's piece?"

"Yeah," Mitch said, fanning at the smoke, his bowels churning. "The plate, too." Pointing at it in Wally's hand.

Miro lit a fresh Newport off the last one, grinding his heel on the butt, watching Wally, the guy smacking gum, eyes peering over sunglass rims with that stupid thing on his head and a three-day growth looking like dirt.

"Think you and Stax owe us a little thank-you," Wally said, holding the plate out to Miro, adding, "That and a few bucks would be nice."

Miro ignored the plate, saying, "You want, I can tell you what to do with it."

"Guys that hit the grow house, came off their van."

"Fucking thing was stolen."

Wally looked at the plate, thought a moment, then tossed it down. Turning, he said, "Hey, Mitch buddy, you know it's raining, right?" Wally wiped at his lenses, looking at the stainless sky, then at Miro like he just beamed in. "Weather chick's calling this 'June-uary.'"

Mitch got up, saying they could go in, then gave another yell to the Tesche boys, guessing their mother was face down on her couch again.

"So, you're Merle, huh?" Wally cocked his hand for a handshake, gangsta style.

Miro corrected him on the name, then on the handshake, taking his hand old-school.

"Miro, okay," Wally said. "That French or something?"

"Not even close," Miro said. "But I'm guessing your Swatch needs a battery." Miro ground his cigarette on the stoop and angled by Mitch.

Wally followed, lifting his sleeve, holding the Rolex Datejust for Miro to see. "Swatch is for losers, Merle."

"That a street model or you going to tell me it's the real deal?" Miro put the bag down in the thrown-together living room and sat on the arm of the sofa, looking around Mitch's dump, the place big enough for Lilliputians.

"Guess I could tell you anything," Wally said, sinking into the cushion, grinning, nothing friendly about it. "Got a spare one of those?" He pointed at the pack of smokes in Miro's shirt pocket, guessing the guy styled his own hair.

Miro reached for his Newports, pegging Wally for thirty, a guy who video-gamed himself into mental lethargy, known to police for small-time shit.

"I got instant if you boys want," Mitch said.

"Long as it's hot," Miro said, tapping the bottom of his pack, the cigarettes popping up, Wally saying who the fuck smoked menthols and reached for one anyway, guessing Miro was from the States, guessing maybe gay, too.

"Heard me say no smoking, right?" Mitch said.

Wally tucked it behind an ear, then he said to Miro, "Okay, how about we get down to it, see what you got?"

51

"What I got is what we're here for," Miro said, wanting to get this over and get in a cab back to his place, slip under the covers with Bruna with the fever hot skin, the paw print tat on her thigh and those perfect tits. He hooked the duffel's strap with his shoe and dragged it close. "Got here on time, too, without any fake watch."

"Makes you feel any better," Wally said, watching Mitch fill the kettle, "froze my nuts blue jumping that piece of shit." Throwing a glance at the Blazer parked out front, he showed Miro the grease on his fingers.

"You jacked that?" Miro said.

"Need her for a job. Got her wired and running about two miles before she starts knocking, alternator light going like it's fucking Christmas. I pull into this Esso, and my foot goes through the floor—fucking hole this big."

"You swiped Fred Flintstone's ride," Miro said, drawing back the bag's zipper.

"Think it's too much to ask people to keep up with simple maintenance?" Wally said, "I mean, what does a tub of fucking Bondo set you back?"

"Guy wears a Rolex and his ride's got a hole in the floor, go figure," Miro said to Mitch, lifting the bag to his lap.

"You didn't get picked for the team much when you were a kid, did you, Merle?"

Miro reached in and hooked a Glock G21 by the trigger guard. "I'm the guy did the picking, still do. One thing I'll tell you, friend, I didn't come all this way to wait while you played at jacking shitboxes."

Wally took the piece, checking it out. "You think a guy that can get any vintage you want and get it going with a screwdriver is playing?" Wally pulled a joint from his pocket, straightened it and stuck it in his mouth, talking around it, waving the pistol all over the place. "Give this old boy an antenna, and I'll give you the Ford it belongs to. Don't believe me, ask Mitch."

"Yeah, makes his momma proud," Mitch said, getting out the mugs, all three of them chipped.

"You say import." Wally took out his Bic. "And I'll crank over a rice burner with just a pair of scissors. That sound like I'm playing, Merle?"

"I ever need a shitbox, you're my man," Miro said, moving the barrel pointing at him.

"Yeah, and you'll have it in about two seconds flat. I never touch the late models. Know why that is?" He flicked the lighter and lit the joint.

"Guess I'm about to," Miro said.

"Late models are for the guys that want to become somebody's hump in the joint." Wally toked, looking at the tat showing below Miro's sleeve. "These days it's all laser-cut keys, high-tech alarms and tracking shit. Freezing an alarm system with liquid nitrogen takes that extra minute, you know what I mean?"

"Me, I just look for one left unlocked, with the keys in it," Miro said, reaching in the bag again.

"Yeah, that could work," Wally said, putting the Glock down.

"Okay, everybody's got a big dick," Mitch said, coming around the counter and snatching the joint from Wally's mouth, going back and spooning Sanka into the mugs, clanging the spoon down. "How about we cut the shit and get on with it?" Mitch felt like giving Wally the bum's rush, Wally telling him to take it easy.

Miro leaned into the duffel and laid a Smith & Wesson .357 on the table, saying they were both clean.

Wally went for the Smith, leaving the Glock for Mitch.

"Like 'em small, huh?" Miro asked Wally.

"Like them fast, but I'm pretty happy with what I got."

"That being Jeffery's hand cannon?" Miro asked, watching Wally slap the blued steel from one palm to the other like some street punk, then aiming it sideways.

"All the gun I need."

"You work with me and Stax, you hand it over."

"Fuck that."

"*Ballistics*, you know that word, Wally? You hand it to me, along with that plate, then we'll talk about doing business."

"Suppose I say no?"

"Then Stax comes to see you."

Wally thought about it, looked out at his ride and said the Python was under the seat. "Sure hope I don't see you with it next time we meet."

"Me, I pack a Ruger, a Vaquero," Miro said, getting used to the new one after the wildlife guys confiscated the one he used on the ram.

"Like 'em old, huh?" Wally said. "A cowboy gun, six-shooter, ain't it?"

"Ever hear the name Bob Munden?" Miro asked.

"That the game-show guy, Merle?"

"The Munden I'm talking about is the guy I'm as fast as." Miro drew two fingers, extending them at Wally's forehead. "Tell you one more time, the name's Miro."

Wally brushed the fingers away.

"Bob was a revolver man, got more trophies than anybody, fastest man alive," Miro said. "Got himself in the Guinness book." ·

"No shit, huh? You got anything else?"

"Think I'm going to carry a Kimber Raptor, a Sig Sauer Combat, a Colt Python and a Walther around with me?"

"You got a Walther?" Mitch brought the mugs over and set them down, picking up the Glock, checking its action.

"Yeah, a P5, same kind the Kraut cops use."

"Not much good to us under your mattress, Merle." Wally flipped open the Smith's cylinder, one-eyeing inside.

Miro went to snatch it from him.

Wally pulled it back. "Just kidding around, Merle. Take it easy and say what you want for these."

Miro looked at Mitch, wondering how you fuck up instant, then said to Wally, "Eight bills—nine if you say Merle again."

Wally let out a low whistle, sipping his Sanka.

"Let's call it six, but I want to take a look at the Walther," Mitch said.

"What I'm not is fucking Walmart. You boys can do better, be my guest." Miro tossed the shells back in the bag, reaching for the pistols. "I'll tell Stax you're out."

"Hey, we're here now, right?" Wally checked his watch, fishing a wad of bills from his stash pocket, counting off his half. "Eight bills, you say. Let's do this; I got somebody waiting." He didn't say Merle again, figuring he pushed Miro's buttons enough.

"Look, I don't know you guys from Adam," Miro said. "But Stax says you guys are right for this job."

"What's the job?"

"One we've got brewing."

"Bank job?" Wally asked. "Surveillance, armed guards, tellers with alarm buttons, exploding dye packs, shit like that?"

"You done?" Miro asked.

"Yeah."

"Tell you this much, what we take we take from those who can't call the cops." Miro wasn't sure which one was Mutt and which one was Jeff, but Stax was right about one thing: here were two losers nobody was going to miss.

SWATTING THE HIVE

Karl picked up his serves at Sea-to-Sky, making chitchat with Bob and Joyce, the two of them exactly as Marty Schmidt had described them, Joyce inviting him and PJ over for drinks and a hot tub, saying she whips up a mean screwdriver, Karl saying he'd get back to her. Getting on the elevator, he checked his watch, pressing the button for PJ's floor, thoughts of an early lunch, treating her while she waited for her new AmEx to show up. Rifling through the serves, he spotted the envelope from Global Trace. The elevator pinged off the floors, and his cell rang. The display told him who it was.

"Hey, Marty, speak of the devil."

"Hey buddy, you get my mail?"

"You're turning psychic on me?" Karl said. "I'm holding it in my hand—just got it." He tore it open.

"Man, wish I could see the look on that Knott-fuck's face when you do your thing."

Karl pulled out the photocopies of the U.S. bench warrant, skimming over it.

"You find out where he is?"

"I'm working on it."

"Well, hey," Marty said, "I hereby volunteer to drag his ass back."

"I'll tell him you said hello."

"You do that."

Hanging up, Karl was feeling the old excitement, the thrill of the chase, the old Lady Luck. How good it would feel to drag Miro across the border, hand him off to Marty. The elevator stopped and he stepped off, seeing PJ through the glass door of Walt Wetzel Legal.

TALKING TWO-BIT

Wally was showing off again, not with the Rolex this time, but with Sunny. Not enough meat on her bones for Miro's taste, but still more than a guy like Wally rated. He hadn't paid her much mind when he was in here with Stax yesterday. To him, she looked like a hooker Barbie with a cute face and perky tits, one of those turned-up noses and big hair like disco chicks wore back in the day.

Setting his pack of Newports on the table, Miro draped his arm over the back of the seat, the vinyl squeaking—everything going to plan, running it through his head: Artie set to bolt with his safe full of cash, Stax sure it was in Artie's house up in the Properties. These two clowns break in, find it, bust into it, steal the cash and end up dead. Miro sets Karl Morgen up to take the fall, and him and Stax end up rich.

"You with us, Merle?" Wally asked.

"Waiting for you to shut up," Miro said, seeing Chickie behind the serving window, sweating and waving his arms like a conductor over his patties and wings—the prices as low as the fare.

Rain beat on the seamless roof, loud enough that Mitch and Wally had to lean in to hear Miro. In spite of the run of bad weather and the Tim's and Wendy's across the street, the usual crowd from the retail stores and the North Van shipyards filled the place.

Wally told them he was getting Sunny to quit this dump, how he was coming in solo one night to catch Chickie with his greasy fingers on the day's take, teach him a lesson for serving this shit. Miro said that was real Robin Hood of him, Sunny scooting back with mugs and a coffee pot, her hair bouncing past her shoulders. Setting the mugs down, she poured and gave their table a wipe, her breasts jiggling inside her uniform. Wally slipped his hand around her waist like he was claiming his territory.

Miro could see Sunny wasn't retarded, so she had to be doing tricks on the side to let a guy like Wally put his hands on her. To him, the girl was no Bruna, but he made sport out of checking her out, liking that it pissed Wally off. Playing with her, asking for a three-egg omelette, smiling as she explained Chickie only did what was on the menu: a one- or two-egg omelette with a choice of topping. He ordered a two-egger and told her for a topping he wanted an egg. Twirling a curl around her finger, she said Chickie would have her for lunch if she asked him that. Miro said so would he, but he didn't see her on the menu, liking that she laughed. Then he ordered a round of cheeseburgers and rings for the table, eyes on her as she went to the pickup window.

"I got to ask again, you with us, Merle?" Wally checked his Rolex, helping himself to a smoke.

"Right here."

"So, how about we get to it," Wally said, tired of Miro's game, pouring cream in his cup.

Miro leaned in, saying, "No offense, boys, but what you're into's a little high school. Pulling B and Es and muling dope, come on, man. You're better than that." He said it but doubted it, getting up, saying he was going to the can, looking over at Chickie through the pass window, the guy tossing patties on the grill, a drop of sweat forming at the tip of his fleshy nose. Coming back, he looked over just as the drop of sweat dripped from Chickie's nose onto a patty on the grill.

Sunny came back and set down a ketchup and vinegar trolley, flicking Wally's hand from her hip, thanking Miro for the twenty he laid down, not saying anything about there being no smoking.

Wally snatched the bill and tossed it back at Miro. "You want to talk talk, just cut the horse shit, Merle."

"What's eating you?" Miro said, winking at her.

"In this country, you eat, then you pay," Wally said, then to Sunny, "Ever have a gunslinger give you a tip before, doll?"

"Not with you around," she said, saying she'd catch Miro later, and walked back behind the counter.

Wally took out a coin and flipped it. Heads, he'd deck this bucktoothed freak, show him a thing or two. Tails. He lit up and eased back, catching Sunny handing a menu to a guy who worked road crew sitting on a stool at the counter. The orange vest, hard hat on the counter, unlaced work boots, jeans riding low showing his crack. The guy was bitching about the piss-poor service, pointing over at Wally smoking. Sunny was apologizing all over the place, saying the other girl called in sick, hurrying to the pickup window and pinning his order to the rack.

"My guess, I'm looking at two guys ready for a bigger slice," Miro said. "Am I right?"

Wally was still eyeing the road-crew guy, then tapping the tat on Miro's forearm, saying, "The kind of slice that gets you one of these?"

"The trick's to minimize the risk and maximize the payoff," Miro said. "What else you need to know?"

"Want to know how do you call this a cigarette?" Wally stubbed the menthol on his saucer.

Mitch asked Miro to go on.

Miro dumped a third creamer in his cup, hoping to kill the bitter edge, saying, "Basically we hit outside the law."

"You mean the burbs?" Wally grinned.

"I mean a place that's got thirty Gs worth of bud." He looked from one to the other, banking that neither of them had any idea what top-grade bud really went for. "It's the new bathtub gin. Maybe you read about it on the net?"

"Sure, customers who bought B.C. bud also bought X and crack."

Sunny came back and set their burgers and rings down, said something to Wally about not smoking.

"Where'd you find this guy?" Miro asked Mitch, then said to Wally after Sunny left, "What you don't know, smart guy, I blueprinted Artie Poppa's grow houses, every one of them, set up the microclimates, retrofit the electrical and ventilation systems, the sequencers, drying systems, everything. Came up with the nutrient formulations, all the bells, all the whistles, all the stuff you know shit about." Looking around, he saw Chickie's glistening forehead, guessed more sweat was building on his nose.

"That'll look good on a resume, Merle, but don't go thinking I don't know shit," Wally said, picking up Miro's cigarette pack, helping himself to another one, throwing a look at the road-crew guy, hoping he'd say something.

"Let the man talk, for fuck's sake," Mitch said to Wally, taking a bite, his stomach churning. He remembered reading about the cops busting a pot operation at the old Molson brewery in Barrie a few years back, something like thirty million bucks of the shit. A handful of arrests for something the cops figured had been running for over a year. Man, what he could do with a piece of something like that.

"Set up the first grow house in a bunker out in Abbotsford," Miro said. "Back when you were in short pants."

"Yeah, yeah, way back, heard about it from my granny," Wally said, squeezing mustard on his burger. "Time of peace and groovy shit, right?" Wally turned to the counter, the road-crew guy giving Sunny flack again on account of the smoke.

"Maybe I'm talking to the wrong guys." Miro pushed his burger away, picked up an onion ring, considered the grease on his fingers and tossed it back.

"Point is, you're not talking," Mitch said, the Big Bowl Breakfast still sloshing around below, making a poor foundation for the burger and rings. He said to Wally around a mouthful, "And how about you let him get a word out, and maybe we'll get somewhere."

"Whatever." Wally wagged a hand, looking at Miro's burger. "You don't want that?"

Miro shoved the plate to him and leaned forward. "Here it is, we're going to hit Artie Poppa again." Miro straightened as Sunny came back, knowing why she was coming, saying to her, "You got an ashtray for your boyfriend here, doll?"

She smirked. "Sure, right out back next to the rolling pins and broom handles. Come on, guys, I'm catching a lot of crap here."

Wally turned, eyes on the road-crew guy, blowing a smoke ring in his direction, grinning as the guy turned away.

Miro took Wally's hand and dunked the cigarette in his coffee, saying as Sunny left, "So, like I was saying, there's thirty Gs of bud waiting."

"Along with armed stoners and pit dogs," Wally said, tossing the soggy butt on the floor, wiping his hand with Miro's napkin.

"I just sold you boys some serious fire power, didn't I?" Miro looked from one to the other. "All Artie's got at this place are two fuck-ups that keep watch, and one of them's a chick." Miro grinned, thinking of Pinkie and Loop guarding the place, Wally right for once about the armed stoners, saying to him, "House full of six-footers, cured and ready for the taking. And we've got a buyer standing by with twenty-five large."

"You just said thirty," Mitch said.

"Yeah, minus expenses."

"Like what?"

Miro waved his hand like that didn't matter, saying, "Look, this place's got sealed ventilation. How we do it is we tap into the air conditioning unit out back, pump in enough nitrous oxide to put anyone inside on their ass. Worst thing they'll do is drool on your shoes while we walk out with their bud."

"Where we getting this gas?"

"All part of the expenses."

"So how come you and Stax don't work for this Poppa guy anymore?" Mitch asked.

"Got my reasons. As for Stax, you'd have to—"

"Hey, if we're going to do this . . ." Wally started.

Miro looked out at the rain. "Okay, I worked a field for him in the Okanagan, another one over in Chilliwack back before the whole works went indoors. When it did go indoors, I put it together for him till the asthma put me out."

"Asthma, huh?"

"Dampness had me going through puffers like a junkie."

Wally asking, "But you still smoke the shit?"

"Bothers some, others not so much. Me, I'm one of the lucky ones."

"Yeah, that's great, Merle," Wally said. "So what's the split?"

"Fifty fifty," Miro said.

"You mean a third each," Wally said.

"No, I mean fifty for you two, fifty for me and Stax."

"And he's doing what?"

"He's the guy who runs things for Artie, our guy inside. You guys were there when Jeffery bought it, right? Figure it out."

"Poppa tied in with anybody, bikers or that Circle gang, people like that?" Mitch asked.

"You been reading the papers, huh? Catch the bit about the politicians and the RCMP cracking down. Look, Artie's an old dude with a pacemaker, more interested in getting his putt right than spending his last days in prison."

"He's just going to stand by and let us take it, huh?" Wally scratched under his do-rag.

"We stick to the plan, we go in invisible and come out rich, and Stax sends Artie in the wrong direction. Again."

They didn't look convinced.

"Look, there's another part to this, even bigger." Miro leaned close. "Artie's planning to check out, and he's keeping a stash of cash at his own place, mansion up in the Properties."

"You want to hit him twice?"

"The mansion first, then the other."

"How much cash we talking?" Wally asked.

Miro said there was no way of knowing for sure, then told them about the drug lord whose house got raided in Mexico City, the DEA and Mexican cops seizing over two hundred million in bills stuffed inside his villa walls. "Only difference, Artie keeps his in a safe."

"Where's this safe?"

"A couple of sharp guys shouldn't have too much trouble finding something the size of a safe, right? You tap out a back window while Artie's getting himself good and healthy down on his nude beach. Hey, why am I telling you?"

"And if there's no safe?"

"There's five hundred bucks in it either way. You find it or not, you make five bills just for showing up."

"Where are you going to be?"

"Getting you the five bills." Miro looked from one to the other and knew he had them. "Just be sure the sun's shining when you go in."

MANO A MANO

Wally flipped a coin and said he was going to hang back for Sunny's shift to end. What he did, he went up to Third for a decent cup of coffee and got himself the bold pick of the day, preferring Starbucks over Tim's, came back and stepped back inside to tell her he'd be waiting. The construction guy was still shoveling it in, bitching about finding one of Sunny's hairs in his rice pudding, Wally figuring the guy should be so lucky.

Turning around, Wally went around to the parking spots, no windows on that side of the diner. The pickup had Karlson Construction painted down the side in orange, a Ford from before the time of alarms and airbags. He tried it—the door unlocked—taking out his all-in-one. If he hadn't downed two orders of burgers and rings, he would have waited and done the guy mano a mano. Getting in, he inserted the screwdriver into the ignition, slapped the handle with the butt of his hand just hard enough and had her purring in no time flat.

Rolling onto Cotton and through the intersection, he

burped up onion and lit a Newport from the pack he'd lifted off the table. Chirping the tires, he coasted along Third to where it became Marine, spinning the radio knob until he found Rock 101, the afternoon DJ putting on "Thunder Road" after saying he was giving away Springsteen tickets to the first ten callers. Wally dialed the station's number, getting a busy signal. The Boss had really rocked that time at the Tacoma Dome. Hitting redial like a Morse operator he slowed along the detour lane, still burping onion, getting a busy tone every try.

The bridge crew was busy slamming the piles for the bridge over the Capilano, Marine Drive reduced to two lanes, Wally checking out the flagger chicks. To Wally's way of thinking, traffic was getting more fucked every time an immigrant stepped off a boat. An extra bridge lane wasn't going to make a shit bit of difference. He drove past Park Royal, remembering the bowling alley, movie theater and driving range, back when there was stuff to do in West Van besides shop.

Pulling into Ambleside Park, he turned past the sailing club, a couple of parked cars and a truck with its trailer. Lining the pickup nose first on the boat ramp, Wally ground his cigarette on the passenger seat, burning through the cheap vinyl.

Nobody around except an Asian guy tossing a crab trap from the pier. Getting out, he took the toolbox from the truck's bed, setting it on the gas pedal. The fisherman looked over, Wally giving him a wave, then he threw the stick into drive. The pickup rode down the ramp until the salt water rose over the Karlson lettering, swirling into the cab before the engine stalled. The guy fishing couldn't believe it, Wally calling to him, "You Chinese ain't the only ones can't drive worth a shit."

Strolling like he had all day, he made his way back to

Marine, happy with the way this day turned out, passing the West Van cop shop, a sign out front warning visitors about swooping birds nesting overhead. It got him laughing— swooping birds too much for the boys in blue. It brought up an idea he had been playing with since he was in high school: decals of a big donut with a hole. The idea was to stick them over the *O* in the word police, tag every squad car in town, give every pig in town a donut.

Fishing around in his pocket for bus fare, burping onion again, he wondered how much was in Artie's safe. Maybe he'd get some wheels with style, something like an Escalade with vanity plates. Good time to pick one up. Checking his Rolex, he figured he'd just catch Sunny if the bus was on time.

The doorbell rang, and PJ
shook her hands over the sink,
wiped them on her jeans and
went to get it. She let Dara in.

NOSEY PARKER

"I'm just here for my stuff" was all Dara said, nothing
friendly in her voice, not meeting her mother's eyes, waiting
for PJ to step aside.

"You didn't have to go, just him."

"Yeah, you're in the clear, Mother, and his name's Cam,"
Dara said, heading for the staircase. "And he's part of my life
now, and for your information, he's doing the best he can."

"Collecting Popsicle sticks?"

"Wrappers, not sticks, and you didn't have to mess with
his self-esteem."

"Okay he messed up my credit?" PJ was doing her best to
keep a lid on her temper.

Dara turned back down the hall. "He's got every intention
of paying you back, Mother."

"He working?"

"He's looking."

"Lucky I didn't have him arrested."

"Oh my God, listen to yourself." Dara walked into the kitchen and stopped, looking at Karl sitting over a cup of coffee. "Who's this?"

"This is Karl," PJ said, right behind her. "I've mentioned him. Karl, this is Dara."

Karl nodded, saying it was nice to meet her, stretched and offered his hand. She was the spitting image of her mother, add a nose piercing, the Joan Jet hair and eagle-claw tattoo on the side of her neck, a big skull ring on her finger. Dara looked at his hand before giving it a shake.

"Better be careful not to spill any of that," she warned him, looking at his cup.

Karl knew when to shut up.

"Where are you staying—with him?" PJ asked.

"Of course with Cam." Dara went to the fridge, got out a bottle of 2%. "We're at a friend's."

"That's ridiculous. Your home is here."

"Rent it out any time you want," Dara said, popping the lid. "I won't be back."

"Fine, tell me where to forward your stuff." PJ stopped herself from telling Dara to use a glass.

"I'd write it down, but you'd pull another nosey parker, get your lawyer boss snooping around like you did with Rudy." She took a drink.

"Rudy was a stalker for crying out loud. God, wake up, Dara."

"Yes, then I'll have a perfect life like yours, Mother? What about you, Karl, are you perfect?"

"Leave him out of it."

"Tell him what you did to Rudy," Dara said, drinking the milk, getting a mustache. "Give him a true picture."

"Just get what you came for, Dara. We'll talk when . . . whenever."

"We're beyond that, don't you think, Mother?" Dara left the bottle on the counter and went up the stairs, calling over her shoulder, "At least until you apologize."

PJ looked at Karl like can you believe this kid and called after her, "You have money?"

"I'll figure something out."

PJ went to her handbag and took out her wallet, frowning at the five-dollar bill. Karl dug the roll from his pocket and peeled off a few twenties. She started to object, then took the money and held it out when Dara came down the stairs, a backpack slung over her shoulder. Dara took it without a word and was out the door.

"Thanks." PJ put the milk in the fridge, sat across from him and drank from his cup.

"No problem," he said.

She looked at him. "I should have sent that kid to Jesus Camp." She knew if she started to cry she'd never stop.

SMALL POTATOES

The reason Mitch was on the Coast in the first place was on account of what happened back in the Hat. Back when he and Tolley were drinking Wild Turkey like tap water. Buddies since grade school, Mitch and Tolley broke into just about every place worth talking about up and down the South Saskatchewan River around Medicine Hat and Redcliff. Some they did twice.

Most of the stuff they sold at Ernie's Second-Hand Shop. Ernie was a cheap geezer but didn't ask questions about the Evinrudes and Colemans and microwaves. Things worked out until Tolley hung an eight-point trophy head they took from Jackson's Lodge over a hot La-Z-Boy, the Cadillac of recliners.

Inviting Ginny McNamara over a week after she said *sayonara* to Mitch undid the partnership. To Tolley, if Mitch was through with her what was the harm? Mixing up a pitcher of syn, equal parts gin and cognac, he got Ginny good and comfy on the chair under the antlers. Mitch walked in on them and ко'ed Tolley with the pitcher, the La-Z-Boy wicking up the syn, broken glass everywhere, Ginny screaming she never wanted to see him again.

Packing up his hockey bag, Mitch took his Washburn down to the bus depot next morning. He got on a Greyhound without so much as comparing WestJet fares, and didn't look back.

Last time Mitch called home, Uncle Harmon told him Aunt Paula was in for bunion surgery, leaving him to choke on his own porridge. Mitch remembered the stuff, the consistency of wallpaper paste. His uncle mentioned he read in the *Herald* how Tolley pleaded guilty to two counts of armed robbery, the judge handing him three to five in Lethbridge Correctional, his uncle saying he always knew that kid was trouble, Mitch saying yeah. When he hung up, Mitch wondered what Ginny was doing these days.

Now here he was with Wally, the two of them not seeing eye to eye on much, Mitch tired of breaking into places, Wally sick of taking the slim jim and jacking shitty rides like the Blazer with the hole in the floor, seeing himself going for prestige autos that get shipped to places like Latvia. Each blaming the other for their light takes.

Mitch's share from hitting Artie Poppa would rent a place on the South Saskatchewan, have him eating at Tumbleweeds and playing golf in the Badlands, start taking care of himself. With Tolley in jail, he could show up at Ginny's door in a new outfit with a handful of flowers.

He filed it away, walking into the Small Potatoes, past the grocery's welcome mat, two minutes behind Wally, one coming in for bagels, the other for Taster's Choice and the morning edition.

Mitch adjusted the shades, his hair combed back, a tie and jacket on, Glock tucked in his pants, looking like he was heading for work down on Burrard. He passed Wally; the ball cap replacing the do-rag and the day-old beard giving him the look of a man who gathered empties and squeegeed windshields.

The tip came from Sunny, one she'd garnered in Chickie's parking lot, same spot Karlson's pickup had stood in, Sunny on her knees in the back of Pimms' Lumina, doing some service providing. Wine-sopped Ray Pimms crowed what a big cheese he was over at Small Potatoes, how the weekend cash stayed in the safe in his office until the Monday morning pickup. That's when the Churchill car would roll in, forty minutes from now.

The store was quiet this time of day, no white-haired security guard until ten, only one cashier and a floater on, the Chinese girl's Coke-bottle glasses distorting her eyes. The braces on her teeth gave her the look of a bot.

A retiree leaned on a walker by the magazine carousel, getting himself a good helping of Hollywood bullshit. Hair tucked under a babushka, a mother pushed her shopping cart to the express aisle. Her boy, about three, sat in the cart kicking his feet, ripping into a Snyder's pretzel bag. The older sister acting like the mother, snapped the bag from his fingers and laid it on the conveyer.

Wally took up his post by the pyramid of bunny-shaped mac and cheese, tugging down the ball cap, feigning interest in the special: three packs for the price of two. He covered the exit, keeping an eye on the Blazer dripping oil in the handicapped spot out front. He couldn't help overhearing the conversation, the mother arguing with the chick that looked like a bot.

Tossing something that looked like yellow sausage into his basket, Mitch went up aisle four, wondering what the fuck polenta was. Checking out the granola and muesli, he got himself psyched, grabbing a bag of Skeet & Ike's Original.

From behind the shades, he made out the window upstairs where Pimms had his office, Mitch practising the scene in his mind: show Pimms the Glock, give him a good dose of piss-your-pants and force him to dial open the safe, crack him over the head and hustle out as Wally fires up the shitbox before the alarms go off. Then six blocks to Mitch's Camry, ditch the Blazer in the alley out back of the Sally Ann and cruise along Marine to his double-wide with Wally lying on the passenger floor. The cops whizzing by would be on the lookout for two guys in a shitbox Blazer.

Mitch angled around a woman taking up most of the aisle. Leaning over her buggy, she studied the fine print on a bag of Dad's, her perfume like repellant.

His eyes were on Pimms' window, seeing him on the phone. Hearing his own name hit him like Iron Mike—that voice and the Yuzu Fou scent. He turned, looking at the hip-huggers, the freckled cleavage and the cauliflower 'do. She'd racked up a couple of dress sizes, her name was on the tip of his tongue, something with an L. Her mouth turned up showing red lipstick on her teeth.

She had been his first mistake after stepping off the Greyhound from the Hat a year ago. A reminder of how much he drank back then. She had called him on a notice he pinned on the bulletin board at the community center: "Need a house painter, call Mitch."

Sitting at her kitchen table with her husband, Lester, and a handful of paint chips, Mitch came up with a price for doing two coats of Whisper White. Lester with his jowels hanging, not giving a shit, told L it was up to her, and he left her to take care of things. And that's what she did. Convulsing and squealing under him, she used her plastic nails on Mitch's cheeks like spurs. Happened every day he showed up for work, Lester leaving for the club on account he hated the smell of paint.

Slipping the sunglasses into a pocket, he gave her a how you doing, babe?

"How you doing yourself, Mitchie?" she said, batting those throw-the-Christians-to-the-lions spider lashes. The plastic fingernails hooked his sleeve. "You lose my number?"

"You kidding?" He forced a smile. "Been meaning to call, but you know how things get." He glanced down the aisle, feeling trapped, searching for her name. "Anyway, what you been up to, babe?"

"Me? Jenny's got me counting calories." She smacked his arm with the Dad's bag. "Eighty calories, just for one fuckin' cookie? You believe it, Mitchie?" She tossed the bag at the shelf and came in and planted a wet one on him, leaving Berry Burst stamped on his mouth. She pulled back. "Into the cleanses and the spas, but I just can't resist the sweet stuff, you know me, Mitchie." She did a half-turn, appraising herself. "What the hell's wrong with being a size *zaftig*?"

He told her she was looking like a million, thinking, yeah pounds, guessing the diet was suet. Looking to the front where Wally was supposed to be, he felt his gut going like a carnival ride. No Wally by the mac and cheese.

"Stomach still acting up, Mitchie?" she said, watching him rub above his belt, taking his clammy hand in hers.

"Ah, gets funny when I don't eat. Ran out of cereal, so I uh . . . came down . . ." He took his hand back and looked at his wrist for the watch that wasn't there. "On my way to work, you know."

"Sure been a while, Mitchie." She stepped in close, turning her face up to his, saying she could use a fresh coat on her trim.

"Yeah, I'm booked up solid, babe."

"Yeah?"

"People getting their places done before the kids are out of school, you know."

"Sure you can squeeze me in, right, Mitchie?"

He said sure he could.

"Working in a tie now?" She flipped the clip-on.

"Threw in with an Italian outfit. Slip on the coveralls at work. You know me, hate walking around like a slob."

"Yeah, you got class, Mitchie. Got my attention right off. Hey, how about Cheerios at my place? You can eat while I show you what I want done."

"Have to take a rain check, doll." He looked at his wrist again.

"How about a juicy chop when you get off then—do some catching up?"

"Les on some business trip?"

"Les? Jesus, he's gone, Mitchie."

"He left you?" It didn't surprise him.

She pouted for a second, then picked up the smile. "Old Les should've gone for the Cheerios instead of wolfing sausages for forty years."

"You mean he's . . ."

"Right up on the mantle."

"Jesus."

"Yeah. Big C got him—those effing sausages."

"Really am sorry, doll."

"What are you going to do?"

Giving her arm a pat, he nodded and locked his cheeks, seeing the washroom sign by the shipping doors, right under Pimms' window, saying over his shoulder he'd bring a bottle of wine, asking red or white.

"Just bring your appetite, Mitchie." Those lashes winking at him. Her cell phone toned, and Mitch was moving, nearly shitting himself, bowels going like a washing machine, that Yuzu Fou scent doing a number. L answered her phone, wagging her fingers after him, a ring on every one, Mitch thinking those chubby digits looked like the sausages that killed Les.

When he came out of the can, he put the shades back on and stepped to the dairy aisle, glancing up at Pimms' window. Wally was nowhere to be seen. Feigning a choice dilemma between soy and rice yogurt, Mitch held the tubs, watching Pimms talking on the phone again, not much time left before the Churchill car showed up.

"You better show up, Mitchie," L called from produce. "You leave me hanging with my stuffed loin, I'll come hunting for you."

He looked over at her, standing by the cantaloupes, the produce guy glancing his way. That was it; it was off. Setting the yogurt back, Mitch headed for the exit, thinking where the fuck was Wally.

"Where the fuck were you?"
Both of them saying it at the same time.

BOTCHED

"You were supposed to be looking out." The pot smell was strong inside the Blazer, stinging Mitch's eyes. He stomped his foot down, felt the hole in the floor.

"Talk to the fucking bitch with the kids," Wally said, opening the glove box, pulling out a Twix. "She gets into it with the chink cashier, waving some fucked-up coupon, twenty-five cents off on Hellmann's. The chink tells her the coupon's expired, and the bitch starts going postal about it."

Mitch cracked his knuckles; no use trying to get in a word, he cranked down his window.

Wally took half the Twix in a bite. "I stepped away from the cash and see you hitting on the *hausfrau* with the jugs." He mimicked the size of L's breasts with his hands.

"Just somebody I used to know."

"So I said fuck it and walked out, called it off."

"And if I got to Pimms?"

"Why you think I'm sitting here? Ask me, looked like you forgot all about Pimms. Eight fucking bills for pistols . . ."

The Churchill car rolled into the lot, fourteen minutes early according to Wally's Rolex. The guy riding shotgun gave them a look, said something to the driver as they passed.

Finishing the bar, Wally put the wires together, and the Blazer's engine cranked over. Neither spoke until they were back at Mitch's double-wide. Calm now, Wally brought up doing this thing with Miro.

Mitch said he was still thinking it over, going down the hall into the can, leaving the door open.

Wally patted his pocket for a cigarette, saying it meant five hundred bucks, safe or no safe.

"Knew this guy Tolley back in the Hat," Mitch said. "Reminds me of Miro.

"Like how?"

"Both of them loose cannons." Mitch told how Tolley waltzed into this place called the Club Foote early on a Saturday with his hand in his pocket, yelling, "Don't stickin' move, this is a fuck up" at a bunch of old posties drinking rum coffee.

"He said it like that?"

"Yeah, was in the paper. My uncle read it to me."

"What'd he get?"

"The bejeezus beat out of him, old posties stomping the shit out of him with those Chukka boots they all wear."

Wally was laughing. "Fucking stupid hick."

"Judge went maximum on him," Mitch said.

"What the hell you doing working with a guy like that?"

"Like I said, he reminds me of Miro."

"So what?"

"So I'm mulling it over."

"What's to mull?"

"For one thing, we do all the work and him and Stax get half."

"Not if we roll the safe out the door and just keep rolling. Fuck half. The only thing we split's town."

GOES WITH LEATHER

"What about this one?" Karl asked PJ, sinking into the cushion, breathing that new-leather smell, checking the tag hanging from the arm. He stifled a yawn, tired from spending half the night tracking Miro's whereabouts, a rental agent Joyce Young knew finally getting him the address, right down to the postal code, Joyce reminding him about coming for drinks and a hot tub.

"You with us here, cowboy?" PJ asked, sensing the distraction.

"Place is like the inside of a giant maze, everything blue and yellow." Karl looked around for an exit sign. "Like buy something or you won't find your way out of here."

"You want to go?"

"No, no. Hey, let's do this."

"So, you like this one?" She pointed to the armchair.

"Yeah, it's good."

"It's got to be better than good."

"It's great."

"And you think it goes with the sofa?" The way PJ screwed up her face told him the answer. He said maybe not, but added it felt good on the back. The address he got for Miro was some flea-dive in Chinatown. He planned to scope it out tomorrow. He took a stab at pronouncing the name on the tag, getting up and angling around a couple checking out a room grouping, the woman correcting his Swedish.

Karl thanked her and sat on the Halmstad, picking up the tent card on the table that said something about a free gift certificate.

PJ sat opposite him on a Stjordal, asking, "Where are you?"

"Sorry—mind's on work. Anyway, okay, so far we like that one, right?" Pointing at a sofa.

"The Bekvam, yeah, it's a keeper. What we do, we focus around that, add accessories that go with it." She gave up on getting him over to Antique Row; he just wasn't ready for it. Probably be happy sitting at home and decorating from a catalog.

Along with the Bekvam, PJ had picked out an oak-veneered dining table and four chairs, calling it a good start, judging by his discreet yawning they were done. Time to go downstairs and arrange for delivery.

She tugged him past the restaurant, Karl saying the Swedish meatballs looked pretty good on the poster.

"You're taking me someplace with chairs that aren't plastic."

DOG EAT DOG

Wally was saying Ambleside was going to hell, counting the hair and nail salons along Marine. "Used to be you crossed the street and cars stopped, letting you walk, courteous as hell, people saying how you doing? Now, you step in the street, you get run over by fuckers never seen a crosswalk before. Racing to jobs they took from us." He turned up Fifteenth, the mountains before them, the last of the snow disappearing from the peaks. He asked if Mitch ever worked a nine-to-five.

"Painted for my uncle back in the Hat," Mitch said, thinking every time this guy got high, his mouth was moving.

"The Hat sounds like where Dr. Seuss lives."

"Fuck you know about it."

"Tried it once."

"Painting?"

"Working. Sold cardboard chairs one time," Wally said, checking street signs, looking for Chartwell.

"Who the fuck'd sit on cardboard?" Mitch pointed left.

"Lot, you know," Wally said, making the turn. "My first outdoor gig I sold fifty of them. Some band nobody heard of, Sailin' Shoes or something like that."

Wally turned into a driveway, parked the hot Caravan with the Mr. Rooter decal on the door. A sprawling Tudor with the crisscross leaded windows and a portico with posts, flower baskets, a triple car garage and a view of Grouse Mountain. Fifteen-foot-high laurels hid them from Chartwell. Garden gnomes with red hats sitting in a bed of impatiens pointed the way up the walk. Right this way, boys; help yourselves.

"Looks like Artie's doing alright," Wally said, tugging at the serviceman blues, checking the clip in his Smith, laying it in the toolbox. Getting out, he wheeled the dolly up the walk, moving like he was expected, taking the soggy newspaper drooping from the wrought-iron railing.

Mitch followed with the satchel and plunger and stuck his thumb on the doorbell, one of those chiming ones designed to amuse the rich. "Been thinking about going back to the Hat," he said, unsure why he would tell Wally, least of all now.

"Need to paint something?"

"I go back, I go back rich." Mitch pressed the bell again.

"Good attitude." Wally put a finger in the air like he was making a point. "Worked for this gimp one time named Ward Clark—had a wife he called Junebug, chunky but a nice pair of tits." He showed the size with his hands, leaning to look in the front window.

"So, what's—"

"I'm talking about attitude. Ward, see, guy put out a rag for and by the handicapped." Wally went down the steps first, pulling the dolly around to the side door, the wheels squeaking, kept right on talking, "Helped him out raising money, calling people from a stack of cards—some we hit up twice a month. Ward being the only gimp that ever saw a cent, minus my commish."

They passed a gate at the side, both of them looking around, Mitch wishing he'd shut up.

"Guy drove a Coupe de Ville, the thing rigged with special hand controls. Had a place like this by some lake, the wife walking around looking fine." Wally glanced at an upper window.

"What the fuck you talking about?"

"Told you, attitude. A guy like that. Come on. Got to hand it to him, being a gimp and all." Wally stepped around the trash can, saying, "Hey, how about we shoot the shit later?" Saying it like Mitch had been doing the talking, Wally got to work with the glass cutter, feeling a good score coming. He'd take Sunny to Umberto's tonight, let the maître d' pull out her chair, put a white napkin in her lap, call him sir. Then take her home, do her on the screened-in porch, all that blonde hair hanging down.

Sunny's leads got them slipping into the homes of Chickie's finest customers. The details came from Chickie's mailing list, the one he used for his Christmas e-cards. The same photo year after year of the diner with Santa Chickie and the plastic reindeer out front of the diner, red and blue lights strung around the windows, tinsel icicles and candy canes. Sometimes Sunny threw in an address because some stingy prick didn't tip her. Have his house broken into, teach him a lesson.

Chickie's diner, it's where Wally first ran into Mitch, the two of them the only customers on a wet Tuesday, doing justice to the all-you-can-eat chili and garlic bread. Mitch needing food energy after working at L's place, putting it to her between coats. It started with small talk, Wally getting around to making easy money. Mitch asked how that would be, Wally saying there was a pancake joint in Deep Cove that did a righteous trade. Mitch said he wasn't into doing dishes, Wally saying it would be tough to do with a gun in his hand and a ski mask over his face.

Sunny overheard them, asking if they ever did more than talk about it, setting down their Jell-O.

♪♪

Pushing the glass in, Wally slid a scrap of tinfoil between the alarm sensors, thinking a palace like this and all that was guarding it was a Radio Shack do-it-yourself wireless, a single sensor any first-time punk could get past. How fucked was that? Likely Artie Poppa figured he was too much of a badass for anyone to break into his place.

The stress showed on Mitch's face, Wally knowing what was coming next. Sliding the door open, his footfalls echoed on the mudroom tiles, the air in the kitchen rank like someone had been boiling gym socks.

Mitch's stomach flipped as he stepped in. "Uhh, man, what do these people eat?" He pulled the Mr. Rooter jacket over his nose, looking past the granite counter at the open door to the basement.

Wally took the Smith and a couple of satchels from the toolbox and said he was going up, telling Mitch to check the basement, tossing him a satchel. Mitch said first place he was going was the can and followed the plastic runner down the hall past a grandfather clock. The living room was a shrine to an old-school widescreen, the thing the size of a Smart Car. Opposite was a shapeless brown sofa and a religious painting over the fireplace. The dining table was set, looking more like Artie was expecting guests than getting ready to flee the country. Wally snapped up an open bottle of Pepe Lopez off the trolley, not booze savvy enough to go for the Chivas. He took the stairs after Mitch, a skylight illuminating the upper hall, rain starting to patter on the dome. Wally guessed they didn't have much time.

Mitch took the bottle, hoping to settle his stomach. Taking a pull and spitting it against the wall, he checked the label, looking for something that read bear lure, handing it back.

Stepping into the master bedroom, Wally nearly drew on the four-foot archangel above the headboard. The wooden figure held its arms out like it was welcoming them, sword at its side, wings spread out above it. Welcome, boys, take what you want.

"How do you do the wife with the Jewish carpenter hanging over the bed?" was what Wally wanted to know, looking at the portrait of the couple above the dresser, a Korean woman gone pear-shaped and an old guy who had to be Artie. Wally thought he looked like Juan Valdez, the coffee guy.

"Isn't Jesus—guy's got a sword." Mitch went to the walk-in closet, looking behind a row of shirts and pants on hangers, a couple of suitcases at the back.

Framed photos on the nightstand on the left showed the couple's plug-ugly offspring in jerseys with Artie's All-Stars lettered across their chests. Pocketing a ten tucked between prescription bottles, Wally checked the labels for anything good, dropping a bottle of Vicodin in his pocket, then a ring, guessing it hadn't dropped out of a Beaver gumball machine. Knocking over a Florida ashtray overflowing with butts red with lipstick, he went through the dresser drawers like a bear at a picnic, clothes piling on the floor. Coming up with a Handycam, he shoved it in his satchel.

En route to the ensuite, Mitch yanked open the other nightstand's drawer. A box of condoms, a bible and a rosary. A key was taped inside the bible. Under it was a stack of hundreds, new bills, banded. Went right in his pocket. He palmed the key and undid his belt, everything below feeling liquidized. He fairly ran for the toilet.

Wally called what he had Mount St. Helens of the asshole, bitching about having to do all the work again. He took the book of matches Miro gave him and dropped them on the rug—Dancin' Bare on the cover, a strip joint belonging to Bumpy Rosco, a guy big into meth, a little flesh trade on the side. The matches would send Artie in the wrong direction, have one of his boys toss a pipe bomb in Bumpy's meth lab, make it look like Bumpy was having trouble finding people who knew to cook that shit.

Tipping the Pepe Lopez bottle, Wally went to the next bedroom, bitching again about working with a guy needing to get his o-ring replaced. The same thing every time, Wally doing the heavy lifting while Mitch left his gravy floating in a toilet, like it was his calling card. The West Van cops sending the forensic guys running to the lab with their baggies.

"Nothing funny about Crohn's." Mitch shut the bathroom door, pretty sure he had it. And if he had any brains, he'd be at the walk-in clinic at Park Royal instead of here right now. Then he took out the banded bills and counted—a thousand bucks. The key had to be for the safe.

Wally poked his nose in the upstairs den, feeling the tequila, looking at a cluster of photos on the wall by the desk: Artie's kids, the girl uglier than the boy, the boy hugging a mutt the size of a mule. "Where you fucks hide your safe?" He came up with a Leica D-Lux in the desk drawer. Sucking back another mouthful, feeling it burn and loop like a midway ride, he slipped the camera in with the HandyCam. Checking the second-floor laundry room, he called to Mitch, said he was going to the basement. Starting down the stairs, he heard a creak from the main level. He froze.

Gassing like a zeppelin, Mitch squeezed and grunted,

tossing his jacket off. He laid the Glock on the vanity, his head between his knees, feeling he was about to throw up and do a rectal tie-in. Rotting from the inside out, it had to be the Crohn's. The whole time thinking about how much was in the safe.

"Get me some TP, man," he called, cursing Poppa for not replacing the roll.

A thump over the patter of rain on the skylight. Wally backed up the stairs, into the master bedroom, looking at the savior with the wings, like he was wondering if he heard it, too. Something stirred downstairs. A footfall. Sure of it, Wally felt his heart going double-time. Had to be Artie home early from the nude beach.

Easing the bedroom door closed, he flicked the lock. Pulling the Smith, clicking off the safety, he backed into the bathroom, locked that door too, raising the barrel to his lips, going *shh*.

"Where's the TP, for Christ's—" Mitch looked up at him, Wally trying to open the window.

A crash and the bedroom doors flew back. Snarling outside the bathroom door. Mitch tugged up his pants, TP or no TP. No mistaking the size of the dog.

Wally tore away the blinds, smacking his palms at the sill. Mitch grabbed his Glock and shoved Wally aside, hammering against the frame, getting the window open. The thing outside was throwing its weight against the splintering door. Mitch climbed, twisting to get his shoulders through.

"Hurry the fuck up," Wally screamed, pitching the Pepe into the shower stall, glass smashing, shoving Mitch by the belt loops. Whatever it was was coming through.

Grabbing a branch, Mitch pulled himself out. Freaking with black fear, Wally fired a round through the door as it flew apart. Jumping on the vanity, he threw Mitch's jacket and the satchel out ahead of him, diving for a branch.

Going out the window, he felt jaws clamp on his heel. Blindly, he kicked his leg and lost the shoe, slipping on the branch, stepping onto Mitch's fingers, losing his handhold and tumbling. Bouncing from branch to branch, he passed Mitch on the way down, landing on his back, the wind knocked out of him.

Mitch shimmied down, bark sticking like quills in his palms. The dog snarling and barking out the window. Mitch dragged Wally past the gnomes to the van, his knee bleeding, both arms stinging. Blood mixed with the rain. His ear felt like it had been ripped from his head.

Wally sputtered, tripping on his torn pant leg, his shoe missing, sock half off. He got in the driver's side, fiddled with the ignition wires and gave himself a shock. The dog barking out the window.

Getting in the passenger door, Mitch clutched Wally's sleeve, the Glock not in his pocket. "Fuck me."

"What, forget to flush?" Wally grabbed the wheel, following Mitch's gaze to the tree. His satchel dangled from a branch, the same branch he left his skin on.

Voices sounded from across the street, and he was backing down the driveway. No safe, no dolly, no satchel, no gun, no shoe.

Driving down Chartwell, they were silent, the rain coming harder now, rivulets rushing along the curbs. Mitch figured now wasn't the time to say he lost his piece, Wally driving with one hand on the wheel, clutching his bleeding leg with the other, foot in a wet sock riding the brake pedal all the way down the hill, nearly side-swiping a Cadillac coming the other way.

IF LOOKS COULD KILL

Miro put on the "my fist your lips" look and told her to get some clothes on, saying, "Don't want to tell you twice."

He liked seeing Bruna frocked out in just his plaid shirt, the paw print tat showing on her thigh. But it was just for him to see, not for Stax banging like an asshole at the door. It was early in their fling, still time to set her straight.

The dysfunction had him worried, Mr. Johnson having trouble keeping the faith. Could be the stress of working with Stax, or mixing weed and meth with the booze. But still, with a number like Bruna . . .

He'd get rid of Stax pounding at the door, get the impending extradition out of his head, toss her on the bed and put it to her. That or start popping those little blue pills.

"Last time I'm telling you," he said, pointing to the bedroom, putting on the pissed look.

Bruna threw him one of her own. "You keep talking like that, you can cuff yourself to the bed next time you're feeling frisky." Ruffling his hair, she topped his mug, told him to drink up like a good boy. She rolled the *Chatelaine* under her arm, leaving the pot of coffee laced with saltpeter, her way of making sure Mr. Johnson took his power nap. "Sorry if I'm pissy, sugar. That prick Leonard sacking me still's got my panties in a twist." She said he was manager of the Bar None, the last place she served drinks and sometimes worked the pole.

His eyes trailed her, that great rack, those tanned legs, that Jennifer Lopez ass. Smooth move, letting her shine his Lamas that first day, getting her drunk, asking her upstairs, listening to how she got fired and took the shoeshine job until something better came along. Miro told her he might be that something better, said if she wanted, he'd go down to the Bar None and teach this Leonard prick a thing or two about employee relations. She clearly liked that he offered to stick up for her, told him she'd think about it, showed her appreciation just that one time with the handcuffs, been hanging around ever since.

The knock came louder, and Miro went and swung the door open, looking at the no-neck, a foot shorter than he should be with his massive upper torso set on stumpy legs. The serpent tattoos over his folded arms. The guy could be Danny Trejo's twin.

"You deaf?" Stax asked.

Miro pulled at his fly, giving Stax the sly grin, the guy with the anger-management issues written all over his face. He guessed his meaning didn't register, figuring it would take a slug from a .45 just to get through the thick hide.

Coming in, sitting on Miro's sofa, Stax said, "Just got word the Task Force is zeroing in on Northside Stevedoring." It was one of the last biker operations Artie had ties to.

"Word from who?"

"From inside 312 Main."

"Meaning?"

"Meaning we got to wait, that or steer our shit through the shipyards." Stax said he could put the oil on board the *Knot So Fast*, the tug owned by the Sanchez brothers, same boat that had run thousands of kilos of Artie's pot from the mainland out to waiting boats. Stax knew the brothers well enough to know they wouldn't say anything to Artie.

"No fucking way we're waiting," Miro said, thinking of his lawyer Cobb with his hand out for a ten-grand retainer to fight his impending extradition. Ten Gs would get Miro as far as an entered plea, Cobb having to convince some judge Miro wasn't a flight risk, no need for an electronic tether. Fat chance after skipping twice in Seattle.

Stax was nodding, saying he'd take care of it. Miro saying he'd oversee the two clowns hitting the grow house on Bowen Island.

"The two clowns that couldn't find Artie's safe," Stax said, frowning, having second thoughts.

"Hey, they're your guys," Miro reminded him.

"Yeah, and I gave them to you."

"Okay, so I'm going with them."

Stax was still frowning, Miro going on, "Should have seen their eyes when I said more money than either of them's ever seen. Got them hooked like a pair of carp."

"Better be," Stax said. What bothered him was the two clowns took a grand in cash and the key to Artie's safe and hadn't mentioned it to Miro. Artie told Stax it was missing, saying Bennie found a Glock and a shoe outside his place, had to get the gardener to use his pruner with the long handle to fetch a satchel out of his tree, the bag holding his Leica and HandyCam.

Reading his uncertainty, Miro said, "I appreciate you being sick of standing over the old man while he's rubbing Banana Boat on his dick . . ."

Stax grinned, letting it slide. It was just a matter of time before Miro got his ass sent back to a fed pen, leaving Stax with what was shaping up to be a pretty sweet set-up. All he'd have to do was find somebody else to cook the oil.

"So, how'd he take it—the break in?" Miro asked.

"Thinks it was punk vandals, fucking teenagers with nothing better to do; still, he wants whoever did it, Artie being Artie," Stax said, easing back in the seat.

"You tell him about Karl Morgen?"

"How about you get me a beer?"

Things were in play; Mitch and Wally would steal the Bowen weed, Miro would turn it into more oil while Stax dropped Morgen's name as a hot-shot tracker. Artie would get him after whoever hit his places. Wearing a wire, Stax would catch the conversation between Morgen and Artie. Then when Wally and Mitch turned up dead, Miro would send the tape to the crown attorney. Except for finding the safe, the pieces were coming together.

He got up and went in the bedroom, Bruna lying on top of the bed, shirt partway undone, a magazine open on her stomach, hands folded under her head. He went to the closet and opened the duffel bag, took out a small vial with a maple leaf on it, and Jeffery's Python while he was at it. She watched him but didn't say anything when he left.

Grabbing two long-necks from the fridge, he came back and sat down, handing Stax a beer and the chrome Python.

"Good old Jeffery," Stax said, weighing the piece in his hand.

"Yeah." Holding the two-ounce vial, Miro put on a lousy Tony Montana. "Say hello to my little friend."

"That's it, huh?"

"Fifty a gram on the street. No shake, no trim, just the best bud along with a few of my secrets."

Stax laid the Python on the table and made a crack about

eleven herbs and spices, twisting the cap off his beer, looking at the vial. "What happened to the Pringles tins?"

"Better to find some empty cases; Pringles come filled with potato chips. What are we going to do, throw a party? Besides, the maple leaf's nice and B.C., don't you think?"

"Think you been testing too much of this shit on yourself."

"A regular Martha Stewart of hash oil," Miro said, admiring the bottle, adding he had four cases, two-point-four kilos, ready to go.

"You got it here?"

"At the warehouse."

"Then I'll call the JayMan," Stax said. "This the bubble hash?"

"Honey oil."

Stax nodded, downing his beer. He didn't get what all the fuss was about, looking into the vial. Why smoke this shit when booze was cheaper and legal? It was purely business for him, kept him in decent cars and with the right kind of women.

"When's he making a run?" Miro asked.

"Maybe tonight, maybe tomorrow. You got a figure in mind?"

Miro worked the math in his head. "Fifty grams at twenty-five per, dozen in a case . . ."

"In English," Stax said.

"We make sixty Gs, we're laughing."

Stax pulled out his cell, punching in a number, figuring out his share of the net. "Hey, JayMan. How's tricks?" He watched Miro go and shut the bedroom door, saying into the phone, "Gonna swing by, take you to lunch, get one of those heart-cloggers you like." The two of them speaking a language they had worked out long ago, Stax letting JayMan know he had two-point-four units he'd let him have for sixty.

JayMan said he could scratch up forty, Stax saying to

scratch harder, JayMan going to forty-five, Stax telling him to go fuck himself, forgetting the code. JayMan said to call back when he got the concept of negotiating and hung up. Stax called back a few minutes later, and they settled on fifty. Hanging up, Stax told Miro the price, Miro throwing his beer, a shower of suds and glass against the wall.

"Time for a Valium, sport?" Stax asked, unimpressed.

"Fuck that."

"I got to explain the concept of negotiating?"

"Fuck me." Miro sat back down, looking up as Bruna came from the bedroom, looking at the beer all over the wall, then at him like he was nuts.

"How about you clean up?" he told her.

"How about you fuck yourself?"

Forcing a laugh, Miro watched her go back in the bedroom all pissed off, then said to Stax, "You say you can get more PVC and butane?"

"I'll get one of the hangarounds to get it. Drop it off when I bring your cut." Stax looked at the dark liquid in the vial again, saying, "Got this guy Vince I want you to meet."

"We don't need another guy."

"Facing extradition not enough for you to worry about?"

"Just saying—"

"Trust me," Stax said.

"It's not that . . ." It was that, but Miro let it go. His eyes traveled to his balled Levi's jacket, the Vaquero under it, thinking it would be dumb to leave it out of reach from here on.

"They get a taste of my oil back in Seattle, they'll be crying for more."

"You say you're the Martha Stewart of hash oil again," Stax pointed his finger at him, "I'm going to hit you."

"Nice to be appreciated."

UNDER THE RADAR

Darkly tanned, rail thin, and naked, Artie Poppa sat on his beach blanket, the old man looking like he owned the whole beach. The guy standing over him today was Bennie, pure muscle under his T-shirt and jeans, dumb as a stump.

"You boys down for some sun?" Artie asked, squinting past the shields at Dom and Luca, two pasty-faced detectives hovering in their cheap suits, both of them sweating from taking the stairs down the escarpment, Dom taking off his jacket, showing the holster and sweat-stained shirt.

"Got a few questions," Dom said, looking Bennie over, sure he had a piece hidden somewhere.

"Four hundred and seventy-three stairs," Artie said. "Could have just called my cell."

"All part of the service." Dom felt his legs burning and his knees wobbling. He looked around at the pink bodies up and down Wreck Beach, the nudity making him uncomfortable.

"Shoot. I got nothing to hide." Artie grinned, his butt on

the terry blanket, his legs wide in front of him, his jewels like a furry rodent curled up and napping. The scar from his heart surgery angry and red against his tanned skin.

Bennie grinned too, like he just got it.

"Want to know about the body we found at your grow house in North Van." Dom looked at his notes. "One Jeffery Potts."

"Like I told the narcs, don't know what you're talking about."

"But you knew Potts?"

"Potts—maybe, maybe not."

"Worked for you for twelve years."

"Not good with names, probably my age."

"What about Wolfgang Klinger?"

"That a Kraut name?"

"Tell us about him."

"Klinger?"

"Yeah."

"Doesn't ring a bell either."

"Found his prints at your grow house."

"Told you—"

Dom put up a hand. "Turned up dead in a Port-O-Potty."

"Look, fellas, aside from some investments, I own a UWager site, and I import mushrooms from China; you guys want shiitake, maybe I can help you out."

"What about Danny Arlis, goes by Stax?"

"That one works for me."

"Yeah, what can you tell us?"

"See him if you want mushrooms."

Bennie grinned again.

Dom checked out Artie's scar, the strange cross around his neck. "Been with you since before Google Earth sent all you boys indoors?"

"Don't know what you mean."

"Busted him coming through a corn hedge around one of your pot fields back in '85, not me personally, but some of the Grand Forks boys," Luca said. "Christina Lake, wasn't it?"

"Boys been doing your homework," Artie said, reaching for his Coppertone, squeezing out a palmful.

"Now he runs your pipeline, taught the border guards at the Peace Arch to wave when he drives by."

Artie smiled and shook his head. "Thirty thousand grow-ops in this province, double the number you guys guesstimate, and you're busting my balls." He held up the Coppertone to Dom, indicating his back. "You mind?"

"We're homicide." Dom took the tube, thought he should toss it to Bennie, instead dropped it in the sand and stepped on it, lotion squeezing on the sand. "We want the guys that took out Jeffery Potts, dumped the load of gravel on Wolf Klinger."

Artie shrugged, the smile still there. "Like I said—"

"Where's your boy Stax now?"

"Boxing up shiitake. Look, fellas, prison's no place for an old man with a heart run by a gadget. I'm clean."

Dom flipped his notebook closed, glancing toward the mountain of stairs. He took out a business card and held it out. "You ever think you need a change of scenery . . ."

The smile broadened. "You boys got more leaks than a Vancouver condo." Artie ignored the card and spread lotion on his arms, rubbing it in. "I ever get the urge, I'll relocate myself."

Dom flipped the card on the blanket. He wasn't ready to climb all those goddamned stairs. "You think of something you want to say . . ."

"Yeah, you're blocking my sun," Artie said.

Dom and Luca walked into the Bean, Dom grabbing a table that looked clean, a dozen other tables occupied, Luca getting Vince to pour a couple of fortes. Dom sat thinking about the new piece to the puzzle: the bumper found out front of the grow house matched a van reported stolen from the construction site where Wolf Klinger was killed.

Luca came with the coffees. "Damn naked people must be super fit. I'm dying here."

"No shit," Dom said, feeling the burn in his legs and the sand in his shoes, fixing his coffee, then talking low. "What I don't get is Artie's got the tax boys sniffing up his ass; Indos, Chinese, Vietnamese, Guatemalans circling like Walmart around a mom-and-pop's; everybody wanting a piece, and he just sits there with his sack in the sand."

"On account he's set to bolt."

"Think maybe he did cut a deal?"

"With who?"

"Drug Squad, Task Force, take your pick."

"Think it would trickle down."

"These guys give up shit these days, every department wanting the glory," Dom said. "Way I hear it, some mystery-man informant got that shit-storm going over in Nanaimo—town where folks were using suspiciously high amounts of hydro. Something like a dozen arrests out of that raid, old church somebody turned into a grow house. Way I hear it, the same source gave up the Sabers' clubhouse in Salmon Arm, one that got expropriated by the crown. That new proceeds of crime legislation." Stirring a plastic spoon around his cup, he said, "Those assholes wear their colors, they're in violation of some new ordinance, painted with the same brush as the fucking al Qaeda."

"Looks good on them, but what's it got to do with Poppa?"

"Maybe he's the snitch, known to have biker ties, sitting on his nudie beach, pointing with his dick." Dom looked at

Vince wiping the next table, straightening a tent card. Sipping his forte, he thought the guy was listening in. "You burn the beans today, Vince?"

Vince looked over, surprised. "Something wrong with it?"

"You tell me." Dom took another sip.

"Roasted them same as always." Vince straightened, looking like a deer caught in the headlights, seeing the black Mustang drive past the door.

The two of them came in and stood on the other side of the oil stain, Ike sitting by the door, above them the bare

DEAD WEIGHT

fluorescents. Stax asked Miro how he could stand it in here, said it smelled like somebody had been cooking road tar. Then said, "This is Vince, guy I told you about."

Miro nodded, said, "Hey."

Vince did the same.

"Guy makes a decent cup of joe," Stax said, smiling at Vince, having a little fun, pulling an envelope from his pocket.

"That right?" Miro said.

"Just got to call it a forte, eh, Vince?" Stax said.

"Call it what you like." Vince pasted on a smile of his own, looking at the envelope, the fucking pit bull by the door, then over at the pans, jars and cases on the workbench, wishing Stax would just pay him so he could get out of there. Or maybe he had something else he wanted done, like maybe this guy Miro. One thing for sure, there was no love lost between the two of them, Stax and Miro getting into bitching about Artie Poppa, Vince just standing there.

"The lay-up after the heart surgery's got him sitting with his ass in the sand," Stax said. "Meantime the Sabers patched over and the 4Play got shut down. New fucking ordinance, and we got bikers looking like yuppie businessmen, driving Beemers with their hair smelling nice, golf shirts with little alligators. They show their colors, they're in jail. A five-million buck pipeline goes to shit, and Artie sits on the beach, acts like nothing's wrong."

"Still say he's doing more than acting?" Miro said.

"Like?"

"Like he's talking," Miro said.

"Somebody is." Stax went to the door, patted Ike, told him he was a good boy, looked out through the barred sidelight, checked the latch on the door.

Miro moved over to his jacket draped on the tool chest, his revolver under it, not sure where Stax was going with this. Uneasy with Vince and that crazy dog in the same space.

"Our boy with the money-laundering unit thought he sniffed out the rat, this trucker in Winnipeg, does a little work with the RagTag crew." Stax stepped around the pooled oil, getting closer to Miro. "Turned out it wasn't him."

Miro put his hand on his jacket, the Vaquero underneath. Two seconds, he'd have it out. "Got to be Artie."

Stax shrugged, lightened up again, saying, "Last week Artie tells me his wife turned her Escalade around, getting halfway to Robson before realizing she left her wallet on the dresser. Walks in on him on their bed with the housekeeper's hand going like a power tool." Vince laughed at that, Stax reaching a Paslode nail driver from the tool bench, checking it out.

Miro forced a grin, eyes on the nail driver. "Right under the archangel, huh?"

"Broad packs up the matching Louis Vuittons and takes the kids on a one-way back to Seoul."

Miro's hand slid under the jacket.

Stax absently flapped the envelope against the nail driver, turning his back on Miro, looking at Vince. "Artie got hold of her yesterday, gave her the moment-of-weakness spiel, how it meant nothing, how it was only a hand."

Vince laughed. "So the broad's coming back?"

"Probably figures Artie's ticker'll quit; why dole out for some divorce shyster. But you could be right," Stax said to Miro. "But to rat out his own operations . . ."

"There something else you need me to do?" Vince said, looking at Miro, holding his hand out for the envelope from Stax.

Stax stepped around the oil stain, offering it to him. "There is one thing . . ." He handed it to him, watched him open it, then grabbed Vince around the neck, clamping his other hand over his mouth, firing the Paslode once, twice, three times. He let go, Vince falling into the oil stain, three inch nails sticking from his head, looking like a pincushion. Ike was up, snarling at Miro.

Backing up a step, Miro said, "What the fuck was that?" Staring down at the dying man, the big pistol in his hand.

"That, my friend, is what I call a good fucking tool." Stax bent and retrieved the envelope.

"Jesus Christ." Miro looked at Vince lying on the oil stain, blood leaking from his head.

"Different than killing a sheep, huh?" Then he told Miro not to point that thing at Ike.

"He's the rat?" Miro said, eyes on Vince, lowering his gun.

"No, just a fuck-up," Stax said. "Asked him to do a job and wasn't happy with the way he did it." He went and tossed the nail driver back on the bench, let that sink in before saying, "Think you're right, Artie's the rat." Then turning for the door, he said, "Come on, Ike, let's go," thinking he'd start leaving Ike at home, nice yard to run around in, get Pinkie and Loop to check in on him from time to time, make sure he had water. At the door, he said, "I'll send someone by to clean up the mess." He looked back at Miro, the guy standing with his cowboy gun in his shaking hand. One thing was sure, Miro would play it his way from here on.

Before PJ came along, Karl had been out of his element, the new town, the new job. Living like a hermit, munching down

WHY JINX IT ?

the daily special at the local in-and-out, spending nights staring at the same flies buzzing around his ceiling light. Missing the old life, hunting down the bad guys.

Elmo's Bohemia was a subterranean club on Broadway. PJ told him she used to hang there after class, back when it was called the Green Lantern, script lettering on a black awning with coach lights flanking the door. The bar was English, the draft was German, and the Buffalo wings were out of this world.

Swiveling his stool, he guessed by the sensible shoes, the young women next to the small stage worked in the medical complex across the street. Laughing like bleating sheep, the three of them were out on the town getting their kicks, ordering drinks with names like panty dropper and buttery nipple. The exec types at the next table sat on either side of a pitcher, putting off the ride home to wives and kids, maybe thinking they had a shot with the women in the sensible shoes.

The doorman was a midget the college crowd dubbed Bit, the guy who looked the other way and called cabs when someone had had too much. Leaning against the entrance at the bottom of the stairs with his pudgy arms folded. Two things were certain at Elmo's: the Buffalo wings couldn't be beat, and nobody messed with Bit, the college boys seeing to it.

Coming down the stairs was the night's entertainment, leather pants and hair gleaming, Billy P. Nunn clapped Bit on the shoulder. The same Billy P. that worked the day pit at the Express Lube on No. 3 Road in Richmond. Dubbed Skytrain Elvis by fellow passengers, he came uptown on the Canada Line, doing a pretty good Elvis knockoff twice a week.

Taking the stage with his Martin, no Scotty Moore helping him with his take on the black leather sit-down show, Billy P. went through his sound check, adjusting the lights and foot pedals. Flipping switches, blowing into his mic, he dropped lines on the women with the sensible shoes, giving them a good look at what Karl bet was a bunched pair of Pantherellas down his leather pants. The business types signaled for their tab.

Karl nursed a beer, thinking of paying Miro a visit, how he was going to handle it, running different scenarios through his mind.

PJ showed up a Thirsty Beaver later, Billy P. saying something Karl couldn't hear. PJ smiled and saw Karl at the bar, Karl's heart going like fists inside an oil drum. Man, she was fine, dressed in a red tummy top and tight Diesels, a string tie around her neck, her hair past her shoulders, making it work. He met her halfway across the dance floor with a hug.

"Sorry I'm late," she said, kissing him.

"Oompa Loompa again?"

She touched her hair, saying, "Hair's fine. Couldn't decide between dressing casual or hot."

"Glad you went for hot." He led her to his spot at the bar.

She said he had all the right words, calling him cowboy. "And I wore this for you." Sitting on a stool, she held out the string tie with a half-moon on the clasp, leaning close to his ear, saying, "It's as close to cowgirl as I get." Talking over Billy P. Nunn as he opened with "That's Alright Mama."

"Put on the Dale Evans for me, huh?" He waved the waitress over.

PJ threw in, "What I've got on underneath would make old Dale blush."

Asking the waitress if they had Beaujolais Cru, he ordered her a glass, PJ adding an Elmo's veggie pizza, telling him it was to die for.

When the waitress left, he slid his hand around her waist, a finger inside the waistband, going for a peek, guessing lace.

"Stay curious, cowboy." She squirmed away, saying, "Just not too many of these tonight, okay?" She had plans for him, picking up his glass and drinking some of his Thirsty Beaver, Billy P. doing justice to the tune, the women with the shoes bopping and clapping along.

When the set ended with "Baby, What You Want Me to Do," and they could talk without shouting, Karl asked if she had any word from Dara. PJ rolled her eyes, saying Dara was willing to come back, but the kid was laying her own cards down, wanting PJ to apologize to Cam for putting him through hell.

"Let me guess . . ."

"I told her when fish fly, and she hung up. You believe it?"

Over the Elmo's veggie pizza, Karl put the business with Miro on the back burner, listening to her talk about the last guy Dara got mixed up with, thinking it couldn't get much worse than the Popsicle groper.

"The one that took the prize went by Rudolph Ernesto Vegas until he chopped it down to Rudy Vegas," she told him.

"Sounds like he fell out of an Elmore Leonard."

"Thought it made him sound cool. Anyway, he followed Dara around, showing up at her classes, coming to the house at all hours—went from shadow to stalker like that." She snapped her fingers. "'Specially after I caught him peeking in my window."

"Come on."

"I was reading on my bed, in my nightie."

"On the second floor?"

"Climbed right up my maple like an ape."

"No way."

"Dara didn't believe me either until he followed her into a school john and confessed he was smitten, saying he couldn't be without her, going to one knee right there in the wet spot."

"The guy said smitten?"

"She swears it."

"What did she do?"

"What could she do stuffed in a cubicle, too afraid to say no? Better question's what did I do."

"Okay, what did you do?"

"I had him smitten alright—with a restraining order. First week at Federman Wetzel, I go to Walt asking for a favor. Walt told me it wasn't exactly personal injury, and I said not yet. Then I asked how his wife was, my way of reminding him about the Xerox machine scene."

"He put the moves on you?"

"Right. Anyway, Walt starts with the jobs-aren't-easy-to-find routine. I asked what he wanted to bet wives were even harder to find. Did the trick. Off he went to the chambers of a golfing buddy, and because Rudy had priors and had done probation, Walt got the order. Any closer than a hundred feet, and Rudy was in breach, fetching him a year in Ferndale. No questions asked. Just wish I could have served it on him."

"So much for old Rudy," Karl said.

"'Fraid it only stirred the pot. I started getting hang-up calls every night, then knicky-knicky-nine-doors at four in the morning, then my recycle bin flew through the kitchen window."

"Tell me you called the cops."

"Dara begged me not to, and I held off till he tried to push her off the Seabus."

"So you called the cops?"

"No, I stabbed him."

Karl just looked at her.

"Just a little. I mean, he took off before the cops showed up at the quay, came by that night and stuck his shoe in my door, yelling and pushing his way in, ready to go off on me for turning Dara against him."

"How did you stab him just a little?"

"Happened so fast, who knows. He slapped me, and I guess I grabbed a ballpoint on the hall table and *whammo*. Rudy's staring at the Bic sticking in his arm while I dialed 9-1-1."

Karl sipped some Thirsty Beaver, regarding her, getting a new appreciation.

She took his hand. "You don't have to worry. You're nice, I wouldn't hurt you."

Karl scooped peanuts from a dish, popping them into his mouth. "You a little wild when you were a kid?"

"Craziest thing I ever did was with this guy Todd."

"You went out with a guy named Todd?"

"Todd Hartwell back at Rockridge Secondary. Word at school was Toddie was a hottie, had the James Dean thing going on, parents were loaded, a mansion in Altamont. His dad was chairman of something or other, sat in the back of a Rolls. Todd got me round the bases and up to my room faster than you, and he was only what, sixteen."

"Where I come from, we're raised to be gents." Karl offered the dish of nuts.

She shook her head, said, "Anyway, there I was, cherry fifteen with dark thoughts in my pink room."

"Nicely put, but too much information there, kiddo." He scooped more nuts.

"Me and Todd put on a hell of a show for my Barbies." She watched him flick a nut in the air and catch it in his mouth.

"And we got a word for making out with fifteen-year-olds." Karl tried again and missed, watching Billy P. get up from the women's table, taking to the stage for his second set, getting ready for some "Lawdy Miss Clawdy."

PJ leaned in, saying, "We were the same age, so it doesn't count. Anyway, Todd had me down to my sensible undies, not like the ones I'm wearing for you, cowboy." She liked the way his brow went up. "We were going to town when my dad stormed in."

"Busted, huh?"

"Sick as a dog from work, Dad takes the stairs two at a time, barely makes it to the throne, Todd going like a crab under my bed, scared as hell. Me, I tossed on my kimono and tended to über-puking Dad. Poor guy was tossing chunks of Frontenac salmon with hollandaise left and right."

Karl pushed the dish of nuts away, PJ saying, "Oh, you should have seen him."

Karl motioned for another round, PJ saying it was Pepto for Dad and a cold shower for Todd. The freckles around her nose showed in the stagelight. "Dad would have shot Todd, sick or not."

"Your dad a cop?"

"No, but he kept a .22 in a drawer, loaded with hollow points. Took it to the Park'N Go when he worked late. Used to tell me about this eight-foot statue of George Vancouver pointing at him all day, telling me old George had his back."

Karl remembered seeing the statue over by city hall.

"My dad was good to me, read me *The Chronicles of Narnia*,

took me to Playland and the zoo in Stanley Park when we had one. Always saw him as a hero, but in the end he was just a real face-in-the-crowd kind of guy, hair thinning, going salt and pepper around the ears. Can't remember when he wasn't wearing that Park'N Go jacket, the one with the crest. Eighteen years of punching tickets and lifting the barrier. Crosswords and a transistor radio for company."

Billy P. did a blow-test into the mic, getting set. The women were up on their feet, clapping their hands, ready to move to Billy P.'s sound. Billy P. making them wait for it.

"Dad only missed one day in all that time," PJ said.

"The day he got sick?"

"Same day he disappeared."

"Disappeared, how do you mean?"

"When he stopped being sick, he said he was going back to the Park'N Go, had nobody to spell him. That was it, never saw him again. Wasn't a great last image of him, but it's all I've got."

Karl looked at her, reading the hurt.

"Mom and I waited up; Mom crying, thinking it was another woman, some trash from the Bay perfume counter. That was up until midnight, then she got scared, thinking foul play, somebody robbing him for the cash in the till. She called the cops, and we sat up most of the night. Not a word from him.

A detective came around with his notepad after the mandatory twenty-four hours and asked a lot of questions. Another one came the day after with pretty much the same questions. Nothing happened till Mom called up and got hold of a supervisor at the Park'N Go, and after doing some checking, you know what he told her?"

Karl shook his head, holding her hand.

"Nobody with my dad's name was or had ever been on the payroll."

That stopped Karl in mid-sip.

"Said there was no such lot."

"No shit."

"The City assumed the lot belonged to the Squamish and vice versa. Microfiche and records were checked. Far as anyone knew, it was just a vacant lot."

"Your dad was running a scam?"

"The signage, the barrier, the booth, right down to the jacket with the fur collar and crest."

"For eighteen years?"

"You believe that? Eight bucks a car, fifty spots on the lot. Stab those numbers in your calculator, see if it makes you whistle."

Karl did the mental arithmetic, coming up with over two million bucks.

"He took care of the mortgage and the house bills, gave my mom enough for groceries, paid for dance lessons, whatever we needed—living the lie. When he left, that was it. We ended up in a bachelor in Richmond, Mom waitressing nights at the Parrot's Perch."

Karl finished his beer. "But he was your dad, I mean, not to ever call or want to see you, make sure you were okay."

"Get this, Revenue Canada came with their hands out, making us prove we never benefited from Dad's ill-gotten gains. Even forced Mom to hire a lawyer."

"Bunch of brown-shoed assholes." Karl brushed oil and salt from his fingers and took her hand again. "You ever look him up, your dad?"

"Used to think about it. I wanted to face him, tell him what he did, mostly for my mom. It made her old, sitting in that same chair looking out like he was coming back. Me, I think about him from time to time, but I was more pissed than anything, probably still am. When I picture palms swaying over surf, him with what's left of his hair all silver now, probably with some tanned tart in a two-piece, the two of them clinking coconut shell drinks with little umbrellas stuck in them, well, I hope he chokes."

"And the parking lot?"

"Turned out it belonged to the city. Had slipped through the cracks all that time. A clerical foul-up, they called it. In the end, consultants were called in, proposals were heard, and a group of Swiss investors bought it to put up one of those taco places—ended up paying a pile more than it would have fetched eighteen years before, so everybody was happy, everybody but me and my mom.

He pictured the statue of George Vancouver pointing at a Taco Bell.

The waitress swooped in, setting down fresh drinks, saying something neither of them understood, then left, the music filling the room. PJ asked if he wanted to dance.

He made a face, scooped the last of the nuts in the dish, saying, "I save that for the bedroom."

"All you do is snap your fingers, move your feet." She pulled him up off his stool. "You can do that, can't you?"

THE BEE'S KNEES

The smug bastard sat there with his pop-eyes and teeth going this way and that. Wally wanted to snatch the menthol from Miro's grinning mouth and stick it in his eye. The guy was nothing without Stax around.

Miro loved hearing it, how Wally lost the satchel with the Leica and Handycam along with his shoe, calling Bruna so she could see the hotshot kid now. To Mitch, he said, "And this guy lost the Glock I sold him not a week ago," telling him he better tie a string around the new gun, the Walther like the German police used. "You know, a string like on dum-dum mittens." The oil he smoked before they showed up made the whole thing funnier, got him away from thinking of what happened to Vince. Choking back laughter, he said, "Hey, there's a bright side, Mitch. The Walther's the one you wanted in the first place."

Wally flipped a quarter, catching it on his wrist, hating this guy, wishing his partner would drop one in the chamber and blow a hole through those laughing teeth. "You didn't say shit about Artie having a dog the size of a fucking horse, Merle."

"Didn't know. But hey, you ever hear of casing the place first?"

"Fuck off."

Bruna smiled from the doorway.

"Hey, you guys are the experts, right?" That got Miro laughing harder, thinking he couldn't feel his toes, seeing them wiggle like they belonged on somebody else's feet. Wiping at the tears, he guessed he made his point, saying, "Okay, let's get serious." He waved Bruna away from the door, then slid Mitch a box of hollow points, telling him it was four hundred cash, same as before. He was thinking he needed another way into that safe.

"How about the five hundred?" Mitch said.

"What five . . . You didn't even find the safe."

"Either way you said," Mitch said. "Means I take the piece plus you owe us a hundred."

Miro stamped his butt in the ashtray, looking from Mitch to Wally, loving how dumb these guys were, guessing how many fingerprints they left all over Artie's, along with a dolly, a shoe, a satchel and a gun. "Alright, forget it, let's move on, next chapter." Miro got up and took a baggie from behind some magazines on the shelf, tossing it to Wally, saying that should put them square.

Wally checked out the bag of buds. Miro told him he was lucky to get it, fucking up the way they did.

"So what about this thing on Bowen?" Mitch said. "We still on?"

"Hell yeah, we're on."

"We?"

Miro stayed on his feet, trying to get circulation back. "No way I'm sending you two alone again."

"So, you two coming with?"

"Just me."

Wally thought about it, guessing Miro by himself wasn't a problem. "Sure hope you're right about the weed being there." Wally thinking he'd empty a clip into him if it wasn't.

"You pay any attention to what I been saying?"

"Heard every word, Merle, still I'm asking."

"Let me tell you boys something, more weed comes from right here than the other Colombia, and I'm hooked up pretty good. So, you two get your heads on right, and we'll do some kickass business. You got any idea how many grow houses we got on the North Shore alone?"

"What happens if Poppa gets wind who broke into his?" Mitch asked, pulling the clip from the Walther.

"Already told you, we'll be dropping a clue, make it look like Bumpy Rosco did it."

"More Dancin' Bare matches?" Wally asked, scoffing.

"Leave that to me."

"Who's this Bumpy guy anyway?" Wally thinking he sounded like a Muppet.

"Nicaraguan, big into meth labs, but branching into bud lately, got some tug with the Nam gangs."

Wally fished out his papers, looking to Mitch, asking what he thought.

"Shit sounds deep, like up to here." Mitch put his hand to his throat.

"Figured it took *cajones* to break into places, but if I got you two wrong . . ."

"You said about pumping in the gas," Wally said. "How about you spell out the rest, how we do this?"

Miro took a Newport from his pack and lit up. "The AC unit's out back of the place. All we got to do is shut it off, tap into the coolant lines, hook up a couple of nitrous oxide cylinders and crank the valves full open. Hit the power back on, and the blower sends enough gas through the vents so anybody inside gets a cabbage for a brain."

"Already said that part," Wally said.

"Then me and you go in with respirators," Miro said to Mitch. "Stuff the weed into Hefty bags. Wally here backs the van to the door, and we're on the four o'clock ferry heading home, up twenty-five grand."

"Thought you said thirty?" Wally said.

"Already told you about expenses. Look, twenty-five worst case, thirty best case."

"Hold on, I'm not sitting in no van. Mitch here's in the van, him with his fucked-up stomach."

Mitch said it was okay with him.

"Okay, hotshot," Miro said to Wally, "'cause when we come out with the Hefty bags, the guy by the van takes aim with the RPG and turns the house to toothpicks."

Wally finished rolling the joint. "You didn't say that part, about the RPG."

"It's how Artie'll think it was Bumpy. The guy had problems with a competitor in Surrey one time. Sent a rocket to straighten things out."

"Okay, so after we blow the place up . . ."

"We're back on the ferry, taking the weed to Stax."

"Suppose gassing doesn't do the trick?" Mitch said.

Miro looked at the Walther in Mitch's hand. "Then you point that and pull the trigger." He looked at Wally and said, "And when you jack a van, get one without holes in the floor this time."

"*Ja wohl*, Merle," Wally said, grinning, checking out Bruna as she came back in, liking that cougar look, her cheeks barely hidden by Miro's shirt tails, the tat showing on her inner thigh.

"Where you going?" Miro asked.

"I need permission to go to the can now?" She looked at

Wally looking at her, liking that Miro was watching this jerk do it.

"Said stay out of sight while I'm conducting business," Miro told her.

"Then your gum-chewing buddy here can't stare at my *tetas*."

"Getting sensitive for a chick that works topless," Miro said. "Don't like him looking, put some clothes on."

"You peel, huh?" Wally asked.

She looked at him with the do-rag on his head and hooked her hands on her hips, the shirt riding higher, showing the paw print.

"How long ago was that?"

She smiled at him, getting close, cupping his chin. "Saying it like you think I can't do it no more."

"Definitely think you can," Wally said it and meant it.

"Work the shoeshine place downstairs." She let go of his chin, straightened and looked down at his new high-tops. "Pop in if you can spare the seven-fifty."

Wally said he just might do that, adding he never carried anything smaller than a twenty.

"That gets you a spit polish. Your twenty got a friend, you get to see if the drapes match the rug." She winked at him and went into the washroom, shutting the door behind her.

Mitch sat there, sticking the clip back into the pistol, pulling it out and sticking it in again, his mind about eight hundred miles away, thinking of Ginny McNamara, wondering if she'd put on any weight since he left.

The reek of dead baitfish rose over the smell of the chicken wafting from the buckets. Stax looked past the terminal area; # DOWN ON THE DOCKS

a container ship showing a high waterline was being loaded, some foreign flag flying from its bridge, the big orange Syncrolift crane swinging overhead, the open warehouses hiding the steel-forming shop beyond.

Walking by the loading area, he looked around until he got in sight of the shop. Its double row of windows was dark like it had been abandoned, some of the panes broken out and boarded.

Beyond the warehouses and the line of containers, waves were capping out in the inlet, the wind bringing a blue sky behind the grey, the rain just starting. An opsrey flying low over the water in search of a meal.

Stax tried the door, knocking on it with his boot. Thinking he should have got original instead of extra crispy, he looked back where his Mustang was parked, nearly hidden by a troller in dry dock. Two guys were working on its bow stem, both of them wearing welder's masks. A six-man crew in yellow hard-hats was working in the open warehouse closest to him, a tow motor driving by. Walking to the door at the other end, Stax missed stepping in one patch of seagull shit only to step in another. The stuff all over the place, looking like egg-mess, the ground slick under his boots. Who could eat in a place like this?

The door at the far end opened, and there was JayMan Healey. His overalls looked like he'd been rolling in soot. Giving a straighten to his Whitecaps' cap, he came halfway, offering his hand, Stax finding it awkward to shake hands while holding two eighteen-piece buckets. JayMan asked how he was doing. As wide as Stax, but a half a head taller, JayMan moved with a slight limp from a bike accident.

A herring gull lifted off from a friction winch. JayMan glanced along the warehouses, looking ill at ease. Most of the guys down here were shitting themselves these days, every-body guessing the Drug Unit and Gang Task Force had every place along the Inlet under the microscope.

Stax told him he got a different heads-up; the cops were poking around Western Stevedoring, not looking at the shipyards.

"Then how come the full-patch guys are keeping away, getting hangarounds to take care of business?" JayMan being the low man on the totem pole from one of the puppet gangs, picked to stick handle the shipments.

JayMan gave a wave to DeJesus Sanchez, the skipper of the ocean tug moored at dock, its rubber tires scraping, *Knot So Fast* painted across the bridge and again along the bow over the tire bumpers. Canadian and American flags flapped from the halyard, the flags used as signals between ship and shore. DeJesus busied himself about his wheelhouse, throwing anx-ious looks at them, eager to cast his lines off, get what was under the floor out to the yacht *Sun Sea*.

"Good and hungry, bro?" Stax said, holding out the buckets.

"That shit'll kill you," JayMan said. "Fuck up your arteries."

"Wanted to spring for burgers at the Apache, remember?"

"And I told you that place is bugged. Don't believe me, ask DeJesus," Jayman said, looking at the tug.

"Relax a bit, dude; you'll like this chicken."

It took JayMan a second to catch on—the hash oil was under the chicken. "Don't fucking tell me . . ." He stopped and turned on Stax, glancing over at the welders, then at the guy driving the tow motor.

"Cost you fifty Gs to find out," Stax said, liking how easy it was to trip this asshole up.

"For fifty, you better have bread and slaw in there," JayMan smiled a bit, still looking at the welders.

Stax shoved the buckets at him. "Be glad I don't tack on a shoeshine for all the dump-duck shit I stepped in."

"We don't do it out here." JayMan pushed the buckets back. "Case you didn't hear about the shit went down at Sea-Tac this morning." JayMan pointed to a trailer with blue barrels stacked along its water side. "Pull your ride around the far side, come through the back door of the shop, and leave your fucking cell in the car."

Stax narrowed his eyes.

"Case it's bugged," JayMan said, holding his hands wide, like he was saying, "What are you gonna do about it?"

Stax had heard about the bust at Sea-Tac, twenty keys of coke and some weapons, half a dozen Asian guys nailed, no bikers even mentioned. "That shit came from Steveston, and one those guys was an undercover cop."

"I'll tell you one more time." JayMan leaned close, saying, "Half the fucking faces down here belong to strangers. So, we do this the way I say, or we don't do it at all. Your choice." Their eyes locked, then JayMan turned and walked back to the open door, saying over his shoulder, "And all I could scratch up was forty-five."

It wasn't his first impulse, but Stax tucked the buckets under his arms and turned for the Mustang, not liking the way JayMan spoke to him, thinking he'd make that plain enough when he pulled around the other side of the shop, get their working relationship back on the right foot, the one he was going to kick up JayMan's ass. Forty-five grand. Even the full-patch guys didn't talk to him like that.

The Mustang bottomed, the undercarriage scraping as Stax drove off the pavement over toward the trailer. Throwing a *fuck this* and *fuck that* to every pothole that ripped his under-carriage like a Croatian mine field, Stax shut off the engine, grabbed the buckets and got out, slamming the door. Glad he left Ike at home, wondering if Loop and Pinkie stopped by to top up his water and kibble like he told them, thinking he should call, make sure. Hearing what he thought was a gener-ator inside the shop, he headed for the door, catching sight of *Air One*, the blue tail with the three stripes coming this way, flying low, its rotors stirring the inlet's water.

Moving, he threw himself against the trailer, rivets sticking out from the corrugated steel catching his jacket. Four marine units raced from the direction of the Second Narrows, cut-ting in, bobbing over the waves. Two cops in each unit with flak jackets and automatic weapons poised.

A line of black-and-whites followed a couple of unmarked cars, coming like a parade through the shipyard gates, the Combined Forces hitting their lights and wailers, eight or nine cars heading straight for the warehouses, fanning out to cut off escape. Some of the workmen stopped, others put up their hands. A few ran.

JayMan stepped from the steel-forming shop, shoving shells into a twelve gauge, yelling for DeJesus to cast off. Officers with high-powered rifles at their shoulders crouched by their units, ordering him to stop and throw it down. Surrounded, he tossed the shotgun down, cops running forward, forcing him to the ground.

DeJesus was screaming in Spanish, the mate throwing off the lines, jumping onboard, DeJesus chucking a box over the side, trying to get his diesels cranked. A shot rang across the water, the bullet buried in the woodwork. A voice piped through a bullhorn ordered everyone onboard the floating towtruck to throw their hands up.

Stax got as low as he could against the siding, his feet slipping on the slick ground. Crawling along the back of the trailer, pushing the buckets ahead of him, chicken pieces falling out. Snatching them, he got behind the row of metal barrels, inching his way, ducking behind a stack of crates. He hoped to hell JayMan left the back door of the shop open. Maybe he could duck in there. Setting the buckets down, he got out his Sig, telling himself they couldn't do jack if he wasn't in possession. Chicken, what chicken? Just a guy coming to take a buddy to the Apache for lunch; no fucking law against that.

Poking his head around the side to the shouts and running feet, he saw more cars coming through the gates, gumballs and screamers going. Helicopter rotors roared overhead as *Air One* circled. Cops searching through the warehouses on foot. Guys with flak jackets and machine pistols coming this way. More yelling.

Leaving the buckets, crawling on all fours, Stax scrambled to the dilapidated shed by the water. The foot-high thistles and weeds did little to hide him. Pulling himself up on a sign reading hazardous waste, he looked back at the buckets. The thought of losing fifty grand had him running back, Sig in hand, ready to shoot the first cop sticking his head around the corner. He dumped out the chicken and crushed the paper buckets down around the vials in the bottom.

He made it back to the shed in time to see the first cop coming round the back of the trailer, an MP5 rifle to his shoulder, looking at the extra crispy on the ground, a black baseball cap backward on his head, making hand signals to the ERT cops behind him, moving for the back door of the shop, the other cops covering him, all in black, all looking serious.

Rivets were missing from a corrugated sheet on the back of the shed. Setting down the crushed buckets, he tried prying the metal away, but couldn't squeeze through, slicing his fingers. Blood dripping, he picked up the buckets and stepped onto the algae and shit-covered dock, the timbers old and rotting. Nowhere to run. Gun up, Stax not going down without a fight.

Snap.

A rotted board gave, both his feet shot out from under him. Arms whirling, the whole scene like slow motion, the Sig and the crushed buckets flipping in the air. Down into the black with a splash. The cold shock, the underwater sound of air bubbles. He came up, sputtering sea water, grabbing for a piling, reaching for the buckets. The first one tipped, part of the Colonel's smiling face on the crushed side, the bucket taking on water, Stax stretching his bleeding fingers, watching the bucket fade into the murk. Then the second one bobbed and tipped. Hearing the cops nearby, he didn't dare to swim for them.

The marine units had pulled their Zodiacs alongside the tug, cops jumping onboard, drawing a bead on the mate, yelling for him to lie down, going after DeJesus in the wheel-house. By some miracle, nobody saw Stax fall into the water, an ERT cop moving above him on the dock, stepping over the broken board, checking the back of the shed, shouting all clear to the cops on the tug.

The pilot and tactical officer looked down from the chopper flying overhead, drowning out JayMan yelling quotes from the Charter of Rights and Freedoms at the top of his lungs, a Mountie butting him with his rifle, suggesting he shut up.

Stax was still weighing his chances of diving for the buckets without being spotted—fifty grand sinking right under him, and nothing he could do about it.

With a bleeding hand, he got a handhold on a rusted spike in the piling, wedged the toe of his boot against the barnacles and tipped his head back, keeping his nose and mouth above water, pulling back as far as he could. Something bumped and circled his leg, making him cry out, rain starting to patter on the inky water.

THE G BUTTON

Miro's address put Karl in a neighborhood local realtors liked to call gentrifying. Truth be told, Strathcona was the kind of place best visited in daylight unless your thing was getting high or getting off. Junkies, hookers and the homeless.

The side street was Princess; just before the Park'N Go garage, he swung the Roadster into a vacant spot at the curb behind a RiseUp bread van stifling in its own funk. Getting out and looking around, he got a whiff of piss as he pressed the passenger door lock. No point tempting fate around here. Gentrifying, my ass, he said.

The four-story rathole had Chinese characters running vertical up the brick, multi-colored graffiti all over the door, on the windows, on the walls. A gargoyle looked down from the roof, its grey eye turned toward the Savoy Pub, ignoring the hip hop braying from the Rise & Shine, the topless shoeshine place two doors up. Karl guessed living in a dump like this was Miro's idea of keeping a low profile.

A guy with wild dreads walked his turf, his sandwich board making known it was seven-fifty a shine—today's special. Bruna James, wearing an over-sized T-shirt with the words "Magic Fingers," came out in thigh boots, carrying a Thermos. She said something to the guy with the board, walking past the piss-stained wall and into Miro's building, not looking over at Karl.

Guessing she did the shining, not knowing a damp cloth from a bristle brush, Karl couldn't see the point—a topless shoeshine chick down there buffing a guy's shoes, blocking the view of what he was paying to see. A case of not thinking things through.

Karl slipped the FedEx shirt overtop his T, the blue and orange logo showing on the chest. Snugging on the matching ball cap, he clipped the envelope with the photocopy of the U.S. bench warrant Marty sent him to the clipboard. Reaching under his seat, he tucked a small metal bar under his arm. Locking up, he stepped by the guy with the sandwich board, saying "no thanks," searching for that Lady Luck feeling, the rush he had always felt during seventeen years of fugitive retrieval, dragging badasses off the streets, going into places that made Strathcona look uptown. Back when he and Marty went after the guys wanted on warrants for unlawful flight, transportation of stolen goods, Class C felonies, theft, kidnapping, assault with deadly weapons, armed robbery, fraud, statutory rape, drug trafficking, and conspiracy to distribute controlled substances. All the lovelies.

He missed the life, thinking about it now as he looked up at the building. The thrill of the chase. A little payback. Maybe even the danger.

The Global Trace office was where they tossed balled paper into trash cans and cracked wise, but on Seattle streets it was all business. The one time he let his guard down was the night his partner Marty stayed holding his wife's hand,

Janet expecting their second baby girl at Northwest Hospital, labor that lasted twenty hours. Acting on a tip, Karl went after an easy one, a bail-jumper on a DUI charge named Benny Bean, catching up with the Bean at a corner dive down in the meatpacking district, a neon light flashing BBQ. Giving the Bean the option of coming in easy, Karl sat on a stool, looking down the bar, late seeing the pipe the Bean pulled from his boot, putting Karl down with a single blow, letting him have a few more, taking it personal that this guy was here to drag his ass to jail. It took a concussion and a few bruised and cracked ribs, but the lesson sunk in.

Taking the Taser x3 out of the closet for the first time that morning since sneaking it into town taped to the inside back of Chip's cat cage, Karl had checked the lithium battery and tucked it in his glovebox. Canadian law flagged the Taser as a restricted weapon, a lesser offense than a restricted firearm, but still likely to fetch some jail time. Back in the Emerald City, ten-year-olds would laugh at a Taser, but Canada was a place where people settled arguments with their middle fingers. He considered bringing it upstairs but decided the glovebox was close enough.

He tipped his FedEx cap and held the door for a gray-hair taking her Boston terrier for its constitutional. Not a cloud in the sky, but the old dear stood in the doorway holding an umbrella, telling Karl not to let the sky fool him. When her joints said rain, you could bank on it. Karl caught a whiff of gin, listening to the old dear tell him the Canucks were going to whip the Ducks tonight, in case he knew a good bookie. Thanking her for the tip (hockey season off by a few months), he patted the friendly dog jumping on his leg. She waved him in—no need to ring up—just asked him to say hello to Margaret when he set up her oxygen. One uniform looking the same as the next to her.

Stepping off on four into a hallway reeking of Scotchgard

masking mold and filth, Karl took the metal bar and slipped it in the elevator's track. It kept the door from closing. Half the bulbs in the hall were burned out, the carpet dotted with burn holes. A shopping cart and a kid's bike blocked the fire exit.

He slipped on his shades and put his ear against the door of 416, listening before he knocked. It was a man's voice shouting about the cops being tipped off, bitching about being out fifty grand. It had to be Miro Knotts.

The voice turned to a whisper when he knocked. Giving the peephole his full-on FedEx smile, Karl bet Miro wouldn't recognize his fish-eye image. Sure enough, the knob turned; the door opened as far as the chain allowed, one eye looking at him.

Taking off the chain, Miro pulled back the door. Hair sticking up, he looked more like a bone-rack than the last time Karl saw him, his Stones tongue T-shirt hanging off him. Not big, but neither was a wolverine. The cigarette in his mouth made him squint, bloodshot eyes darting to Karl's clipboard, saying to whoever was on the phone, he'd call back. He clicked off, keeping his hand on the door, asking, "Aren't you guys supposed to buzz first?"

"The thing's on the fritz. Nice lady let me in, but you know, you haven't changed, not a bit." The smell of pot was strong coming from the apartment.

"I know you?" The eyebrows bunched, the door opening narrowed.

"See, I wasn't asking who you are," Karl said, enjoying the moment.

"Don't know any Miro," Miro said, starting to close the door. "Got the wrong guy."

Karl stuck his shoe in the door and held up his cell phone. "Now, I haven't said your name yet, right?" Snapping a photo of Miro, he punched in a number.

"What the fuck . . ." was all Miro got out before the phone

in his hand rang. Karl shrugged like it was cute, clicking off and dropping his phone in his pocket. He pictured Marty at his desk, getting the email with the pic of Miro opening the door.

"So, what's that make you, a smartass delivery boy?" Miro snapped his fingers for whatever Karl had, tired of this guy's game.

Karl took off the shades, hooked them on his collar, looking at Miro. "Makes me the guy that grabbed you by the hair and dragged your sorry ass off that sofa in Belltown, you screaming like a girl all the way to the cop shop, remember?" Karl held up his palm. "Should have seen all the hair came off in my hand."

Miro blinked like he'd been hit, ash dropping from his smoke, everything going too fast. This was the guy, the guy he was setting up: Karl Morgen, the fucking bounty hunter. The Vaquero hung in its holster on the coat rack, one in the chamber, just out of reach. The aluminum Combat bat was closer, just inside the door.

"The family of the fifteen-year-old you molested wants to meet your ass in a Seattle court," Karl said, his voice loud in the hallway. "Coming after you for psychological and emotional trauma to their little girl, but that's not why I'm here." Karl slid the envelope from the clipboard, the copy of the U.S. warrant. "Lucky for you, I don't have a license anymore, otherwise I'd do you for free, drag your sorry ass all the way back, snatch another handful of hair."

Miro's hand was moving for the bat.

"I'm serving paper these days, thanks to you." Karl smiled as he slapped the envelope against Miro's chest, catching a glimpse of the Hefty bag with bud sticking out the top. The envelope landed in Miro's hands.

Karl hustled for the elevator, saying, "They're going to deport your ass, Miro, get you registered as a sex offender—I don't know, I'm just guessing. Anyway, you've been served, big guy." He was halfway to the elevator, its doors banging against the metal bar, its chimes going off. "Oh, and you might want to stash that shit somewhere other than by the door when the Mounties come with the real warrant."

"Goddamn it." Miro threw up his hands like the envelope had leprosy, like if he didn't touch it, it didn't count. He jerked the door all the way open, screaming, "You fucking fuck, get back here." Miro spat out the Newport, grabbing the bat, wielding it shoulder high like he was taking the plate. "Hey, hold on, delivery boy, forgot your fucking tip." He came at a run, winding up. "You get out of emergency, you'll want to find a new line of work."

Karl was fast enough, ducked and twisted away, his glasses flying off, the bat taking out a wall sconce and a foot of drywall, Miro ripping it from the wall, winding up again.

Karl was diving for the elevator, hitting the floor hard, grabbing the steel bar out of the door, Frisbeeing the clipboard at Miro, gaining that extra second. Miro swung again, smashing the clipboard out of the air. Bruna, came running out of 416, powder around her nostrils, the Thermos in her hand.

The shoeshine chick. Karl caught a glimpse of her as he rolled, swinging the bar, cracking it like a tomahawk against Miro's knee. The crazy bastard shrieked, dropping the bat.

Bruna was yelling for them to stop, waving the Thermos, Miro pushing her back. Karl jabbed Morse code against the panel's G button—faces poking from apartment doors—Miro grabbing for the Thermos, throwing it against the closing elevator doors.

SHE'S GOT THE SPIEGELANTENNE

Bypassing the lobby, taking the side door out onto Princess, thinking that went better than expected, Karl poked at the ragged tear through the first E in FedEx. His elbow was scraped, knee throbbing. His cap was gone, clipboard and sunglasses gone, but he made the serve and snapped a pic.

Reaching for his phone, he started punching in Marty's number, spotting a guy by his car looking all wrong. The guy was bending with the do-rag on his head, giving the Roadster that this-is-my-kind-of-ride look, fingers testing the passenger door handle. Karl angled and came up behind him, spotting the second guy looking all wrong on the corner. "Help you, bud?"

"This your ride?" Wally straightened, smiling like a kid caught with his fingers in the candy jar, favoring his injured foot as he turned.

The second guy was in jeans, redneck rube written all over him. Karl kept him in view, dangling the Porsche fob to answer Wally's question. Angling by him, he unlocked the passenger door and sat on the seat, still catching his breath, his back hurting, eyes on the building's door in case Miro wanted to go another round. The second guy was limping, coming his way, slipping a hand in his jacket, the pocket looking heavy.

"Looks like FedEx's improving the fleet," Wally said, admiring the car, running a hand along her quarter panel. "You guys doing the thirty minutes or it's free deal?" Wally talking like he had all day.

"Yeah, copying you pizza guys," Karl said, pointing to the do-rag.

Not sure what he meant, Wally took a glance, Mitch shaking off the crackhead with the sandwich board. Turning back to Karl, he said, "Fifty-nine replica in sand grey lacquer," showing what he knew.

Karl nodded like he was impressed. "You know your bathtubs, only this one's ivory."

"So she is." Wally tipped the tinted shades, saying, "Super 90 with the Solex carbs. Zero to sixty in what—about nine flat."

"Something like that, yeah."

"Not a rocket, but still, you got yourself a head-turner."

"For me it's more about the handling. That zero-to-sixty thing's kind of high school, don't you think?" He looked past Wally, Mitch's hand still in his pocket, still coming this way.

Wally leaned close, thinking why not have a bit of fun with this delivery boy before going upstairs. "Yeah, this is class. Full leather, removable hardtop—got the Blaupunkt, fully loaded."

"And she's got the Spiegelantenne built right in," Karl said, tapping the rearview.

"Read about that in *Road & Track* one time, but never seen one," Wally said, bending, checking it out, saying, "Now that's some rare shit."

"You bet. Set me back a fair bit, too, but you want to see my favorite?" Karl clicked open the glove compartment and laid his Taser across his lap. "Anti-theft device. Taser X3; it's fully loaded, too."

Wally backed up a step. "Light your fags with that?"

"Just fry assholes with it. Fifty-thousand watts' worth, bites like a bitch."

Mitch stood next to Wally now, saying, "Think you got the wrong idea, amigo. My friend here's just a car nut. Anything on wheels, you know the type, always got grease on his hands, been that way since Hot Wheels."

"An enthusiast, huh?"

"Right. First guy on the block to get his driver's license." It wasn't just the Taser, it was in the guy's eyes; he'd been in this kind of situation before. Mitch tugged Wally by the sleeve.

"Yeah, no need to pull the bug zapper on me, friend," Wally said, holding up his palms. "Auto aficionado's no kind of crime where I come from."

Mitch and Wally kept stepping back.

"Have a nice day, boys." Karl waited till they turned before tucking the Taser back in the glovebox. It wasn't like his .40 caliber Smith, but it got the job done. Climbing over the stick shift, he knocked against the horn with his knee, pain shooting through him like a current.

"'Have a nice day,' the smug cocksucker says to me," Wally said. "Sitting there with his fucking ray gun. Should have shown him what a real man packs."

MUDMEN OF ASARO

"Nothing like the asshole I just ran into." Miro took the facecloth off his forehead, looking at Wally at the far end of the sofa, Mitch in the armchair. The bleeding had stopped, but his knee hurt like hell. Still rattled by Morgen showing up, still not believing Stax let fifty grand of his oil sink to the bottom of the inlet, he said to Wally, "Just so you know, pretty much every smackhead down here packs a piece, in case you're new in town."

"Yeah, nice digs, by the way," Wally said.

Miro throwing it back, "Got to say, the guy practically catches you breaking into his car. Man, my grandmother jacks cars better than that."

"Told you, I wasn't jacking it, just having fun. One call to

FedEx HQ and that prick's out a job," Wally said, looking at the Hefty bag with buds poking out the top.

Miro stiffened like he'd been poleaxed. "What the fuck you say?"

"What?"

"Said FedEx guy."

"Yeah, fucker comes out the side door," Wally said, surprised by the way Miro was looking at him. "But the way he did it, he—"

"That's the fucking guy," Miro yelled, jumping up and kicking at the envelope on the floor, then wincing, grabbing his knee. "Fucker who laid this shit on me." He got in Wally's face, pressing the ice pack against his swollen knuckles, the hand that would look like an eggplant by tomorrow.

Wally looked at Mitch, wondering what the fuck. "Hey, I see a knockoff Porsche out front of a place like this, and it doesn't fit. Then this FedEx guy comes up behind me, giving me lip for looking at his ride, and that doesn't fit. Like how many deliveries he got to make to afford a ride like that?"

"You're a fucking idiot, you know that?" Miro was seeing floaters in his eyes, sucking air, three inches from Wally's face. "The fucker's not FedEx," Miro said, spit flying from his lip.

"Take it easy, man." Wally leaning back.

"Guy's the bounty-hunting asshole that dragged me off the sofa in Belltown." Miro had to sit again.

"And I'm supposed to know that?"

"Snuck up on me making it with this babe. What kind of asshole does that, comes up on a man like that, slapping those nylon things on my wrists?

"What's he doing here?"

"When I got out of the Ridge I went after him, him and his fucking partner. Got them shit-canned from their jobs."

"Shit-canned, how?"

"Got their licenses revoked. Can't bounty hunt unless you got one."

"What did they bag you for?"

"For bullshit."

"That where you got the tat, the Ridge?"

Miro looked at it, the clock with no hands, saying yeah.

"How long you in for?"

"Three months."

"You got a tat just for three months?" Wally looked over at Mitch.

"You got any idea what they do to a man up there? I'm taking that fuckhead down."

"What did he want?"

"Laying this shit on me." Miro's face was red as a radish; he got up again and ground the envelope underfoot, crying from the pain. "Guy's got hell coming, I tell you that."

Wally was laughing, looking at the envelope. "So, you got served by some guy used to be a bounty hunter, busted you for something you don't want to say, like what—mail-order bride want a divorce?"

Wally was pushing his buttons; Miro was clutching the ice pack, veins popping at his temples, blinking to clear the floaters.

Bruna came in with two bottles, one of Tylenol, one of Dead Frog. Wally leaned into the cushion, away from Miro and checked her out—a bit old, but still . . . the woman had the kind of headlights that talked to a man, Wally guessing they were the real deal, no tit-plants.

Setting the bottles down, she wheeled around barefoot, Wally thinking she liked being checked out.

"Still got the wrong shoes," she said, looking at his high-tops, giving him a smile.

Miro popped the childproof lid, shaking out a palmful,

clapping them into his mouth, chewing them, twisting open the beer and knocking the bitter taste down in a swallow.

"Only supposed to take two," Bruna said.

"I got more pain than you can believe."

"Like the shirt by the way," Wally told her.

"Let me guess, Karl Lagerfeld, right?" she said.

"Name's Wally," he said, reaching for Miro's pack of Newports, watching Bruna disappear into the kitchen. "Nice girl," he said to Miro.

"Think you get a rise out of me with that shit?" Miro said, getting himself in check.

"What do you call what you did at the cafe?"

"What are you talking about?"

"Talking about the way you were playing Sunny."

"Who, the hooker?"

"That's my girl, Merle." Wally considered adding to Miro's cuts and bruises. "Throwing your money on the table, acting cute with the three-egg omelette bullshit. See why people line up to beat the shit out of you."

"Yeah, Sunny, right, your rent-a-girl. Sunny side up. Okay, whatever." Miro looked at the envelope, calmer now. "For the record, I'm far from done with that asshole." Miro threw back his beer and let go a corner-of-the-mouth belch, thinking about facing Morgen with his Vaquero strapped down, the hand-tooled holster, doing his Kirk Douglas from *Last Train From Gun Hill*, see the fear in the guy's eyes as Miro put one in the crotch, one in the heart, and one in the head.

Wally settled into the cushions and nodded toward the Hefty bag. "Got any of that ready to twist up?"

Miro reached the baggie off the bookcase and tossed it on the table, swallowing, feeling bits of lodged Tylenol in his throat. "This bud's for you." Grinning, thinking this was from the same batch of pot these two idiots were supposed to mule the day Jeffery Potts took a shotgun blast to the chest.

"Now you're talking." Wally forked a pack of ZigZags from his shirt pocket and set to work. "Sorry, I didn't bring the flavored kind," nodding at Miro's pack of Newports. "Blue JuJu or Purple Thunder."

Miro drank some beer, watching Wally roll; odds were he'd end up shooting him too before Stax got around to it. He flicked his lighter, Wally leaning in with the joint in his mouth, Miro guessing the do-rag was flammable.

Wally drew in a lungful, that staircase feeling creeping in right away. Offering it to Mitch who waved his hand, Wally passed it to Miro, saying, "Good shit," on the exhale, adding Mitch was into booze because he liked waking up next to ugly chicks.

Feeling it ease him, Miro took another hit before passing it back and getting down to business, bringing the conversation around to Bowen Island. The weed at Artie's second grow house would make up for the oil that sank in the inlet. "When we do Bowen, we go in like the Mudmen of Asaro."

"The who?"

"Primitives from Papua, New Guinea. Lived smack-dab in the Indonesian archipelago."

Asking if this was the one about the where-the-fuck-are-wes, calling Miro Merle again, Wally checked his watch, pretty sure it was Sunny's afternoon off.

Mitch pointed at Miro's beer. "I'll take one of those, if you got?"

"Go ahead, but I ain't your maid." Miro shot a thumb toward the kitchen, taking the joint from Wally. "Cold ones are in back."

"So what the fuck's with these mudmen?" Wally said, looking at his watch again.

"Yeah, see, these hostiles from the other end of the island came to kick the shit out of them, but the mudmen were savvy, see? They spot these guys with spears and warpaint coming and hightailed it into this swamp."

Wally sank back, trying to picture the scene.

"The hostiles knew the swamp to be full of evil spirits, so they stayed the fuck out, letting the spirits take care of business. Job done, so the hostiles paid the lady mudmen a visit. But when night came, the mudmen crept out, covered head to toe in swamp mud. They hightailed it back to their village, the mud drying white, making them look like ghouls."

Wally nodding now, getting into the story, saying, "Let me guess, the hostiles were banging the mudmen babes, their spears laying on the ground. Nobody on watch."

"One look at the mudmen all white in the moonlight and the hostiles took off screaming and running, never to return."

Taking the joint, Wally thought about it, then asked what the fuck it had to do with hitting a grow-op. Mitch came back with three longnecks, setting them down, said he didn't get it either. Wally took a beer, looking at Bruna walking from the bedroom, offering her a toke. His eyes on her as she leaned in and made a circle of her lips, drawing in the smoke.

"It's just to illustrate . . ." Miro started to say, thinking these people were too stupid for analogies. "Fuck it."

"Look, Merle, in spite of what happened at Artie's, me and Mitch know our business."

"Sure you do, but this is a different game, boys," Miro said.

"A game with a chance of getting smoked," Mitch said, twisting off the cap.

"You got your P5 in your pants, don't you, Mitch?" Miro asked him. "What you do is point it, and take what you want."

"And going in armed gets us extra jail time."

"In this game, nobody's going to call the cops. No chance of doing time."

Wally peeled his eyes from Bruna as she left the room, asking Miro, "You ever do any real time, I mean other than three months for bullshit?"

"Too smart for that, but let me ask you one, what's the most you two ever took breaking into places?"

"No matter what I say, you're going to say what you got's better." Wally glanced around the apartment, sucking on the spent roach, saying, "Guess that's why you live in the Dump Towers."

"Getting real sick of your shit," Miro said.

"Then how about you cut all this mudmen crap, and get down to it." Wally reached for the baggie of Miro's weed on the table, then the papers. "I'm up for anything worth being up for. Don't need your pep talk." Wally crumbled bud onto the paper, rolled it up and licked the edge. "Thing I want to know is how come you got a hate on for this Artie Poppa guy?"

Easing back, Miro flicked the lighter for him, then got into telling them how he and Stax worked for Artie at the Christina Lake plantation before it all went indoors, how he perfected the strains, adapting silent diesel generators to keep the hydro usage down, setting up the high-tech hydroponic environments for dozens of operations, all of them mid-sized with five hundred to a thousand plants to keep them flying under the radar. How it was the high temperatures and humidity that left Miro with a puffer in his mouth and asthma in his lungs. Artie showing no consideration, Miro not mentioning how Artie nicknamed him Popeye on account of the puffers looking like pipes. When the asthma became full-blown, Artie tossed his ass out in the street.

"No Workers' Comp, huh?" Wally said.

"You fucking asked."

"Yeah, so you're a disgruntled employee," Wally said.

"How about you let him tell it," Mitch said, wishing Wally would shut up.

"How about the part he's not saying, the part where this Poppa guy sends his goons after us?"

"That being Stax," Miro said.

"Other goons." Wally offered Miro the joint, Miro saying no, Wally asking if there were space cakes or something to eat.

"Cheezies above the fridge." Miro turned to Mitch. "Look, Artie's an old dude, health is the shits—under the eye of the fucking Task Force. Believe me, the guy's more interested in playing with his grandkids than taking care of business, but if he does go after anybody, it'll be Bumpy Rosco." Miro lit a Newport, saying as Wally searched for Cheezies, "I'm telling you boys, it's just waiting for us."

"Yeah, so, let's get to it." Coming back in, Wally ripped into the bag, stuffed some in his mouth, offered the bag around. "One thing I want to know," Wally said to Miro. "How come you hold your cigarette like this?" He held the joint between two fingers. "And you hold a joint like this." He put three fingers around it, grinning, mouth Cheezie orange.

Miro reached his ringing phone off the coffee table. The display showed it was Stax, Miro switching it off. He didn't need another asshole to deal with right then.

Karl flipped through the travel brochure, stepping from the display rack to the counter. Photos showing a coral sea

NOT A STITCH

and a white strand with palms swaying had him thinking of a week in Costa Rica, feeding white-faced monkeys from a skiff, horseback riding along the dunes, making love to PJ on a moonlit beach. He held the image of her coming toward him barefoot in the sand in a two-piece or something lighter. The voice interrupted his thoughts.

The blonde behind the counter was asking if she could help, eyes smiling at him, watching him close the brochure and hold it over the envelope, the papers he was there to serve, a bouquet tucked under his arm. Bob and Joyce at Sea-to-Sky gave up trying to nail this guy Melnick, and it landed in his in-basket. Holding up the flowers, Karl smiled at her. The nameplate said she was Helen Jackson. Nobody needed to tell him she was a knockout.

Helen's eyes lit up at the sight of the roses. She said, "Mr. Melnick doesn't come in on Mondays, but I can sign . . ."

"They're not for him, they're for you." Karl turned on what Jerry his ex used to call his Clooney.

Her painted mouth formed a perfect O.

"Yeah, I'm told yellow's for friendship, and I'm hoping that's where we're headed." Handing them to her, he set his elbows on the counter, wondering how much the rock on her finger set some guy back.

She thanked him, eyes playing over the blooms, making like it wasn't every day Giovanni Casanova breezed through her door.

"I'm Karl, with a K."

"Helen," she said, Karl thinking, with a double D. She pointed an acrylic nail at the brochure. "And I'm guessing this isn't about booking the trip of a lifetime."

"It could happen, but right now I'm just asking if Marv Melnick is behind that door."

"I already told you . . ."

"I know, he doesn't come in on Mondays, or he wants you to say that."

"I don't lie for Marvin, Karl with a K." She was playing, putting her nose into the flowers, looking at him over the petals, guessing Karl's game. "Wish I could help."

Karl produced a roll of bills and ironed one flat on the counter. Helen's eyes drifted to it.

"Just want to hand him this." Karl held up the envelope, not hiding anything.

"He going to want it?" She walked her fingers over the bill.

"Not likely, but either way. I'm going to serve him."

"There were a couple others, came with an envelope," she said, remembering Bob and Joyce, the envelope marked Personal and Confidential. "I guess it's the same one."

"It is."

146

"Only you seem pretty sure of yourself. Kind of cocky."

"They send me when the others come back still holding it. See, I don't take no for an answer."

"That makes you Special K."

"It's how I do it. See, I like to give the guy the option of taking it the easy way. No running, no hiding, no need to be embarrassed when I serve him at his place of worship, or while he's putting the eighteenth hole or sitting over his Cornflakes with the wife and kids. But like I said, either way."

The bill disappeared below the counter, and she said, "So long as Marv won't find out."

"My lips are sealed." Again with the Clooney. Karl peeled off another bill, setting it down, keeping a finger on it this time, asking if she could point him in the right direction.

"Like I told you, Marv never does Mondays and he doesn't play golf." Her fingers walked over his, the nails like high heels, the big rock catching the light.

"Yeah, that narrows it down," Karl said. "But what does Marv do when he's not golfing on Mondays?"

"He likes to watch," she said, smiling, batting her eyes, letting him roll that around.

Karl's finger stayed on the bill, his eyes on hers, waiting.

"You know the Paramount?"

Karl shook his head.

"So-called gents' club in New West where the raincoaters go for a lap dance—girls from all four corners."

Karl got the picture.

"Marv's partial to the Platinum Room; he likes a nice air dance while he's chewing his clubhouse, getting a little girl-friend action from a redhead named Sinnamon. Spells it with an S."

Karl guessed Helen's last job involved a G-string and a pole, back before she started answering Marv's phones, maybe before the rock on her finger. "He there now?"

"Why don't you go find out?" She pinched the bill from between his fingers. "Same time every week, when the missus visits her daddy in Westside."

"That's a nursing home, huh?"

"You bet."

That second twenty got Karl the color and plate number of Melnick's Beemer. It also got him Helen's home number scratched on the back of the brochure. Before PJ came on the scene, those dark eyes and double Ds would have kept him up nights.

He pocketed the brochure, thinking Bob and Joyce will love this, seeing it going down like this: Karl sneaking up on Melnick under the mirror ball, the Spice Girl doing her thing in his lap, Melnick telling him to go fuck himself, putting on the big man. Karl apologizing, saying he could see Marvin was busy, saying he'd just pop over to the nursing home and hand it to the missus instead. Melnick chasing after him, pleading for the envelope.

Miro and Wally argued most of the way to Horseshoe Bay, Mitch thinking who gives a shit whether Jack Daniel's is a bourbon. He was on the Sunny D these days.

THE BROUHAHA

The argument shifted to which lane would get them onto the ferry faster. Mitch tuned them out; the important thing, they were doing it. Miro and Wally up in the front seats of the big Chevy van, puffing away on weed and Newports, Mitch in the back, holding his stomach, wondering what asshole designed this thing with the tinted windows that wouldn't open. He thought about the key he took from Artie Poppa's, wondering if it opened his safe.

A sedan pulled up next to them, the passenger with her hair in a pixie cut like Ginny's, bangs down in her eyes. It got Mitch wondering if she stopped in at Lethbridge Correctional from time to time to see Tolley on the other side of a partition, pretty sure she'd have to be a legal spouse for a conjugal visit.

They stayed in the van on the ferry ride over, the first sunny day in a week, nobody interested in catching the sights of Howe Sound, the island in the distance, the snow-capped mountains to the north.

Miro went from bourbon to faster lanes to bragging how he got the THC up to the point of creating his own super-strain, declaring he was to B.C. bud what Owsley Stanley was to white lightning, Wally asking if this Owl guy was a Native.

Snug Cove was coming up, looking more like another Shitstain than a weekend destination. A long line of cars waited to get on the ferry at the other end, packed with kids and dogs, topped with kayaks and coolers, some pulling campers, all smogging up the cove.

"Emerald Isle my ass," Mitch said as they drove off the ferry, passing the welcome sign.

Wally looked at him in the rearview, grinning, turning on Miller, rolling past a shop with a sign that said Pottery and Crap.

"Who told you to turn on Miller?" Miro asked, telling him to swing around and get back on Grafton.

"*Ja wohl*, Merle," Wally said, angling the rearview, adjusted his do-rag, turning the van around, asking Mitch, "You feel the turds coming yet, buddy?"

Mitch told him to get stuffed, adding, "You know that thing on your head looks like it belongs to Lucy's friend Ethel."

Miro laughed until he was coughing, saying that was a good one. Wally reached under the visor for a joint and stuck it in his mouth, saying he needed to get his game on, pressing in the lighter, pointing out the RCMP detachment as they passed it.

"Not to worry," Miro said. "The island squad's a bunch of Dudley Do-Rights. Got their hands full with speeding logging trucks and bear sightings."

Heading west on Grafton, Miro told Wally to go straight till he got to Adams, reaching for the joint.

After turning onto Sunset, they passed a lone Jeep coming the other way. Once past Josephine Lake they had the road to themselves all the way to the southern tip of the island, pines a hundred feet tall, the odd house here and there.

The place they were looking for was a graying board and batten facade with the blinds drawn—moss growing on the walls and roof. The only sign that anybody came by was an axe buried in a stump, a flower box under the front window that used to contain geraniums until the deer got them. Deer all over the island, eating everything in sight, leaping the six foot fence behind the shed, the building used for supplies and sleeping quarters. A Pinto wagon that survived countless recalls stood in the tall grass, the front quarter panel rusted through, the door in primer grey, the rear quarter in faded green.

Miro pulled the holstered revolver from under the seat, checked the rounds and strapped it on, telling Wally again to stay with the van and keep his eyes peeled, asking if they needed to go over it one more time. He nicked his head to the ordnance crate holding the RPG-7.

"I got it," Wally said. "Stick the rocket in, hit the button and *whoosh*, you got a building lot."

"Remember the part where you stand away from the van when you go *whoosh*, or we're walking back." Miro nodded to Mitch, and they were gone, leaving Wally drooling over the crate.

They came low among the ferns, brown and dead, the fronds sending up clouds of flies. Along the blind side of the house, they crossed a broken section of fence, each cradling a cylinder of nitrous oxide, the Hefty box, a bag of tools slung over Mitch's shoulder, the flies swarming, getting in their ears and eyes.

Around the back, Miro tapped the AC line and connected the cylinders via flex hoses, leaving Mitch to swat flies and keep lookout. The grass out back was patchy, tall in spots, bald in others, the color all gone from a kid's swing set, a tangle of blackberry and rusting paint cans by a potting shed. He thought he caught a glimpse of a whitetail moving like a ghost among the trees, bringing visions of Tolley's eight-pointer, making him think of Ginny again.

Mitch flicked his tongue the way he did when his nerves started taking over. Deciding which way was up, he took the Evirstar gas mask, fastening the strap behind his head, catching a flash of the Chevy van's chrome through the pines, the very model Uncle Harmon used for hauling his paint cans and ladders between job sites. Pulling the goggles down, he hoped Wally wasn't smoking more of that shit, thinking of doing something stupid with that warhead.

♪♪

Drumming his fingers on the steering wheel, Wally relit the joint and cursed the morning DJ, telling him to shut the fuck up and play some Sabbath or Zeppelin, "War Pigs" or "The Immigrant Song." Next time he stole a ride, he'd get one with a CD player, treat himself to something cool like that FedEx guy drove. He checked his Rolex, itching to open the crate.

He picked up Mitch's Sunny D bottle from behind his seat and unscrewed the blue cap, looking into the liquid, considered the last few swigs. Recapping it, he tossed it on the floor and checked the glovebox for something to eat, thinking he caught a whiff of Sunny's perfume on his sleeve. Was she up yet, teasing her hair, getting ready for her shift at Chickie's? Thinking of her in that red thong. Then he was comparing Bruna, decked out in that plaid shirt she had on the first time he saw her, that paw print tat on her thigh.

Unzipping himself, he slumped back in the seat, guessing the boys should be pumping in the gas by now.

Fifteen minutes since he turned the valves full open—time to do it. Pulling a pry bar from the bag, Miro moved to the side door, leaving the cylinders and tools behind. Back in the van, he had told them how he rigged Artie's front doors with spring-loaded knives and spike rigs, leaving the back doors for coming and going, told them about the narc that kicked in the wrong door that time in Maple Ridge, left him shish-kebabbed to the door, making the world a better place.

The two of them looked like something out of a Japanese sci-fi, the masks giving them bug eyes and long muzzles. Miro flapped his jacket behind the Vaquero, ready to go Wild West in case Loop and Pinkie weren't out on the floor with stupid grins.

The brief thing with Pinkie was long ago, back before Artie cut him loose on account of the asthma, back before Pinkie settled for Loop. The guy was half her age, freebasing his pimpled face off most of the time. It would do Miro good to put a bullet in him. He nodded for Mitch to ease back the storm door.

Mitch's breathing sounded like he was underwater, the screw-on cylinder on the end of the mask weighing heavy. He ignored his rumbling gut, got ready to tape up anybody inside, mouths, wrists, and ankles, then stuff the pot into bags, the Hefty box and duct tape jammed under his arm. Get out before Wally got into the hundred-percent range and let the warhead fly, Miro dropping the Dancin' Bare matches in the yard. The three of them would be back on the ferry and heading home, reading about it in tomorrow's *Sun*.

Wedging the pry bar between the wooden door and frame, Miro set his feet, looking into Mitch's sci-fi eyes, then he counted three. Splintering wood tore from the frame, Miro bucking his shoulder at the door, ripping out the chain, stumbling into the dark, Mitch right behind him.

The storm door's glass shattered, Miro and Mitch whirled on the landing, both looking out at the spring-loaded blade stuck in a pine twenty feet away. The knife had passed between them, no more than an inch from either one.

The pit bull jumped a child's gate at the top of the half flight of stairs, snarling, leaping at them, both men turning into each other. Throwing his arms up, Mitch knocked Miro's mask. Snapping its jaws on the cylinder of Mitch's mask, the dog snarled, shaking it.

Dropping the pry bar, ripping off his mask, Miro drew and fired. The pistol shot was deafening. The dog was pitched down the basement stairs, an explosion of dark wet on the wall. The handrail leading down kept Mitch from falling after it; he stumbled into Miro.

Loop showed at the top of the stairs, bringing a carbine level to his hip, working the bolt. Shoving Mitch aside, Miro moved, bringing the Vaquero up when an animal trap snapped into his ankle. He screamed, the pistol dropping from his hand.

Loop fired as Miro fell. Missed. Mitch jumped past Miro on the stairs and rushed Loop as he worked the bolt, bringing his Walther hard across Loop's head, Loop falling, knocking down the child's gate.

The ringing in his ears gave way to Miro's screaming. Mitch told him to hang on, kicking the gate out of the way, jumping on Loop, ready to strike him again. The racking of a slide stopped him. The light clicked on in the kitchen, making him turn his head.

"Get off him." The woman's voice was cool, the black hole of a slug barrel staring Mitch in the eye, same as the one that took out Jeffery. Behind the barrel stood Pinkie Fox.

Mitch let the Walther drop from his fingers. Lifting his

knee off Loop, he raised his hands, Miro still bawling on the stairs.

"Shove it with your toe—slow," Pinkie said, "because I hate the way this thing kicks." Pinkie stood in the middle of the kitchen, raw-boned with short-cropped hair, gelled in spikes like a pineapple, ghost white hands on the Mossberg. "That all of you—just two?"

Mitch nodded and made a V with his fingers, showing two, shoving the gun toward her. He saw the knife rig mounted above him where the doorbell box should be.

She told him he'd go first if he was lying, then told him to go back down and lock the door, watching Mitch step past Miro and the fallen child's gate. Padding forward, slippers on veiny feet, a granny dress with a camo pattern, she picked up the Walther, helping Loop to his feet, pressing the pistol into his hand. Top of the stairs, she looked down at Miro lying in a ball, smiling as she recognized him. "Miro Knotts." She laughed. "You old son, you should have called first; I'd have baked a cake."

The pain was unlike anything Miro had ever felt, hands hopeless on the steel jaws, the teeth feeling like they were sheering through to the bone. He begged Pinkie to get it off.

"Number-four coil-spring, best thing for vermin," she said, looking at his ankle. "Stax wanted to up it to a sixteen. Lucky Loop is Loop and never got around to it—would've left you with a stump." She lifted the trap's chain with the end of the shotgun barrel, making him scream. "That's Victor traps for you—the best there is, sharp as hell." She looked to Mitch, taking the friendly out of her voice. "Told you to go lock the door."

Telling Loop to watch them, Pinkie cradled the shotgun on her arm, went and took her cell off the kitchen counter and punched in a number.

At the side door, Mitch looked at the dead dog at the

bottom of the stairs, its tongue lolling, its eyes lifeless, an ugly, wet crater in its side. The jamb was splintered away, nothing to close the door on. His heart was punching at his ribs, his breath coming like he just dashed the hundred. He turned back with his hands held wide. Loop asked if the dog was dead, and he said yeah. Loop motioned for him to come back up.

Miro squeezed away tears, prying at the steel teeth, the blood puddling into his Nike, looking at his gun on the stair, then at Mitch, hoping he'd do something.

"Loop, where's your head's at, you old son?" Pinkie asked from the kitchen, waiting for someone to pick up the other end of the line.

"Getting careless I guess, Pink," Loop said, leaning his carbine against the wall, the Walther in his hand, checking his teeth with his tongue, a couple feeling loose. He wiped blood from his mouth, saying, "I got no excuses." He waved for Mitch to hurry up and come up the stairs.

"Guess it's a lesson then," Pinkie said.

"Yeah," Loop said, then to Mitch, "Help him out of that thing. I'm sick of his whining."

Loop called Miro Popeye, telling him if it was up to him, he'd have him chewing through his own leg to get free.

"Stax? Pinkie," she spoke into the phone, leaving a message. "Seems we got company over here. An old friend's come to call, and brought a buddy with him. We're having a nice chat about old times. Right now, they're admiring my Mossberg. Me, I'm wondering how you want to play it. Oh, and I hate to do it, but I got to tell you . . ." She sighed, saying they shot Ike, waiting a moment before adding she was real sorry about that, nothing she could have done about it since Loop insisted on bringing poor Ike, then flipped the phone closed and laid it back on the counter.

Loop said thanks a lot.

Coming into the back hall, Pinkie watched Mitch hunch next to Miro, saying, "Stax got him as a pup from someplace called the Paw'd Squad, outside of L.A. Rescued him from some asshole raising dogs for sport. Where's the sport in dogs tearing each other up, tell me that?"

Looking up at them, Mitch said he was sorry about Ike, said he grew up with dogs.

"You got five more seconds to get that off his leg, Sunshine," Pinkie said to Mitch, "or you'll be joining Ike."

Mitch took hold of either side of the trap. Miro clamped his eyes and teeth together, Mitch pulling the steel jaws apart. Miro couldn't swallow the scream, Mitch lifting his bloody foot out, inching the pistol with his own foot, sliding it close to Miro's hand.

It dawned on Loop, he only had the one gun, guessing what was happening in front of him. Taking a couple of stairs, he swung the pistol, hitting Mitch across the spine, shoving him with his foot, Mitch falling back down to the landing. Getting down and sticking the Walther against Miro's ear, Loop reached for the Vaquero, saying, "Still playing John Wayne, eh Popeye, you little freak?" Grinning when Miro told him to fuck himself, Loop grabbed him by the hair, reminding him there was a lady present, sticking the Walther in his belt and pressing the big revolver into Miro's cheek. "What do you think, Pink, do a little root canal with Popeye's own gun?"

"Think we wait for Stax."

"Hey, I know Stax," Mitch said, pleading in his voice.

"That so?" Loop pulled Miro up the stairs by his hair. He was enjoying this, saying to Mitch, "Come by just to help Popeye take Pinkie on a date, did you? Him not being man enough to do it on his own."

"Get fucked," Miro said through all the pain.

Loop bashed the barrel into Miro's face, breaking his

nose, letting him fall, saying, "Warned you about the mouth."
Loop smiled over at Pinkie, then told Mitch to get his ass
back up here, bring that duct tape with him and get in the
kitchen unless he wanted some of the same.

Mitch wanted to run, wishing he could go back to an hour
ago, his eyes on Miro, seeing the blood flowing from his
nose, giving him a slick goatee, his pant leg bloody and torn.
Pumping nitrous oxide through the air conditioning, Miro
talked like he knew what he was doing, and Mitch had been
dumb enough to buy it.

Stepping over Miro, he handed Loop the tape and went
into the kitchen, wondering if Wally was waiting for a printed
invitation. Feet on the dash, smoking that shit with that stupid
do-rag on his head, rock blaring loud enough to drown out
the gunshots.

Pinkie nodded to the custom-fit plastic door sealing the
living room archway, ushering him by wagging the Mossberg.
"What you came for's in there."

Mitch unzipped the plastic door, stepping through. The
marijuana stood in plastic tubs in even rows, flowering under
more lights than the Vegas Strip, heavy black sheets over the
bay window, Mylar on the walls, twin propane tanks fueling
the heaters. The walls had been opened to the dining room
and the bedroom behind it, making a long L-shape. The air
was humid with that skunk smell.

"Nothing like a few potted plants to spruce up the place,"
Pinkie said.

Mitch nodded like he was impressed, telling her his name.
Not surprised that the weed wasn't cured and compressed
into bricks like Miro said it would be. He hadn't got anything
right so far.

"Want me to say it's good to meet you, Mitch? 'Cause I
don't see it as that kind of situation."

"Look, it was all him, Miro there. He worked for you guys, for Artie Poppa, at least he said he did, said he set all this up."

"True."

Mitch looked around at the six-foot forest rooted in rock wool, tubing running to the hydroponic pots.

"Don't get me wrong," she said. "Miro's the shits as a human being, but when it comes to growing, he knows a thing or two. When he crossed the Bob Marley with the Maui Wowie . . ." Pinkie said, her head going side to side, holding the barrel level with Mitch's bubbling gut. "It was a thing of beauty, I must admit."

He nodded like he got it.

"Never saw a guy so dedicated," she said. "Worked around the clock when Artie moved the works inside. He tweaked it, got the high so there wasn't so much couch-lock, not too much head-stone either so you're asking questions all night, just a good balance."

Mitch kept nodding.

"Even came up with framing in the false living rooms, making a three-foot wall behind the picture windows, nail up some pictures, leave the drapes open, and from the street it looks like a normal place." She said it was sad to see old Miro slide down the shitter like this. "What did he figure, Artie owed him one?"

"I don't know what he figured. I just—"

"He seeing anybody?"

"You mean like a doctor?"

"Like a woman—he got one or still renting them?"

"Some chick comes and hangs around."

"Yeah?"

"Works at this topless shoeshine place downstairs. Guess she's like a girlfriend."

"Topless shoeshine, huh?" Not surprised, Pinkie nodded,

then was laughing behind the Mossberg, getting the picture, asking, "This topless shoeshiner got a name?"

Mitch had to search for it. "Bruna, I think it was, something like that."

"Bruna, huh? She young?"

"Not too, I guess maybe forty."

"Good looking?"

"Guess so."

"Huh. Not like him—used to go for the young stuff, I mean bobby-socks young. Had a hard time with a grown woman." Pinkie was thinking for a moment, then asked, "Bruna, what's that, Russian?"

"I don't know, Italian maybe."

"Don't get me wrong . . . what's your name, Mitch?"

"Yeah."

"Well, Mitch, my hat's off to him. It's on account of guys like him, the shit we're growing these days blows the rest away, better than any Kush, Haze or Thunderfuck I ever smoked, better by a mile."

"Yeah. Listen, think I could use your can?"

She went on, "Yeah, the guy was part of the vision alright, a big reason why bud's right up there with lumber and fish, far as industry goes."

"And I'm why assholes like you have jobs," Miro called from the floor in the back hall, catching Loop's foot to his ribs.

Pinkie said that was true, telling Mitch they'd all have jobs until the feds decided to legalize it. "That's when a seven-billion-dollar industry does a crash and burn." She snapped her fingers. "Thousands of us in the UI lines. The whole West Coast'll go bust."

Mitch nodded.

"Don't think it can't happen. Lucky for us, the premier's an imbecile, not a storm trooper like that guy they had in New York." Pinkie took her cell phone, crooked the Mossberg under her arm and hit redial. "You know, I read where this professor in Colorado figures pot's like oil to a car, slows down human aging."

"That right?"

"A joint a day keeps the nip-and-tuckers away." She let it ring until Stax's answering machine came on again. She hung up.

"Look, Pinkie, is it? I suffer with the Crohn's disease, irritable bowel syndrome, and—"

"Wouldn't be good for that."

"I mean, I really got to use your can."

"Which one of you shot the dog?"

Mitch pointed in Miro's direction, Pinkie nodding, motioning him through to the kitchen, saying it was right down the hall, reminding him how he could be peeing out of a giant hole in his chest.

He lowered his voice, looking in her blue eyes. "I owe Miro some dough on account of my treatment for the Crohn's. You know how he gets, had my feet in the fire . . ." Ducking through the plastic door, Mitch didn't see Loop coming past the stove, raising the revolver and cracking the butt across his head. An explosion of pain and down Mitch went, looking up at Pinkie's mouth moving, words coming through a funnel, the room swirling.

"One thing I can't stand is a whiny snitch," Loop was saying to Mitch. "Think you're talking your way out of this? I don't think so." Then to Pinkie, "I say we do them both, show Stax some taking-care-of-business." He aimed at Mitch.

"How about you settle for beating on them till he calls? No point pissing him off more than he'll already be."

Loop thought about the dead dog at the bottom of the stairs. He tore a sheet of paper towel from a roll on the counter, dabbing blood from his mouth, sure Pinkie would be reminding Stax it was his idea to bring the dog. "We could take them out by the blueberries. Nice and private there."

Mitch looked at Miro laid out in the hall, the fear rocking him. "You already got Miro. Me, I'm nobody. I'm on the next train out of here; you'll never see me again."

"You hear that, Popeye?" Loop went and flipped Miro onto his stomach. Climbing on him, putting the gun on the floor, he asked if he was still breathing and twisted his hands, starting to wrap the duct tape around his wrists.

"I got a kid and an old lady somewhere," Mitch said to Pinkie. "Miro there, he's got nobody."

"The shoeshine chick," Pinkie said.

"That's nothing real. You said yourself he pays her. I mean, I hate to see anything happen to him, but he's—"

"Tell you what," Loop said, "you don't want to see anything happen to him, I'll do you first, how's that?"

"Fuck you all," Miro said, his voice a croak, his face pressed against the floor, blood smeared across his face.

Loop grabbed a fistful of hair, loving this, slamming Miro's head against the boards, once, twice—the sound of a coconut getting cracked. "Didn't I just tell you to watch your mouth?"

Miro curled his fingers, leaving the middle one up. Taking out a knife, Loop yanked off a yard of tape, slicing it and mummified Miro's head, broken nose and all, cutting off his air and bashing his skull on the floor a couple more times. His nose gushing blood, Miro kicked out his good leg, his Nike marking the oak with a blood trail, Loop riding him like a Brahma, having fun with it, counting off steamboats. He ripped off the tape when he got to ten, Miro screaming and moaning.

That was it; Mitch made a break for the front door, got as far as clamping his fingers around the door knob before Pinkie swung the barrel, clipping him on the ear, sending him tearing through the plastic wall, fighting like he was caught in a web.

"I got money," Miro wheezed. Where the fuck was Wally? Where the fuck was Stax?

Loop's face was one big grin. "Like how much?"

"Got a hundred on me." Miro couldn't seem to get enough air, the pain in his leg unbearable.

"That's already mine, plus I leave more than that in the collection plate."

"But there's more, lots more."

"You got the floor, Popeye." Loop got off him, rocking on his haunches, pressing the Vaquero under his chin, lifting it, wanting to pull the trigger, watch this guy's head do zero to sixty.

"Ten GS in twenties," Miro said. "And I got some oil stashed away."

"You back doing the oil, huh?"

"And a bunch of pistols. Whatever's there's yours. You go help yourself, then let me go," Miro said through gritted teeth, glancing at Mitch. "You can do what you want with that piece of shit."

Pinkie fetched a pen and paper from beside the phone on the counter, the Mossberg hooked under her arm, waiting for Miro to speak.

"Back of my bedroom closet there's a box of LPs, mostly James Last."

"Who?"

"They were my mom's. The oil's behind it in a box marked 'xmas,' not Christmas spelled out, guns are in the hockey bag, money's laid out under the mattress."

"You still over at that place on Homer?" Pinkie remembered where he used to take her.

Miro spelled out his address since coming back to town. "Key's in my pocket."

"This Bruna chick live with you?" Pinkie asked, Miro

saying no, she was just a hooker that worked downstairs, meant nothing to him.

Loop dug into Miro's pocket, coming up with a key ring, asking, "Which one?"

Miro nodded when he held up the right key, Loop asking what the other keys were for. Miro told him most were from Seattle.

"And the car keys?"

"My Challenger."

"You mean my Challenger."

Miro said sure, it was his, not saying it was back in Seattle.

"That his right address?" Pinkie held the paper down to Mitch, Mitch looking at it, nodding.

Loop said to Pinkie, "Still say we should do these assholes."

"Do it then," she said, her eyes going to Miro. "But you answer for it, along with the dog."

Miro called her a bitch, paying the price, Loop grabbing his hair, slamming his head down again, yanking him to his feet, slamming him against the wall, sticking the barrel against his broken nose. This was the moment: he was going to shoot him.

"On the way back, stop at the Ruddy Potato and get a bag of French ground; we're out." Pinkie said it like she didn't care what Loop did.

"Me and Stax are like this," Miro said to Loop. "Fuck with me, you fuck with him."

"You want the fine grind?" Loop asked her, pressing the barrel against Miro's nose, making him scream.

Pinkie's cell rang. She hooked the shotgun and reached for the phone.

The side door flew open with a crash, the knob gouging into the wall. Wally threw himself at the stairs, pistol in both hands in front of him. Pinkie was swinging the Mossberg, Loop turning. Wally fired first.

Loop was slammed back into the wall, blocking any clear shot Pinkie had, Miro dropping. Pinkie pumped a round over the counter, taking out the broom closet and the railing, racking and firing again.

Loop pressed back against the wall, trying to stay on his feet. Wally shot him again, jumping up and grabbing him as he fell, getting behind him and firing into the kitchen, taking out the Florida light. Bakelite and glass rained down, the room pitched in darkness.

Backing into the grow room, Pinkie racked the slide, Mitch kicking out a foot, causing her to stumble, the Mossberg going off, blasting out the bank of thousand-watt grow lights, punching holes through both propane tanks.

The fireball matched anything the warhead would have done, rocking the house, blowing out the windows, blasting Pinkie through the grow room like she was on guy wires, her body slamming into the far wall. The plants fueled the flames that ate the house, spreading to the shed and ferns and brush and pines.

WHO DID IKE?

"Bitch said you were upping it to a bear trap," Miro said to Stax, gritting his teeth, looking at the mess of his leg resting on the coffee table, the pain incredible, shooting up into his knee. The dried blood and ripped flesh looked right out of *Jaws*. His broken nose made him wheeze, sounded whiny when he talked. He gripped his thigh while Bruna swabbed cotton against the raw meat.

"Jesus, take it easy," he cried out, twisting his face at the sting of hydrogen peroxide, growling like an animal.

"That stupid bitch was stoned half the time," Stax said, sitting on the sofa, unconcerned about the leg, thinking Miro was a wimp, watching Bruna play nurse with the swab. "And you go believing the shit coming out of her mouth."

"How about your spring-loaded knife for fuck's sake?"

"Yeah, Loop changed that a while ago," Stax said. "Forgot about it."

Miro flinched, slapping at Bruna on account of the stinging.

"How about you drag your whining ass to emergency?" she said, slapping back.

Stax got off the sofa, easing her aside, getting in Miro's face. "And who the fuck told them to take Ike?"

"How should I know?" Miro grabbed the swab away from Bruna, told her she was done, told her to get something to wrap the leg, saying to Stax, "I told Artie long time ago, those two were worth shit. He ever listen? No, he did not." The scene at the grow house flashed through his mind: Pinkie firing the Mossberg, the fireball, Pinkie hurled through the living room, Wally dragging him and Mitch out the back door, the whole place going up, all that weed feeding the flames.

Stax leaned close, clapping a hand above Miro's ankle, inches from the raw meat. "So, tell me again, who did Ike?"

Miro cried out and tried to twist away, but couldn't. "Already told you, as soon as we go in, Mitch knocks me down the stairs, goes all nuts and starts shooting, puts one in Ike."

"With the gun you sold him?"

"Then he got Loop; who knows, maybe Loop hit Ike?"

"And you weren't shooting?"

"I told you I got pushed down, lost my piece. When I got back up, got my leg in your fucking number four trap. Look at this hamburger. Jesus."

"The perfect stupid guys, you said."

"They were your mules, remember? And who told you the shit'd go down at Western? Me, *aiiyyeeeee . . .*"

Stax squeezed the leg, saying, "That was the word I got from inside, yeah." Then he thumped a finger against Miro's chest. "Ike never did nothing to nobody."

"Yeah, he was a sweet guy," Miro said, thinking if he hadn't shot it, the psycho dog would have had Mitch's arm down to a stump.

Bruna came back with Polysporin and a Telfa pad, wedging herself between the two men, telling the big man to go sit down over there, let her do her work. Stax stepped back, and Miro knocked the stuff out of her hand, telling her to stop with the Florence Nightingale horseshit and go get some beers, Bruna telling him to fuck off, saying she hoped they amputated the leg, told him if he wanted beer to hop to the fridge. Then she went in the bedroom, slamming the door.

"Girlfriend's all heart," Stax said, and went and got the beer. "So it was this Wally guy, huh?"

"I told you it was Mitch." Miro took the can, popped the tab. "Wally was in the van drooling over the fucking rocket launcher."

"Right, Mitch," Stax said it like he was being handed a load of crap.

Funny time to be thinking about her, on his way to see Artie Poppa on a nude beach. But Karl was thinking about

WRECK BEACH

her all the time now, drawing her face in his mind, the sea-green eyes, the auburn hair, the way their bodies came together, realizing he was in love with her.

A name on the Vancouver drug scene, this Artie Poppa had ties to the Mexican drug cartel, networked into a web of biker distribution all down the coast. What Karl didn't know was why Artie wanted to see him on a nude beach. But what do you do? A guy like that has his goon call and wants a face to face, you don't say no. Karl guessed Poppa must have heard about his reputation, heard the if-your-man's-breathing line. Truth be told, Karl missed the excitement of playing with the bad guys.

He threw the Roadster into park next to the "clothing optional" sign on top of the bluff. A notice waved next to it, announcing something called the Bare Buns Run coming up.

Stax had called in the morning, told him Artie wanted to see him at two, Karl asked why and why there, Stax repeated the time and place, asked if he got it and hung up. Karl guessed it was the kind of place that made it tough to wear a wire or hide a piece.

Pine trees hung over the bluffs, blocking the view of the Pacific, swaying in the breeze coming inland. Cold for this time of year. Parking next to Artie's Cadillac, Karl left the Taser under the insurance papers in the glovebox, guessing he'd have the naked folk edgy—a guy walking around with fifty thousand volts of frying power.

Letting Johnny Cash finish "Hurt," he switched off the Blaupunkt, locked up and started down the escarpment, over four hundred and seventy stairs. The same stairs Bob Young took when he made the serve with the envelope between his cheeks. He told Karl his thighs ached for a week.

Nearing the bottom, Karl understood what Bob meant, his own thighs felt on fire. Doughy bodies, some sitting, some lying, the odd one baked leather brown. Karl thinking it was a world of its own down here, quiet and hidden below the university lands, away from the city's static.

Along the tree line stood Vendors' Row, a stretch of umbrellas and portable tables. Sandwiches and drinks, Native blankets, Swedish massage, pot and X under the table, whatever you wanted. The place reminded Karl of a time of free love in the sixties, a time before his. There was a vibe about it he liked.

His sneakers brimmed with sand by the time he spotted them, the grit getting between his toes. An old man on a beach blanket with his goon standing over him. A middle-aged guy looking like Ray Winstone in dreadlocks sat on a Coleman near them, banging on a conga, his gut jiggling, his wife strumming on a six-string. Eyes squeezed shut, she dished up a Ziggy Marley number about sailing to Jamaica.

Their towheaded twins were busy building a city in the sand, looking up as Karl approached.

The goon was Stax; he stepped over to the Ray Winstone guy and said something to him. Ray and his wife stopped playing and packed up the kids and moved down the beach. Artie peeled off his shades, Ricardo Montalbán looks with the coldest eyes Karl had ever seen framed by a uni brow. A silver cross on a chain hung around his neck, the cross looking upside down, with the cross tie closer to the bottom than the top.

"Karl Morgen?" Artie said it was good of him to come, his accent barely there.

Karl offered his hand, surprised by the grip of the gnarled hand, guessing Artie knew hard labor in a younger day. Standing behind Artie, Stax was dressed in jeans and a T-shirt, fitting it like liverwurst in its casing. Karl checked himself in the goon's wraparound shades. The twin images were distorted, leaving Karl wondering was he really that white.

"Good place to get your vitamin D," Artie said, Karl's paleness not lost on him, motioning for Stax to stop blocking his sun.

"Get it places you don't even want it," Karl said, taking off his sneakers, shaking out the sand.

"Good place to see if anyone's got bugs, too," Stax said, motioning for Karl to turn around, his own wire sewn inside the pocket of his jeans, Miro listening in. Nothing special about this guy. Middle-aged and going bald. No big deal he dragged Miro off some couch in Belltown. The cockiness reminded Stax of the guy who owed Artie ten grand two days too long, Stax going to collect it, the guy telling him to come back when he finished lunch. Stax knocked away the guy's grilled cheese, dragged him over and pressed his head against the stove's coil, turned it on, saying to let him know when he was ready to pay up. Branding a spiral across the guy's cheek, he got Artie's ten grand just like that.

Karl held his hands out and did a turn. Stax patted him down, hoping he'd try some shit like he pulled on Miro.

"Stax tells me you're good at finding people," Artie said.

"Heard that, huh?"

"Yeah," Stax said. "Some shyster lawyer in Seattle says you got a reputation like that TV guy, Dog."

"Gave that up. Got myself a healthy line of work."

"Ah, a man's health . . ." Artie shook his head. "Without it he has nothing." Artie tapped his own chest, Karl seeing the two-inch scar on the left breast. "Have a cardioverter-defibrillator planted here, keeps me ticking."

"That like a pacemaker?"

"A pacemaker corrects the heart rate. My little friend gives a jolt if the beat goes too fast or slow. Never ate a donut in my life, you believe that?" Artie looked to the sun and shrugged. "Now I eat like a rabbit, take meds and I'm in bed by ten."

"Maybe just bad luck," Karl said.

"Cardiologist says it's bad genes; me, I blame stress in the workplace."

Karl looked at the waves rolling onto the sand. What did Artie expect, a cushy life with a pension?

"So now I breathe the sea air, feel it tickle my balls."

"Guess there are worse things," Karl said, his eyes going to Artie's upside-down cross again, wishing he'd get on with it, knowing he wasn't here for a dick-swing and a reminisce.

Artie noticed him looking at the cross, asking if he was a religious man.

"Not so you'd notice."

"It's a Peter cross," Artie said and held it up to Karl. "On account they crucified St. Peter head down."

"Head down, huh?"

Stax told him yeah, those Romans could really torture a man, make it last for days.

"Guess Jesus got off lucky," Karl said.

Artie said it was no joke, tapping the scar on his chest. "Things become clear to a man after he comes this close."

"Yeah, look, I don't mean to be rude, Mr. Poppa," Karl said. "But see, I burn easy."

Artie told him about Jeffery Potts getting killed at a place of his in North Van, then what looked like a pair of plumbers broke into his own house up in the Properties, shot it up while his useless dog stood by. "Then two nights ago, some *cabrónes*, maybe the same ones, broke into another place of mine, burned it to the ground." Artie glanced over his shoulder in the direction of Bowen Island. "A small fortune went up in smoke."

"Think I read about it," Karl said, remembering the headlines in the *Sun*. "Take it the place wasn't insured?"

Artie's tight grin said he was getting tired of Karl being cute, saying the ones that did it took the spoons from the mouths of his children and left him with one associate dead, another in the burn unit at Vancouver General.

"And killed my dog," Stax said.

"This the same dog?"

"Different one," Artie said, looking to Stax, then saying to Karl, "You get me the names, you make me a happy man."

"Why not let the cops handle it?"

Stax asked if he was kidding.

"Okay, let's say I find them, then what?"

"You point your finger and five grand lands in your hand," Artie said. "Five a head if you're pointing more than a finger, fact, make it an even twenty."

Karl knew Artie was telling, not asking, but he asked him anyway. "Why not use your own people?" Nodding at Stax.

Down the beach, a fat couple walked along hand in hand, their stomachs hanging like inner tubes. They stopped over by the Ray Winstone clan, all of them glancing over, then quickly away.

"To the authorities I am a man of interest, that is how they say it." Artie's eyes followed the fat couple as they continued over to the vendors' tables.

"Not sure I'm your best bet," Karl said. "I mean, I'm retired from all that."

Artie snapped his fingers and said to Stax, "What's that name?"

"Named him Ike."

Artie looked up at him like he was an idiot.

"PJ Addie," Stax said, reciting her address, adding it was right off Commercial, liking the way the smug melted off Karl's face.

Karl's stomach gave a growl, he picked at the shared anti-pasto. Pissed at the way Artie and Stax played him, he

BOTTOM FEEDING

wanted to tell PJ about the meeting on Wreck Beach, wanted to have it all out there, wanted her safe—but couldn't get a word in edgewise.

On her own tangent, she was excited about the gifts she brought, eager for him to tear away the gift wrap. The *Neck and Neck* disc was her way of weening him off the hardcore hick tunes. She loved Knopfler's licks back when he was with Dire Straits, this album with Atkins every bit as good, only mellow in an old-school sort of way, right up Karl's alley. The second gift wrapped in red tissue was the Jamie Oliver cook-book, the one with the tikka masala recipe.

He kissed her, feeling kind of bad, had no idea six months was an anniversary.

Lunch arrived, the waiter holding the plates, asking her, "Gnocchi?"

She answered, "Who's there?"

Karl was still laughing when the waiter left, gagging on his calzone, the mushrooms he asked the waiter to hold tasting like earthy cardboard. Chasing it down with some of PJ's Beaujolais Cru, he tried again to tell her about Artie. But PJ was on her second glass, loose talking about a case Walt Wetzel had her working on, filing punitive damages for some granny shopper that went down on a wet Safeway floor, not an orange pylon in sight. Karl grimaced at the thought of the old girl needing a double hip, PJ saying her boss Walt was doing his personal crusader bit, getting a little media out of it, a total ham in front of the Global News camera.

"Walt wear a cape and tights when he talks out of both sides of his mouth?" Karl liking the guy less every time he heard his name.

"Does it as easy as breathing," she said, sipping her wine, pulling the pimento from an olive and popping it in her mouth. "Walt sniffs out negligence and lost wages like a police dog. No stopping him—acts like he's doing people favors, and all he gives a shit about is maximum compensation."

"Sounds like you need a break." The pieces to a dead lawyer joke came together in Karl's head, but this wasn't the time. PJ went on about how Walt sued the city for negligence last year for not posting warning signs about waves at the aquatic center. Won two hundred K because his ten-year-old client swallowed water other kids allegedly peed in.

"Lot of dough for an alleged *schluck*," Karl said, letting her unload, still aiming to tell her, topping up her glass for the third time. "How do I explain to Mother my girl works for an ambulance chaser?"

"Your girl, huh?"

"Yeah." He looked at her, liking the reaction.

"That's got a ring."

"Could be one. We'll see how it goes."

It got her smiling, saying, "And I'm going to meet Mother."

"You'd love Bovina."

"That her name?"

"Where she lives, in the Catskills—beautiful this time of year."

It scared PJ a bit, thinking of herself as his girl. Taking his hand, she dropped the pimento into it, folding his fingers over it and squishing it. Then she was back to Walt, telling Karl they were suing the Playhouse Theater for inadequate security on seniors' night after two old-timers pummeled the bejesus out of each other in the line-up. She went on about nailing some waste management company for eight figures after some environmentalist photographer fell from the top of one of their garbage trucks, Walt arguing his client couldn't have known the truck might move.

Karl reached in his pocket, pulling out the travel brochure, pretending to ignore her, opening it to the picture of a couple feeding white-faced monkeys, saying again she needed a break. Artie Poppa's money would land them in a five-star and leave enough for IKEA.

Seeing the phone number and Helen's name on the back, she asked what his mother's name was.

RAIN · CHECK

"Got it," Miro said into the phone to Stax. The audio surveillance recorder worked like a charm. The guy at the Spy Shop assured him it was the latest thing, undetectable, voice activated, time and date stamped, the very thing the feds used. The bastards could listen through the cell phone in your own pocket, eye you from a satellite, tap into your home computer with their spyware. Can't be careful enough, the kid told him, throwing in a discount for paying in cash.

The tiny wire Miro had Bruna sew into Stax's jeans did the trick, the audio perfectly clear, Artie's voice, Karl's voice. Their words enough to incriminate both of them. Worth every cent Miro paid, everything on track until Stax called, throwing a wrench in the works, saying there was a change of plans, wasn't going to take out the two clowns, at least not now.

"What're you talking about?" Miro's euphoria popped like a bubble.

"Too much heat since the raid—my car the cops found at the docks, not yours."

"So, your car was there."

"Means they're watching me."

"So, be careful."

"Here's how we do this, we forget about the Burnaby house, lay low a bit, leave the personal shit out of it." Stax thinking of the JayMan, DeJesus and the hangarounds that got busted. The cops tore the *Knot So Fast* apart, pulling eighty keys and a couple dozen G36 automatic rifles from the false floors. Banging on his door, they wanted to know what his car was doing at the docks. Stax saying he loaned it to a friend, JayMan saying yeah. With nothing to hold him on, they released his car and promised they'd be watching.

"Either way, the two clowns got to go," Miro said.

"In due time," Stax said and hung up.

With Karl Morgen and Artie Poppa on tape, they were going down. Miro ached to stop by whatever prison they threw Morgen in, do a little visitation, dangle the recorder the kid at the Spy Shop sold him, tell the fucker through the glass who set him up, ask how it feels. Do it before the feds came with their extradition papers.

Bruna came in the living room, handing him a coffee, fifth one today, checking out his squashed nose, saying it was time to change his dressing, the bottles and gauze under her arm. He lifted her shirt tails, giving her a pat, saying how about it, raising a brow. Bruna pulled a face, saying sorry, sugar, she was already late getting back downstairs, thinking Miro was looking worse for wear every time she looked at him.

THE NURSE THAT SUCKS LEMONS

Leaning against the juice machine, Karl made like he was intrigued by getting the low-down on Valerie Bertinelli's engagement. The security guard passed on his rounds, Karl saying hi to him again, face buried in the old issue of *People*. When the intercom called the nurse at the station over to psychiatric, Karl tossed the magazine on the table, ducked past the empty station for the third time that morning and poked his head into Pinkie Fox's room, hoping to catch her awake this time.

She lay in the air-chamber burn bed under the fluorescent lights, drifting in and out of consciousness, hooked to a series of tubes for fluid resuscitation. Blue eyes nearly swollen shut, a gauze pad over one cheek, a cravat bandage around her forehead, her hair singed off. She spoke, her voice belonging to Phyllis Diller, barely audible, complaining about no peace in this dump, adding, "I already told you guys I was picking berries, just stopped to ask for directions . . ."

Karl held up the bouquet. "I'm not a cop."

She checked him out, just her eyes moving. "You always dress like that?"

"I get that a lot, probably the haircut."

"No, hon, it's the shoes."

He looked down at the Oakleys, realizing she couldn't see his shoes.

"So, if you're not a cop . . ."

"Guy you work for sent me."

"With flowers?"

"Wants to know who blew up his place." Karl laid the flowers down. "And the big guy that eclipses him, the guy you phoned from the house, wants to know who shot his dog."

"Stupid thing wasn't even housebroken."

"So you shot it?"

"Think Stax ever cleaned up after it?"

"That what you want me to go back with?"

She blinked at him like it didn't matter what he went back with, saying, "Who's picking up my tab?"

"You mean for here?" Karl had to lean in to hear her.

"Think Blue Cross covers getting blown to hell in a grow-op?" Her voice a whisper, she turned her head to the wall like she was talking to somebody. "Guy sends me flowers."

"The flowers are from me." Karl picked the bouquet off the bed. "Yellow, you know what it stands for?"

"Yeah, means we're friends, means you give a shit—like if I call up, we can catch a show or a bite like old buddies, and you won't expect a blow job."

Karl raised a brow, and she said, "That's what pink's for."

"You know your flowers."

"And I know this guy I'm supposed to work for didn't send lilies for Loop." She coughed.

"Sorry about your friend."

She closed her eyes to the pain, and Karl waited, watching the readout on the machine, hearing her breath come in rasps, wondering if she dropped off again. Then her eyes opened, and she asked if he'd heard about this cat that lives in a ward someplace back east, New England she thought it was. "Cat comes in and sits on a patient's bed when it's their time, curls up right through the family tears and last rights. Cat never gets it wrong. Thing sits on your bed, you're done."

"Some cat, huh?" Karl thought about his own cat, Chip, the way his eyes moved, like he was seeing things Karl couldn't. "Yeah, why not? An extra sense or something. I've got a cat that's pretty tuned in."

She said good for him and closed her eyes against another wave of pain. "Prick could've sent some methadone, not even a fucking Hallmark card." She looked at him, saying, "Still say you look like a cop."

"Think you know I'm not," Karl said and turned as the nurse walked by the door, going back to her station.

"What I told the ones this morning, the guys that dressed like you: look for a couple of guys with assault rifles, Vietnamese guys, something like that."

"Cops'll dig out the slugs, match them up, dust for prints then they'll ask you again, maybe get you under oath."

"I'm hooked to wires, eating painkillers like candy, second- and third-degree burns all over, just had a friend shot. Think I give a shit?"

"Sorry, Pinkie, I really am."

She drew a long breath. "How about you go find the nurse that looks like she sucks lemons, tell her her painkillers are worth shit."

"That it?"

"No. Take your flowers and your cop shoes and go fuck yourself."

"Nice."

"Oh, it's white for that."

"White, huh? I go back with that, you'll be seeing the big guy with the sour face. Don't think he'll be bringing flowers."

She was quiet a moment, knowing the kind of guy Stax was, then said, "The one guy's name was Mitch. The one that came in and shot Loop had one of those rapper things on his head."

"Okay."

"But the one you really want's a bug-eyed runt with bad teeth, goes by Miro."

It hit him like a punch. "Miro Knotts?" His mind flashed to the two guys standing by the Porsche outside Miro's the day he made the serve. They had to be the other two.

"Got a new way of walking after stepping in my Victor trap." Trying to smile, she started hacking, trying to tell him to get lost.

Saying thanks and wishing her a speedy recovery, he placed the flowers on the table by the door and went looking for the nurse that sucked lemons.

LADY LUCK

It was mid-morning when he got back to her place, tiptoeing in, PJ sleeping in on her day off, told him she felt like she was coming down with something when they got back from Elmo's Bohemia last night. Karl spooned her, feeling her warmth, wondering how her old man could just take off back when she was a kid, thinking of his own dad, the way the two of them got along. His dad would have called PJ "a keeper," saying something like she'd still be a beauty twenty years past drop-dead, the old man's way of talking.

When he did get a chance to tell her about the meeting on Wreck Beach, she asked if he was nuts, loud enough for all the heads in Elmo's to turn, the two of them at their spot at the bar. Karl said Artie wasn't asking as much as telling, PJ saying the problem was Karl liked rubbing up against danger, pushing it to the edge. "When a naked guy tells you to do something like that, threatens you if you don't, that's when you dial 9-1-1."

Karl promised to sleep on it, guessing by her look, he'd be doing it alone. But here they were in her bed, her sleeping in his arms, him lying awake, the trip to Costa Rica rolling through his mind again, seeing her on that white sand.

Lying there, thinking things through, he was wondering what happens to Miro Knotts when he gives him up to Artie, sure it wouldn't be pretty.

She turned toward him, awaking and giving him a smile.

Filing away the early visit to the hospital, he kissed her forehead, feeling her fever, asking how she was feeling.

"Like crap. You call yet?" She waited, glassy eyes looking at him. "You know who," she said, pulling the blanket around her neck.

"You scare me when you do that."

"Don't do that," she said.

"Do what?"

"Change the subject."

"You said sleep on it."

"Yeah, now it's morning." Looking at the bedside clock, she cursed how late it was.

"Thing is I hardly slept."

"That's the guilty conscience."

"What can the cops do? I mean, a guy asks to see you on a nude beach, offers you money to find somebody. Where's the crime in that?"

"He offered you money?"

"I tried to tell you, but—"

"Tell me now."

"Five grand to point them out." He didn't mention it was twenty if he pointed more than a finger, didn't mention one of them was the same guy he cuffed and dragged to jail in

Belltown, didn't mention he went to see Pinkie. "Artie just wants names. Right up my alley."

"The alley they'll find you in."

He put the back of his hand to her forehead.

"Nice try, cowboy." She play-punched his chin. "Go make the call."

He sat up, fishing for his pants. "You're sounding more and more like a wife."

"Logical?"

"Comes to things like this, I've always had this Lady Luck thing."

"She in the john when that Bean guy decked you with the pipe?"

He said good point.

"I mean, why you?" PJ asked. "He hear the 'if the guy's breathing' line?"

"Artie's being watched, playing it like he goes to church on Sundays. That's why me."

"Why not this Stax guy?"

The front door opened, and Dara called a hello through the house. PJ shot out of bed, grabbing her bathrobe, waving for Karl to hurry and get dressed, a glimmer of that long-ago time: her dad chasing up the stairs, narrowly missing her and Todd getting into things.

PJ was going for composure, scooping French roast for a pot of coffee, not sure if she put eight or nine scoops in the

PLEDGIES

grinder. Whatever she was coming down with was getting worse by the minute; the fever high, her eyes burning, her head in a vise.

Karl offered the plate of muffins he ran out to get from JJ Bean's, saying the very berry were to die for, everybody in town said so—trying his hand at small talk with Dara, a punk version of her mother.

"So, the two of you coming down the stairs means I have to call him Uncle Karl?" Dara bit into a muffin, her eyes sparkling, loving the moment, catching her mom in the act with her new boy toy. She said to Karl, yeah they're good, licking a bit of berry from her lip.

Cam the purple-haired groper sat on the counter in the corner, the KitchenAid mixer poking at his back. Acting like he wasn't high, checking out the muffin in his hand, the Visine doing nothing for his doll eyes.

"You think about it?" Dara knew she had her mom on the ropes, picking another muffin for later.

"About you coming back?"

"No, the other thing."

"Not now, Dara." PJ dumped the beans back in the bag and started recounting.

"Why not now?" Dara took another bite.

"Because now's not the time."

"The money's mine though, right?"

"The money's for college. We collapse the plan for something else, we get taxed and lose all the interest."

"But I'm not going back."

"Maybe you'll change your mind; you're young . . ."

"What about him—Karl, right?" Dara said. "He was young once; let's ask him." She smiled at Karl, saying again his muffins were good, crunching the paper cup and tossing it on the plate.

"Alright." PJ folded her arms and faced Karl. "Dara and Cam are off the Popsicle wrappers. The new thing's bigger tits."

"Mother!" Dara feigned outrage but was loving this.

"What suits you then, sweater melons?" PJ turned to Cam. "Cam, what do you call them, dear, your little rack of lamb?"

Cam was tongue-tied.

"You wanted me to ask, I asked." PJ switched on the grinder, counted to ten, turned it off and said to Dara, "Honey, there's nothing wrong with your original equipment. We should all be so perfect." She shot Cam a look, shaking coffee into the filter.

"You know your problem, Mother? You can't accept change—freaked when I dyed my hair, freaked when I got the eagle claws, freaked when I lost my . . ." She looked at Karl, let that trail off.

"One minute you're getting a BA, now, you've got D cups on the brain. Two-thirds of all boob jobs burst, you know that?

"Where'd you get that?"

"Where's he going to be if one pops?" PJ looked at Cam. "How about it, Cam—you wake up one morning and one of the rack's strayed to her naval, leaking like a sieve, what do you do, call Popsicle Pete?"

Cam was sure he saw the veins throb at PJ's temples. He put the muffin down, trying to hold it together.

"Come on, Cam. We're out of here." Dara shoved her muffins in her jacket pockets, tugged him off the counter and steered for the door. "It's Boobs-dot-com. Screw the college fund."

"Oh, for Christ's sake, Dara," PJ said.

Dara waited for Cam to stuff his feet in his skate shoes by the door, saying to him, "We'll go online."

"Online?" PJ followed them to the door.

"Yeah. Boobs-dot-com. Bountification of Our Boobs. They've got pledgies sponsoring girls like me."

"Dara, you've lost your mind."

"Come on, Cam." Dara was out the door.

Tugged down the steps, Cam turned and said to PJ, "Going up from a B is a big thing, believe me, Mrs. Addie."

PJ was looking at an idiot, then turned to Karl. "This from the man who collects Popsicle sticks." She watched them go, Dara tugging Cam, saying she knew this was a waste of time, PJ yelling after them to get their pledgies to go feed some Africans, they want to help people. "Cup size isn't a world issue for Christ's sake."

Two doors down, Mrs. Bennett raised her head from tending her geraniums. Closing the door, PJ went back in the kitchen, grabbing the coffee pot that was still dripping. The vise was tightening, her temples throbbing. She just wanted to crawl back into bed.

Karl held up the plate, offering her the last muffin.

PJ poured a cup and put the pot back. Twisting off the muffin top, she bit into it. She asked him to get an Aspirin from the bathroom.

He got up. "Sweater melons?"

She waved it off. "I've got her Barbies and her bear with the button eye in a box in the back of my closet." She dropped the rest of the muffin on the plate. "Now this, Jesus."

Karl went for the Aspirin, then held her until the coffee finished dripping. He told her she needed a change of scenery, meaning his place, along with a bowl of his famous chicken soup. His phone rang. The display told him it was Stax, probably wondering how he was coming with those names.

She couldn't sleep on account of the pounding outside, the windows rattling and Karl's bed feeling like it was vibrating.

LOUDER THAN WORDS

The garbage truck four floors down made more noise than the bridge crew, the driver rolling the metal bins to the truck and hoisting them up. She should have stayed home last night, but Karl convinced her it would do her good to get out of the house, stay at his place. He was being a sweet guy, wanting to take care of her. Made her a decent bowl of soup. She ate and tried to believe him that things with Dara would turn around.

He went to Sea-to-Sky early, saying he had a couple of serves waiting, told her to take more of the NyQuil, told her there was more soup in the pot, told her to get some sleep. Nice that he cared. She lay there knowing he was getting the names for Artie Poppa.

Wrapping the pillow around her ears like a wonton did no good. Her mind fluttered with thoughts of Dara, Popsicle wrappers, a boob job, and mother and daughter like oil and water.

She couldn't picture Patrick's face anymore, the senior who took notice of her so long ago at Rockridge Secondary, offering her rides home in his mom's Regal. All it took were a couple of sodas and tickets to the Five Man Electrical Band. PJ went from the front to the back seat to breastfeeding and changing diapers. And in the same wink, Patrick dropped out of school, got a job, got canned, got another job, got canned again, then dropped out of sight, borrowing his mom's Regal and driving to Calgary, starting life fresh, stocking Save-On shelves. The next nineteen years left PJ putting the ends together, alone, living from one child support check to the next.

She rolled one way, then the other, the pillow feeling like second base under her head. "Who can sleep in this place?" she asked Chip, sat up, kicking off the blanket, wrapping herself in Karl's robe, tempted to go on the balcony and throw a finger at the guys in the hard hats working the heavy machinery. The steam whistle sounded from over in Gastown, barely audible over the pounding. God, it was noon already.

Going into the bathroom, she guessed what she stepped in before she looked down. A flick of the light switch showed her foot well-coated in cat puke, squishing between her toes, cold, wet, and sticky. Nothing cute about her pink toenails now, the furball looking like a hair-encrusted kabob under her foot.

"Believe this belongs to you," she said to Chip, sitting by the door with his yellow-eyed indifference, licking a forepaw. PJ was pissed, but it wasn't Chip, and it wasn't the fever or the bullshit with Dara or the pounding from outside.

It was Karl. More cocky than cute, thinking he had things with Artie Poppa under control—the macho gene's dark side. From the start, he was all sweetheart and good looks, charming her pants off with those Clooney eyes, turning her inside out. Now she was looking at it, thinking maybe he was like the rest.

She stiff-legged it to the sink, lifting her foot under the spray, balancing herself, the water's jet giving back her pink toes. No towel on the rack, she just let her foot air-dry, thinking Karl was right about one thing: a vacation sounded pretty good.

Out the window, swallows darted between the buildings as a siren wailed over the pounding. Chip rubbed himself against her leg, his motor purring. She wondered how long before Karl got back.

A CAFÉ CON LECHE THING

"The kind of guy who would roll over and plead down," Miro said. He got up, hobbled to the fridge and handed Wally a beer, then sat on the arm of his sofa, his leg throbbing and stinging. "Tell you the guy's a chickenshit, and what the fuck was he doing on the ferry, man?"

"Does it every time we get in a tight situation," Wally said, choking back a laugh, thinking Mitch was right about the flattened nose giving Miro a gay Rocky look, made him sound funny, too.

"How you mean, he shits himself?" Miro asked, thinking Wally was laughing at Mitch.

"Yeah, but you fucked this up," Wally said. "Pumping in gas, telling bullshit stories about mudmen."

Miro kept it in, saying, "You want to frag a place with a rocket launcher, you can't have a candy-ass around. Hey, I admit, maybe I fucked up, but shit happens, and when it does, it's the weak links that get you screwed. Am I right?"

Wally couldn't argue that one.

"I mean, hey, if you hadn't kicked the door in . . ." Miro offered his hand, saying his ears were still ringing.

"Yeah, mine too," Wally said, shaking his hand, not sure why.

"Compared to Pinkie, guess we got off lucky," Miro said.

"The broad with the shotgun? Yeah. Man, *whoosh*, like she got shot out of a cannon—clear across the room."

"Used to go with her."

"No shit? Ah, sorry, man."

"It's okay. Didn't end well between us. Still, good to put some closure to it."

Wally picked up Miro's Newports, tapping one out, asking, "You mind?"

"Go ahead, keep 'em. I got a carton," Miro said. "What we're going to do now, you and me are going to get this right."

Wally squinted as he lit up.

Miro said Artie's other place in Burnaby was good for a thousand plants, cured, all pressed into bricks.

"We struck out twice already. And there's your leg."

"I'm a good healer." Miro smiled, eyes glazed from the Oxy he got from the guy downstairs with the sandwich board.

"And Mitch?"

"No Mitch, just me and you and the rocket launcher." Miro reached and pulled the baggie from the shelf and tossed it to Wally, liking how easy this was. "This place is bigger than Bowen, and no Loop or Pinkie watching it."

"Thousand plants, what's that, like twenty pounds?"

"Try over thirty," Miro said. "Figure about fifteen hundred a pound, wholesale. You and me split it down the middle. No Stax, no Mitch."

Wally was working out his share, the knock at the door making him drop the ZigZags, Miro getting off the sofa's arm, reaching for his holster.

"Probably just Mitch," Wally said, his voice low.

"You tell him we were here?"

Wally shook his head, forgetting he called Mitch earlier.

Miro snapped his fingers, waited, then did it again, Bruna poking her head out from the bedroom. He motioned for her to get the door, her mouthing for him to get stuffed.

"Don't want to tell you twice." He fairly hissed the words, sticking the four-and-five-eights barrel to his lips, motioning for her to get to the door.

Bruna did up a couple of buttons and went through the living room, Wally seeing the tat one more time, betting Bruna's olive skin felt as hot as it looked.

The recliner became Miro's cover. Wally left the makings on the table, crouching beside the sofa, fumbling the Smith from his jacket.

Putting an eye to the peephole, she took in Karl's smile. She turned and mouthed that it was the FedEx guy.

"He alone?"

She made a face and shrugged.

"What's he want?" Miro whispered a little loud, steadying his aim across the chair, thinking Morgen was out there with a sheriff, ready to drag his ass back to Seattle.

"Like a word with Miro Knotts," Karl said through the door, his hand on the Taser in the messenger bag.

"He's not here," Bruna said back, looking through the peephole, guessing he wasn't holding a bouquet behind his back.

"Here's a thing I like to do, Bruna, is it?" Karl asked. No answer. "See, I do my homework, that's how I got your name." He waited a moment before saying, "What I like to give the guy I'm coming after is fair warning, try to do things the easy way."

"You want your bogus papers back? 'Cause if you do, I got to tell you, Miro wiped himself with them."

"That's real nice, Bruna. Something like that doesn't surprise me, but that's not it. See, what it is, there's a guy wants some names."

"So he sends FedEx?"

"Sent me on account of how he's funny about people burning his places down and stealing his stuff."

Miro was aiming past Bruna, a foot below the peephole, right about where Karl's throat ought to be, remembering that stupid line: if your man's breathing, Morgen would find him. He wanted to, but despite the painkillers making him high, Miro knew it would be stupid to shoot him here. The recording he made would have to do, enough to get his ass sent to Kent Maximum for taking out Mitch and Wally, something Miro planned to take care of personally. He got up, slung his hand tooled holster over his shoulder, grabbed his jacket and went to the window, shoving it open. It hurt like a bitch, but he stepped out onto the fire escape, looking back at Bruna in his plaid shirt.

"When I give Miro up," Karl said through the door, "I don't want sleepless nights. Even a dirtbag deserves better."

"Let me get you right, you're the clown that dragged him off that couch in Belltown?" She didn't wait for an answer. "And you pulled your FedEx stunt, served up your papers, just to piss him off."

"Maybe that time in Belltown I got a little carried away, seeing him, two in the morning, wrapped around a child."

"Went from a bounty hunter to process server. Now you're a boy scout," she said, turning to see Miro climbing down the fire escape, Wally right behind him.

"Came to give him an hour."

She was sweating under the arms, about to do something that could backfire in a big way. She flicked off the chain and pulled the door open.

His eyes darted past her.

"They went out the window."

"They?"

She turned for the kitchen. "Going to put on some coffee."

Karl ignored her, half-expecting an ambush, he looked around the apartment, his hand on the Taser.

"You take cream?"

"No, but I'm glad to see you're a grown-up."

"I'm a lot more than that."

"Yeah?" Saying he'd take a rain check on the coffee, Karl turned for the door.

She called to him. "I'm not the kind of girl who takes no for an answer."

"Honey, you want company, switch on *Oprah* or go knock on a door."

She followed him into the hall, enjoying this. "Got me figured out, huh?"

"I need my shoes shined, I know where to find you." He was reaching for the elevator button.

"Didn't guess I'm a cop, huh?" She liked how that stopped him and the dumb look that followed. She wagged a finger at him, told him, "Come on back in, and I'll flash my badge at you."

Karl stood dumbfounded, the elevator door opening with a *ding*.

"It's just Nescafé, but I do a kind of *café con leche* thing. It's not half bad." She turned and went inside, knowing Karl would follow her.

The first day he laid eyes on her, she was waving a Thermos. Today she flashed her badge.

FLIPPED OVER

Sitting him down over the *café con leche*, Bruna told him he was playing a game that could get him being charged with conspiracy. She knew about Artie offering him money, telling him how Miro had Stax tape the conversation down at the beach, trying to frame him for a double homicide, telling him it was Artie she was after, how she suspected Artie was wearing a fed wire. Not telling him about the two detectives who busted the warehouse Miro and Stax had been using, finding a quantity of marijuana along with a bloodstain on the ground, along with a witness that put them there. Meaning time was running out and everything she had done here could end with her back in a uniform, or worse.

"Why you telling me?" Karl asked.

"Here's your chance to put yourself on the right side of things."

"How?"

"You drive over while I take care of the warrant for my own wiretap, keep your phone in your pocket, on or off it doesn't matter. Wait till I call you, then go down, give Artie the names and get him talking. We'll be right behind you."

"You just said Artie's good as wired. Can't you people share?"

"What I can do is charge you with obstruction right now. Can have a black-and-white here before you finish your cup—tack on a weapons charge."

Karl made the call in front her, telling Stax he was on his way, said yeah he had the names.

Leaving her to make her own calls, he stepped back on the elevator and pressed the button for the ground floor. The elevator dinged off the floors, Karl looking at his phone, hoping her tap worked better than the wireless router he got from Shaw, the piece of shit cutting out at random. The elevator stopped at the lobby, and the door slid open. There stood Mitch, eyes going wide, his hand reaching inside his jacket.

"Don't do that, man." Karl put up his hand. "Look, Mitch, right? I'm going to tell you the same thing I came to tell your buddy, Miro."

"Don't know any Miro." Mitch put his hand on the Walther.

"Guy who went out the fire escape." Karl stepped past him and spoke over his shoulder, "Artie sent me to get your names, all three of you."

"Don't know what you're talking about, man." He had the gun out, pointing it at Karl's back.

"Guy whose house you broke into—grow house you blew up." Karl was moving for the door. "Want my advice, turn around and split town before the shit truly hits the fan."

"Suppose you don't make it to the door?" Mitch waited

for Karl to half turn and see the Walther, the lack of conviction in Mitch's eyes.

"We both know that's not what's going to happen." Feeling the tingle at the back of his neck, he opened the door for the grey-haired lady coming in with her Boston terrier, hearing the elevator ding behind him.

CHANGE OF PLANS

The alley smelled of puke. Trash cans and ripped chunks of drywall piled against a Dumpster, a scaffold up against the side of the building. Sections of stucco had been patched with concrete. Pigeons pecked at a clamshell, going for a bit of chicken nugget.

Miro lit a smoke, thinking this through. Wally had hit Loop dead center, clipped him with three rounds. Pinkie must have survived the blast, and Morgen got to her lying in a hospital bed, getting her to give him up along with Mitch and Wally. Morgen at the door, Miro not sure why, maybe to have it out, something Miro would be happy to oblige, guessing Morgen would be heading to Wreck Beach next for his sleazy reward.

Taking out his cell, Miro punched in a number, limping past the Dumpster out of Wally's earshot. His leg was hurting like a son of a bitch, the Oxy doing dick for the pain but turning his stomach and putting his head in a fog. He picked up a length of two by four, paint splattered on it, using it like a crutch, careful of the rusted nails sticking out. He waited for Stax to answer.

"Think Morgen's coming your way," he said, the reception crackling.

"Artie's farming this one out," Stax said.

"Fuck that."

"You need to get this revenge shit out of your head, brother," Stax said. "Get your head on right and no more screw-ups."

"Who the fuck let fifty grand of my oil sink?"

Stax hung up, leaving Miro looking at the phone, throwing it against the Dumpster.

Wally lit a Newport, watching Miro have his Oxy tantrum, then hobble back with the two by four, Miro asking, "You any good in a fight?"

"Me? Hell, yeah. Why?"

"What kind of ride you say Morgen has?" Looking down the alley to the parking garage.

A COP WHEN YOU NEED ONE

The bank of fluorescent lights was out near the Porsche parked between the two pillars at the end of the parkade's main level. Karl held the ring of keys so the ignition key stuck out between his index and middle fingers—learned that when he was a kid growing up on the tough streets. He kept his other hand in the messenger bag. Call it a feeling. Aside from the junkies and hookers down in this part of town, Karl guessed Miro would be looking to square things, sooner than later.

He passed the booth, the teenaged attendant reading a Justice League comic, headphones on his mohawked head. It got him thinking of PJ's old man working the Park'N Go all those years ago, raking in the chips and leaving his wife and kid, never showing up again.

Karl's footfalls echoed on the concrete, his car at the back. Stepping on broken glass from the smashed fluorescents, he took out the Taser and got as far as sticking his key in the lock.

"Hey!"

It was the years on the hard streets that got him ducking instead of turning. Jumping out of the shadows, Wally swung the two by four with the nails, knocking the Taser away. Karl kicked, catching Wally on the backswing. Wally's next swing took out the side view. The sucker punch had him doubling up, the board clattering down.

Hobbling in from behind a pillar, Miro pulled his piece, Karl feinting right, stepping in, blocking the gun hand, catching a fistful of Miro's hair, twisting and snapping him over his shoulder. The gun flew from his hand, hitting a Volvo, its alarm going off, Miro crawling for it, Karl stomping it from Miro's fingers, sending it spinning under his car.

Wally grabbed him from behind, Karl sending back an elbow, turning and jabbing, landing a straight right, Wally tumbling over the back end of the Roadster. Boxing moves Karl learned at Cappy's Gym back in Belltown. Catching hold of Miro's bum leg, he dragged him away from the pistol, Miro screaming, kicking his other leg out at him.

Snatching the two by four again, Wally waded in swinging, putting him down; Wally hitting him again, the nails biting into his shoulder.

"Police!"

The shout and running feet had Wally dropping the board, Miro grabbing for the gun, the two of them hurrying through the parked cars.

The attendant with the mohawk ran up, fire extinguisher in hand. Looked to see they were gone, then he knelt next to Karl, seeing the blood spreading over Karl's shoulder, telling him he needed a doctor, wanting to call the cops.

"Let's skip that part," Karl said, touching his bleeding shoulder, opening his car door, letting the light spill out. The kid's name tag said he was Norm. "Far as I'm concerned, I owe you, Norm."

"Forget it."

Finding his keys on the ground, Karl asked if Norm saw the *Late Show* where Letterman let Richard Simmons have it with a fire extinguisher. Norm said yeah that was a good one, adding he had a first-aid kit in the booth. Karl shook his head, picked up the Taser, looked around for security cameras. Not seeing any, he tossed the broken side mirror into the car, asking, "Know anybody at ICBC, Norm?" He started the car.

Back in his booth, Norm raised the barrier, waving Karl through, saying the seven-fifty flat rate was on the house.

Karl parked in the same spot above Trail 6, next to the same Cadillac, the pines along the top of the trail making a

RIDING THE LIGHTNING

perfect spot for another ambush. What the hell had he been thinking giving Miro and his crew a heads-up?

A lump was growing like a tumor on the side of his head, blood dripping down his sleeve. No guilt now about giving up Miro and his merry band of assholes. He checked the Taser's AAs and air cartridge.

Going down those stairs was slow murder, each step hurting more than the last, four hundred and seventy-three of them. At the trash can at the bottom, he caught his breath, spotting Artie and Stax near the shore, one sitting, one standing, a beached log and a hamper next to them.

A few vendors stood by their folding tables and barbecues, waiting for naked diehards to brave the unseasonable cold. Whitecaps rolled in, churning the water brown.

Artie was sitting on his beach blanket, lathered in lotion,

waiting for the sun to poke out from behind drifting clouds. He was letting Stax think it was business as usual, making like he cared who robbed him, burned his place down. Tonight he'd stay at the Fairmont with the twin suitcases in the trunk of his Caddy stuffed with hundreds, over 1.2 million in each. Tomorrow he'd board the Korean Air flight to Seoul with the money and a fake passport. Half his holdings had been sold off, the proceeds transferred to his bank in Gyeongju; the rest could be handled offshore.

Stax stood in his jeans and T-shirt, showing off the serpents, watching Karl walk up.

"How you going to work on your tan like that?" was Artie's greeting, noting the bloody jacket, the way Karl was holding himself.

"Sign says clothes are optional."

Stax got in front of Karl, motioning for him to put his arms up.

Karl drew the Taser. "Had enough of people putting hands on me for one day."

"You want to play Flash Gordon?" Stax guessed he could stand a little jolt before ripping this guy a new one, looked like somebody already got the job half done.

Walking around them, his back to the water, Karl pointed it at the big man's chest, "Brought it in case the assholes who just jumped me want to go another round."

Artie motioned for Stax to ease up, saying, "Saw on the news when the cops used one of those on that Russian guy at the airport. Killed the poor fuck."

"Tasered him like five times, and I think the guy was Polish, but anyway, I got your names. You bring my money?"

Artie motioned to the hamper, and Stax reached in and came up with Jeffery's king of handguns, not aiming it, just holding it at his side.

Artie snapped his finger like he was trying to remember something, asking Stax, "What's the girl's name again?"

Stax looked at Karl, saying, "PJ Addie."

Karl lowered the Taser.

"Your names pan out, Stax forgets hers," Artie said. "Then you get your cash."

"My names'll pan out alright," Karl said, then started grinning, nicking his head, wanting them to turn and look, saying, "Fact, you don't believe me, ask this guy." Karl was looking toward Vendors' Row, Miro stiff-legging it over the sand, blood crusting on his face.

His jacket hung open, showing the old-time gunfighter rig. Miro could have made the shot from the trash can at the bottom of the stairs, even with his leg unsteady, but he wanted to look into Artie's eyes when the light went out of them. The asshole bounty hunter, too. Nice and close. If Stax made a move, he'd kill him, too.

Artie's face tightened, the unibrow bunching. Stax tucked the Python in the front of his pants, stepping to the side.

The vendors didn't see a movie crew filming the guy with the greased hair acting like a gunslinger with his black eye, flattened nose and the hitch in his step. After the gang shooting there last spring, they knew better than to stand around, so they scattered into the pines, abandoning their grills, leaving a dog tethered to a chair leg.

Wishing he had his old Smith, Karl half-turned, hiding the stun gun along his leg, not sure about the range from where he stood. Watching Miro, he missed seeing Stax step in and snatch it, shoving him into the sand.

"Popeye—thought you were in Seattle," Artie said, greeting Miro, playing the man in charge.

"Got business here." Miro's hand swept the jacket back, making sure Artie saw what was coming.

"What business is that?"

"The unfinished kind." Miro was set, looking into the old prick's eyes. Naked or not, didn't matter.

"Well, you look like shit," Artie said to him, then looked at Stax, the Python tucked in his belt, the Taser in his hand. "What do I pay you for?"

That's all Artie got out; Stax raised the Taser and fired, the probes biting into the old man's tanned chest. Artie's eyes went wide, his face contorted, and his body flopped backward into the sand.

"Fuck!" Miro yelled, rushing forward, looking at Artie twitch in the sand, then at Stax. "What the . . . He was mine."

"No way I'm doing time 'cause you want to put on a Wild West show." Stax looked down at his boss, electrodes sticking in his chest.

"After what he did to me?"

"You got to see him ride the lightning, that's as good as it gets." Stax motioned at Karl. "Shoot this asshole you need to shoot somebody so bad."

His pistol still in its holster, Miro looked at Karl.

"But not in front of me," Stax said.

"What the fuck are you going to say when he wakes up—'Oops'?" Miro said.

Stax turned to leave.

"Suppose I do him anyway?"

"Do what you want." Stax looked back at him. "I'm out of here. Going to see a man about a dog."

Miro couldn't believe this guy, thinking about the dead dog again, saying, "Toss him the gun."

"Like fuck."

"It's Jeffery's."

"With my prints." No way Stax was giving up the gun.

"Then that thing," Miro motioned at the Taser still in

Stax's hand. "And I'll tell you where to find Wally, guy that killed your dog."

Stax thought a second, bent and checked Artie's vitals.

Miro told Karl Stax had been wearing a wire all along. "Got you and Artie on tape first time you came down here, making a deal to find the guys robbing him. Been setting you up for a double murder. Wanted to see you doing time, but now I'm thinking your time's up."

Karl checked around, nothing but abandoned tables and grills, the dog tugging and barking.

Miro got himself set, saying, "Still owe me for that date you fucked up, dragging me off that couch. Why I'm going 'round to your girlfriend's when this is done, drive up in your car, slap the cuffs on her and take a spin someplace quiet. Show her a good time." He said to Stax, "Gonna throw him that thing or what?"

Stax came up with a bewildered look. "Fuck me."

Miro's eyes flicked at him.

Stax looked at the spent Taser in his hand, the probes still sticking in his boss. "Fucking things are supposed to be safe now." Wiping it, he tossed it at Karl's feet, thinking it was discharged, telling Karl, "You live, you got some explaining to do, asshole."

"Forgot the goddamn pacemaker," Miro yelled at Stax, getting set to make this a three-way killing.

"Just tonic-clonic seizure," Karl said, bending for the Taser. "What?"

"Just got to jump-start him."

"And what the fuck are you—"

Karl was swinging the Taser, Miro drawing as the copper probes shot out, biting in. Miro's body jerked, his piece dropping from his fingers.

Karl was whirling and firing again as Stax rushed in, head

lowered like a tattooed rhino, both of them going down in a heap. The wind knocked out of him, Karl pushed Stax off, the guy stinking of sweat, mouth foaming and his eyes rolled up, showing just the whites.

Getting to his feet, Karl spit sand and stumbled over to Miro. A dark urine stain was spreading over his crotch, the scrawny bastard still breathing, blood blotting the gauze on his leg. Sand stuck to his greasy hair. Fishing out his cell, Karl punched in the number Bruna gave him, then walked over to Artie, the St. Peter's cross around his neck.

"You get all that?"

"Still waiting on the warrant," Bruna said, then hesitated. "Get all what? What's going on?"

"You're kidding, right?" Karl rifled through the hamper, guessing she thought he'd actually waited at the top of the stairs till she got her warrant. No cash in the hamper. He started back for the stairs, coming up with a new deal for Bruna. "I'll fill you in, maybe even testify, but I get to snap the cuffs on the runt, read him the you-have-the-right-to shit."

"Keep talking like an asshole," she said, "and I'll be cuffing you."

He told her how it just went down as he climbed the stairs. "I'm guessing you've got five, maybe ten minutes before the two assholes come around," adding, "and better bring a stretcher and one of those Ziploc bags for Artie." He kept climbing, filling in the details.

Bruna ordered him to stay where he was, said she was en route, told him units were on the way. He clicked off.

PJ jerked awake, her head and
heart pounding. Wet with
fever. In the stupid dream Cam
and Dara stood in a mortuary

PJ'S PARTS

facing Karl in front of refrigerated doors, Karl acting like
Carol Merril in front of the three doors on that game show,
rolling a gurney out, drawing the zipper down. The corpse
was PJ herself, peaceful and serene, once pretty.

First time her mother's lips had ever been sealed, Dara
said. Karl yanked the zipper and parted the plastic, asking
them to guess what these babies set him back. Cam said nice
rack, Dara saying she'd take them, asking how long to pop
them out. Karl pulled a watch and chain from his pocket, and
the dream dissolved.

God, even in a feverish dream the kid was a bitch. Getting
out of bed, PJ went to Karl's bathroom, careful where she
stepped, head feeling heavy. Splashing water on her face, still
wondering how anyone slept with that noise outside. Then
she smiled at the mirror, thinking of Dara coming to identify

her mother's body, bringing a date, harvesting implants like they were organs. She put a hand to her forehead. Man, that NyQuil was something. She was toweling her face when the phone in her handbag rang.

It was Karl on his cell, tension in his voice, asking how she was feeling. Traffic sounds in the background.

She put a hand over her other ear to hear him over the bridge construction, told him they needed to talk. What she wanted right then was for him to stick his key in the lock, wanted his lips to get in the way of her giving him hell for lying to her, knowing he wasn't out serving paper, worrying about him and the people he was mixed up with. Karl told her he was on his way, said he'd explain things, and then he was gone.

His phone rang. It was Bruna, standing on the beach, a dozen uniforms working the scene, no sign of Miro or Stax, just

A MAN ABOUT A DOG

tracks in the sand of a struggle and the hamper with sandwiches and lotion.

"How about those stairs, huh?"

"Where the hell you get off leaving a crime scene?"

"Things to do." He rolled through an amber light, traffic ahead getting heavy.

She ordered Karl to get his ass down to 312 Main, told him to wait at her desk till she got there, told him she wasn't asking.

Karl hung up, thinking she made a better skank than a cop. He dialed PJ back, told her to get out of the apartment, wait outside for him, then told her to call Dara and get her out of the house in case Miro showed up there first. He gave PJ the short strokes of what went down on Wreck Beach, Artie getting tased, Bruna turning out to be a cop, Miro and

Stax getting away. Cutting off her questions, he promised to tell her the rest when he got there, said he just wanted her safe, and hung up.

⚡

They had trudged up the stairs, both of them out of it. Stax helped Miro, taking a hold on his arm, minimizing the risk of getting shot in the back, Miro holding the railing. Focusing on how bad he wanted to kill that fucker Morgen got him to the top.

Hearing distant sirens, Stax, nearly at the parking lot, had pulled Miro off the stairs, the two of them hiding among the ferns. Cars swept in and doors slammed, then voices, then more doors. Keeping low behind a burned-out tree trunk forty feet from the stairs, Miro and Stax watched and waited as a dozen cops hurried down, Dom and Luca the last to arrive.

They climbed up the rest of the way through the trees. Motioning Miro to stay still, Stax crept past the "Clothing Optional" sign and came up behind the lone cop waiting by his unit in the lot. Doubling his fists, he clubbed the cop on the side of the head, the cap tumbling off as he fell. Stax took the service SIG from the holster and threw it into the trees, reached in the cruiser and yanked the handset from the radio, threw it too. Climbing into Artie's Caddy, he looked at Miro, then at the parked cruisers, saying, "Take your pick." He cranked the Caddy to life, then said, "Better pray Wally's at that address."

Miro watched him squeal away, stepped over the cop, looked inside the cars, finding keys dangling in an unmarked Chev minivan. Man, he wished he had his radar-red Challenger. Still, with any luck, he'd get to Morgen's right behind him and get it done. Couldn't believe the guy beat him to the draw, even with the swollen hand and bum leg.

SUNNY WITH A CHANCE OF BLOW

The rain tapped like fingers on the standing-seam roof, the screened-in porch letting the cold damp bite. It brought Wally around, the ratty sofa's springs poking his back. He must have nodded off, waiting for Miro's call, his phone on the glass coffee table. No messages.

No fouler taste than that after-the-party mouth. Reaching the bottle, he swished a mouthful of wine like it was Listerine, moving his jaw, giving the FedEx guy credit for knowing how to throw a punch. He would have shot the prick in the parking garage if it wasn't for Miro screwing it up, wanting the guy for himself, the hotshot getting his cowboy gun knocked away.

Miro's last word was for Wally to go jack a van, sit tight and wait for his call while he took care of business. Wally was pretty sure the business meant round two with the FedEx guy. The plan was to lay low until later, then hit Artie's place in Burnaby.

Fingers spidered on the floor, he felt around for his Smith.

Then checking his Rolex, he looked at Sunny curled up at the other end with a magazine, hair smelling of Suave, the same brand he was using these days. He laid a hand on her thigh, guessing they were good together.

Her eyes flashed, blue and pissed off, and she shoved his hand away. "You mind?" Wet landed on her lip, and she sat up.

"What?"

"Stick them down your own pants; see how you like it. Fingers like goddamn frozen fish sticks."

Wally straightened his do-rag, thinking fuck this, he may as well go see about that van. Working through the coke, smoke and wine fog, he couldn't remember screwing her. What he did remember was telling her about the construction guy at the diner, how he took care of business for the way the guy ragged on her. He didn't say exactly what he did to the guy, only that he took care of it. Point was, he showed how he felt about her. And here she was playing the bitch.

He patted his stash pocket for the folded tinfoil that wasn't there. Tossing the magazine, leaning forward, she picked the foil off the table and opened it, shaking the last of the coke out, tapping the razor, her hand shaking and making a mess of the lines on the glass top.

"Here," he said, sitting closer and taking the razor from her, telling her she wasn't chopping wood. "Nice and easy like this, this shit's the real deal, not that lactose and talcum crap you're used to." Probably why he couldn't remember getting it up, pure coke mixed with red wine and a couple of joints. Should have popped a couple of zoomers instead of the wine. Go in clean, put it to her, then guzzle some wine.

She grinned at him like she knew what he was thinking and snorted a line, saying, "Beam me up, Scottie," handing him the rolled Post-it note. She watched him do the other line. "You were so wasted, you couldn't . . ." She draped her forefinger and laughed.

"Uh huh."

"Then you just passed out with your eyes like this."

"Like I said, the real deal."

"Blow makes you horny, not . . ." she said, crooking her finger again, knowing she was pushing her luck.

"One of your hooker buddies tell you that?" The coke rush saved her from having her finger broken, Wally easing into the sofa. "How about now—now's good?" He wiped his nose, sniffing.

"You still owe me."

"Owe you what?"

"For the first one." She eased into the cushion, enjoying the rush.

"You just finished saying nothing happened."

"Hey, that's not my fault. You know how this works. You want to go again, peel off another hundred and slip on a raincoat."

"After the kind of day I had," he said, pointing to the welts on his own face. "You know what, fuck you, Sunny." He tried to get up.

She grabbed for his arm, but he pulled away.

"Not till you pay me."

"In your dreams." He stood.

"Think I'd learn to get it up front." She balled the tinfoil and threw it at him.

Wally lit the last of Miro's Newports, crumpling the pack, dropping the match in the wine bottle. The two of them had split up after jumping the FedEx guy at the Park'N Go, Wally running along Hastings, sure the cops were chasing him. Flagging a cab to Chickie's, he took it over the Second Narrows to the North Shore, catching Sunny at the end of her shift. He wanted her, said it didn't matter that she was sweaty from being in that greasy hell all day. They had the cabbie stop for a bottle of Asti, then rode to her place, got in the shower together and got a good buzz going. Wally passing out.

And here he was, dropping the cigarette in the bottle, the menthol taste twisting his stomach. He reached for the strap of her bag.

"Hey," she said, grabbing for it, raking his arm with her nails, thinking the jerk was ripping her off.

He slapped her mouth, hard, saying all he wanted was a decent smoke, fishing out her Rothmans pack with one left. "This it?"

"Yeah, I was saving it." She grabbed her bag and hugged it to her, putting a hand to where he hit her, giving him the hurt puppy look.

He lit the cigarette, looking at the hand print on her cheek, saying he was sorry, then, "I'll share it with you."

"Great," she said. "I get stiffed, slapped and fucked over—second time this week."

"Somebody else hit you?"

"The Small Potatoes guy—told me to put it on the tab."

"You want me to go see him?"

She took the cigarette from him and dragged on it. "I'm a big girl, take care of myself."

"Told you what I did to the construction guy, right?" On her exhale, he came in for a kiss, caught her on the cheek as she turned her head away. That was it; he got up and went through the door without another word, letting the screen slam behind him. The rain coming down at an angle.

The screened-in porch ran across the front of the two-story. Standing on the stoop, he looked around, every house on the street the same. Like the street he grew up on in Riverdale, back when that part of Toronto was a slum, except the houses there were brick. These were all wood. Inside, he heard her phone ring, heard the floorboards creak as she went to pick up and say hello. Probably another john.

He was done with her. What he needed right now was to get his head around jacking the van for the Burnaby job. The street was Sunday-morning quiet, a dead zone of cars lining both sides. Looked like the top of a green Chevy Express parked on the next block.

The screen door squeaked open, and Sunny stepped out beside him, arms folded around him. "Sorry, guess I'm a bitch sometimes." She dropped her head on his shoulder.

The smell of her hair, the warmth of her body disarmed him. Hearing the rain patter, he turned and slung an arm around her. "Coke mellowed you out."

She slipped a hand under his jacket, touching the Smith tucked in his belt, playing with him now. "That a gun or are you glad to see me?"

"Funny."

"It's kind of . . ."

"What?"

"I don't know . . . a turn on." She was giving him that look.

"Yeah?"

"You any good with it?"

"The gun?"

"Yeah, the gun."

"Not into the quick-draw shit like my man Merle's into, but . . ."

"This the guy you work for?"

"Working with, not for. Yeah, the jerk with the three egg omelet—that day in the cafe."

"Right, the tipper."

"Guy likes to twirl his cowboy gun around his finger, thinks he's Roy Rogers or somebody—likely blow his dick off one day—no great loss. But yeah, I'm good with it. Why you asking me that?"

"Told you, it's a turn on." She drew closer, pressing against it, put her lips on his, worked her tongue into his mouth, pressing her thigh against him, knowing what he liked, making like she did, too.

The van could wait. Wally got into it, ran his hands under her top, feeling her, not hearing the rain, not hearing the car pull up to the curb, the door open. Steering her hand down the front of his pants, he was rocking his hips to the rhythm, reaching for the screen door behind her.

"You like surprises, baby?" Her voice was a whisper. She pulled back from him, taking her hand away, looking into his eyes.

Wally saying, "Yeah, love a good—"

The big hand clapped his shoulder and spun him around. The swipe from the open hand felt like a punch, knocking the do-rag from his head.

But Wally was quick; he had the Smith pressed against the big man's gut, Stax in his T-shirt and leather jacket. Snorting snot back up his nose, Stax grinned at him, took hold of him by pinching thumb and fingers around his collar bone. Shaking his hair back, Stax didn't bother about the .38 against his gut.

"Wally, you the fuck who shot my dog?"

"Let the fuck go of me, man." Wally clicked the safety off, looking at Sunny, saying, "Better tell him I ain't . . . ahhhhh . . ."

Stax pinched harder, like he was disjointing a chicken.

"You crazy fuck." Wally's words came through clenched teeth; his knees buckled. It felt like he was being ripped apart.

Sunny retreated behind the screen door, couldn't take her eyes off what was going on.

"Bowen Island. One of you assholes shot Ike." His fingers dug in like a vice grip, the fingernails all white. "And I'm thinking it was you."

The pull on the trigger brought a dry click.

"You or your fucking buddy, Mitch—which one?"

Click. Click.

"Who's Ike?

"Which one?"

Click.

Stax ground his teeth, growling and digging in harder.

"Miro. Fuck! It was Miro." Wally was crying out, realizing Ike was the dog, almost on his knees, his collar bone feeling broken.

Click.

"Miro, huh?" Stax straightened Wally up, taking hold of his arm.

"Yeah, that gun-crazy fuck."

Click.

"You see him do it?"

"Mitch told me about it after."

"And you were where?"

"In the van."

"So how you know it wasn't your buddy Mitch?" Stax pinched the flesh at the back of Wally's arm, making it hurt.

"Mitch doesn't shoot anything but his mouth, plus Miro's been dying to kill something since I met him."

Stax eased the grip, but held onto Wally, knowing the truth of it, saying, "I promised your girlfriend here I wouldn't make a mess, blast your guts all over her walls."

"I appreciate it," she said through the screen. The call came when Wally was out cold, Stax saying he got her number from Chickie, asked if she was interested in a reward, telling her what she had to do to collect.

Wally looked back at her, then said again it wasn't him, that he loved dogs.

"Okay, so, let's go for a ride, find your buddy Mitch, see what he says," then to Sunny, "You got something for me, doll?"

She reached in a pocket, opened the screen and handed Stax the shells she took from the Smith, Wally looking at her.

"When you were passed out," she said to him, shrugging. "Sorry."

Aiming at her, Wally pulled the trigger one more time. *Click*.

"Gonna fuck up the firing pin you keep doing that." Stax jerked the Smith from his hand, dropping it in his own pocket with the shells.

"I didn't shoot your dog, man. I swear. Talk to Miro."

Stax nodded like he believed him, snorted again. "Right now Miro's gone to square things with the asshole who dragged his ass to jail."

Wally nodded. "Miro and me got something going. Come with, you can talk to him about the dog."

"Grow-op in Burnaby? Said that to set you up." Stax turned Wally for the steps. "Right now, you and me are going to see what your buddy Mitch says. Where do we find him?"

"Try his double-wide."

"His what?"

"Place like a trailer where he lives."

"This double-wide got an address?"

"Don't know off the top of my head, but it's in that RV park by the Capilano, under the Lion's Gate."

Stax nodded, "Indian reserve, ain't it?"

"All I know, there's an old shitbox Camry out front—used to be red."

"He got a cell?" Stax told Sunny to get a pen and paper.

Sunny turned from the door, and Wally said, "Look, give me five minutes, and I'm on the first thing smoking."

She was back with a stub of a pencil and a pad.

"Write," Stax said.

Wally jotted the number down, and Stax reached in Wally's pocket, took his cell and punched in the number. No answer. He said, "Let's take a ride." Fishing out his keys, he asked Sunny, "You go through this guy's pockets like I asked, doll?"

She shook her head, and he nodded for her to do it now. Coming back out onto the stoop, she dug around in Wally's pants, pulling out a few crumpled bills, the all-in-one and the fresh pack of Newports he lifted from Miro's jacket. "Took my last one. You cheap prick." She handed the stuff to Stax.

"I don't get you," Wally said to her.

"Did it on account of the G-note on your head," Stax told him.

"Every time I looked at you, my hand was in my pocket," Wally said to her.

"Earned every cent, so spare me your bullshit." Then she did look sorry. "Look, this guy was going to catch up with you one way or the other."

Stax ripped off the cellophane and tapped out three smokes. He flicked a lighter and got a flame like a blowtorch, lighting all three, handing her one and one to Wally. He said to her, "You keep the bills, doll."

She counted them, saying, "You're short like nine hundred and forty."

"You're looking at the wrong guy. See, the guy paying the reward got fried on Wreck Beach."

"He's dead?" Wally asked.

"Very."

"By the FedEx guy?"

Stax said yeah, Sunny bitching about getting fucked over again, tucking the money away.

"Shit happens, doll." Stax reached for his wallet, pulled out some bills and handed her what he had. "Understand, this comes out of my own pocket." Then he said to Wally, as she counted, "You, in the car."

As Stax turned, Wally jumped the railing, falling into her rose bushes. Going and lifting him out of the bushes, grabbing the do-rag, Stax marched him to the curb, opening the door and shoving him in, catching Wally's head on the frame.

Standing on the stoop, Sunny went on about the two hundred and twenty bucks and her broken rose bush, Stax looking at her through the slanting rain, going around to the driver's side, saying, "You keep running your mouth, doll, you're gonna be standing there with nothing."

"What about the rest?"

"Just had a pretty shitty week myself, but try me again in a couple of days. Meantime, we weren't here, right?"

"Where do I find you?" she called, not liking the look on his face when he said not to worry about it; he'd come see her.

Halfway across Sixteenth, Karl cut up to Broadway hoping the traffic would thin. Raining like a bitch. He was heading

THE RUSH

toward the Causeway, zipping from lane to lane.

His cell rang again; it was PJ saying Dara wasn't answering, worry in her voice.

"Probably sees it's you on the call display and won't pick up."

"God, that kid."

"Cam's with her," he said.

"That supposed to make me feel better?"

Karl was thinking there was a good chance Miro would head to PJ's house first. Shit. Karl checked his rearview, pulling a Steve McQueen move, drifting the Porsche around, vehicles honking at him from all four lanes, Karl telling her he'd swing by, check on Dara, then come get her. "Get downstairs and wait for me."

She said she was going out the door now.

HAIR OF THE DOG

Pulling a couple of Buds from the pack on the backseat, one he picked up while chauffeuring the old man around, Stax tossed one in Wally's lap. Wally popped it open, watching Sunny disappear into her house. Pulling a rose thorn from his palm, he knew it was the last time he'd see her.

"Hair of the dog," Stax said, pulling from the curb, hitting the wipers, taking a sip and pulling out the CD hanging from the player, looking at it, saying Beyoncé like he had shit in his mouth. Pressing the window down, he sailed it out like a Frisbee. He couldn't believe Artie listened to shit like that.

Wally said the chick had a nice ass, trying to make conversation. "This the DTS?"

"The what?"

"Cadillac DTS."

"A couch on wheels, you ask me."

"You jack it?"

"Old man left it to me," Stax said, asking if Wally was high, Wally saying yeah, a little.

They passed Attic Treasures and a bead shop, Wally asking what anybody would want with beads. He looked into the back seat, hoping for a tire iron or something heavy, nothing but the beer and a beach blanket with sand sticking to it.

"Popeye said you got a knack for jacking cars, that right?" Stax asked.

"Who's Popeye?"

"What we called Miro back in the day. You want to piss him off, call him that."

Wally filed it away. "Said I had a knack, huh?"

"That and you were dumb as shit." Stax turned east on Venables, waiting on a white-haired couple to cross to the Baptist church, the two of them arm in arm under a giant umbrella. The sign outside read "Get high Sunday, my place—God."

"So, tell me about jacking cars," Stax said.

Wally shrugged. "Snatched my first one at sixteen back in Toronto, fired up this Aerostar with nothing but a roach clip, right by the Eaton Centre. I'm pulling out of the Express Park and got cut off by some asshole in a Suburban. Guy gives me the finger. Followed him home, waited till he went inside, broke in his tuna boat, touched a screwdriver to his solenoid, left the fucker against a pole down by the racetrack. Fucking airbag nearly knocked me out. Surprised the hell out of me. First time I ever seen one."

"Popped your cherry, huh?"

"Yeah. Two in one day. How about you, ever jack a ride?"

Stax pulled out a key ring, holding one up, asking if Wally knew what it was.

"Think I don't know a master key when I see one?"

"Opens any Ford truck made before '03."

"Broke into a tow truck one time, not long after I hit town." Wally swallowed some warm beer. "Got a bunch of them. Ford, Chev, Dodge, you name it. Those tow-truck fuckers got master keys to everything."

"Still got them?" Stax pinned his beer between his thighs.

"Lost them going over the fence at the old police impound."

"Stealing from the cops?"

"Candy red Vette caught my eye." Wally rested his hand on the door handle, betting he could roll out without breaking his legs, thinking his chance was coming at the next light. Then thinking they were getting on, him and the big man, the two of them telling each other who they were. Besides, he didn't shoot the dog. Mitch would back that up.

Stax looked at him. "You bozos find the key to Artie's safe when you broke in?"

"Found shit on account of the dog Popeye didn't know about."

"You the one shot at it?"

"Fucking right." Wally realized his mistake as he said it.

Offering Wally one of his own smokes, he took one and pushed in the cigarette lighter. Stax pulled around the bus, chirping rubber, stopping for a red, listening to Wally saying how it was just a warning shot, meant to scare it. Wally mouthed the word help, the bus driver looking down at him as friendly as malaria. Stax looked over at a Japanese family at the opposite bus stop, each wearing an umbrella hat, looked like aliens with dangling Nikons. The husband called to Stax, unable to make sense of a map.

"*No capisce*," Stax called out the window. The light changed and Stax stepped on it, regarded the Newport in his hand, tossing it out the window, the pack along with it. "You lift those off Popeye?"

"Yeah."

Stax looked at Wally's do-rag. "Worked with this Jamaican guy back when I was jacking rigs, wore one like that."

"Yeah?"

"Till the night he got up on the step of a Peterbilt in Vernon, showed the trucker his sawed-off pump. Trucker pulled a .45 from under the seat and blew it off his head."

Wally touched a hand to it. He should have jumped back there.

"That real or a street model?" Stax said, checking out the Rolex.

GOOD TO GO

Cinnamon and pastry. The smell brought on the juices, Mitch passing the patisserie's window. The sign under the Visa and MasterCard stickers said a ten-dollar minimum credit card purchase was required. Mitch bet if he flashed the Walther, the woman behind the counter would oblige him with any cruller he wanted. But he still had the thousand bucks he'd lifted from Artie's nightstand on him. A bell tingled over the door, Mitch going in, telling the shopkeeper to fill a box, asked if she could break a hundred.

Wally had called in the morning wanting to meet at Miro's, talk about hitting the next place. Fucking Camry wouldn't start, the engine always iffy when it rained. Mitch thinking he should have taken that as a sign. No way he was hitting another place with Wally and Miro, wondering why he hauled his ass down here at all, guessing he needed to tell Wally face to face he was through. That was before running into the FedEx guy coming off Miro's elevator, telling him Wally and Miro split.

Standing in the middle of Chinatown eating a cruller, he rang Wally's cell, Wally telling him how they ducked out the fire escape, split up, left a squad of cops banging on the door.

"Merle just called me," Wally told him. "Said the FedEx guy put out Artie's lights down on the nude beach."

This was getting more fucked up by the minute, Mitch saying, "I'm out." Mitch's mind was set; forget telling Wally face to face, he was leaving for home—the gas city, Wild Rose Country. Even painting ceilings beat chasing pipe dreams.

"I'm cool with that," Wally said. "Fact, what d'you say the drinks are on me?"

"Quit drinking," Mitch said.

"Yeah, right, the stomach—coffee then—end things in style."

"I don't know."

"Order milk if you want. Tell me where you are, I'll swing by in the Caddy I just jacked—give you a lift any place you want to go."

Mitch told him thanks anyway, said maybe he'd see him sometime and hung up.

A chill was blowing rain clouds in from the Pacific, bringing unseasonable cold, the sun dropping behind the mass of grey. A call to information got him the number of the Greyhound office on Station Street. The next dog for Medicine Hat was scheduled to roll out at quarter past ten the next morning. With his Visa maxed out, he'd have to pay the fare out of the thousand.

Maybe Artie was dead, maybe he wasn't, but if the FedEx guy had told him straight and gave up the names, then Artie would have sent people looking for him. Could be someone hanging around his double-wide right now.

Leave his stuff, find someplace to crash for the night. The

L woman came to mind. Find her place in Delbrook, say sorry for standing her up, get that Yuzu Fou scent on him and wait till she dropped off to sleep, reach into her purse and take out a loan.

He felt the Sentry key in his pocket. It got him thinking, if Artie Poppa was dead, and his wife was gone, the house was empty, nobody there but maybe the dog. All he had to do was get inside, deal with the dog and find the safe, open it with the key. Make what he had in his pocket seem like an appetizer.

Crossing Pender, eating a third cruller, he pictured himself back in the Hat with pockets full of cash. His cell rang again, the caller ID showing it was Wally. This time he let it ring.

His denim was useless against the angling rain, his teeth chattering, box of crullers getting soggy. A bus shelter allowed him a break, every inch of the glass tagged in graffiti, scribbles of black and green and red like what the Tesche kids sprayed on the train trestle down river from his easy-wide. Needles, broken glass, butts and used bus tickets all over the ground. His toes felt frozen inside the wet leather.

A car alarm squawked down a lane between tenements, a couple of punks running the other way. Up on the second story, a guy with a muffin-top gut was turning meat on a grill smoking like a two-alarm blaze under an awning. He yelled inside for Peaches to get him the HP, watching Mitch like he might climb up and swipe his T-bone.

The door to the next tenement flew open, and a crumpled old man in a porkpie hat stumbled into the street, looking down the alley at the car with the alarm and parking lights flashing. Holding the neck of a bottle inside a bag, he took a drink and flagged a florist's van, calling it a taxi. The driver swerved wide and drove on, water splashing off his tires. Porkpie threw him the finger, cursing gibberish.

Mitch looked at his ringing cell—Wally again. He

switched it off and started west. Porkpie kept pace, making conversation, offering Mitch the bottle. Mitch picked up the pace, pretty sure Porkpie wasn't on Artie Poppa's or anybody else's payroll. Stopping out front of a butcher's, he pointed at hanging sausages and slabs of meat with rivers of fat veining through them. Porkpie ran his tongue across his three yellow teeth. The universal language of meat. Mitch tugged the door handle that boasted Coca-Cola Refreshment, gesturing Porkpie in, the guy's shoe sole flapping up water. He handed over a couple of small bills and kept going. Hunching against the rain, he kept a steady pace until he was long past the Savoy and the Husky station.

Guitar strains rang from the doorway of the Commerce Bank, the singing coming from behind a nest of grey beard. No telling how old the guy was looking out from under the JG ball cap, his guitar case open, a few coins in the wet lining. The old Barry McGuire tune about the eastern world explodin' brought Mitch back, had him thinking about his old Washburn in the pawn shop window, wondering if it was still there. Fishing change from his pocket, he dropped it along with the box of crullers in the guitar case, the guy calling thanks.

The Eastside gave way to downtown, the rain letting up as he passed the new Woodward's Building, getting on the 254 bus at West Georgia, shivering like a junkie. Mitch sat in a wheelchair seat behind the driver, not wanting to miss the stop when they came up to it. The guy across from him took up two seats and spread out his *Province*, glancing at him now and then. Riding up the Lions Gate bridge, Mitch grabbed the bar and pulled himself up. Looking down, he hoped to catch a glimpse of his double-wide, see if anyone was hanging around. He barely made out the rooftops from this angle.

He wouldn't miss the double-wide, cramped and depressing. He just wished he wasn't paid up till the end of next month.

A phone call to Tesche and maybe the old man would get his boys to box up his stuff and walk it over to the post office in the mall, forward it to the Hat. Maybe get a few bucks for the Camry.

Getting off a block before Poppa's Tudor, he flipped up his collar and shoved his hands deep in his pockets, the air cold enough to bring snow. He walked by the house a couple of times, no paw prints or turds on the lawn. No sign of life. Sure would be nice to get out of the wet clothes, fill Artie's tub good and hot, maybe catch a nap under the archangel, the blanket pulled over his head.

A key stuck in the lock, a fob with a skull dangling down. Dara pulled the door open, put on the bored look, her hand staying on the knob, blocking him from coming in. She called him Uncle Karl and said, "Thought you were the guy with the moving truck."

COFFEE'S ON KARL

"Afraid not." Karl fought to play it calm, thinking how Bruna fucked this up, not getting to Miro and Stax in time.

"You bring any of those muffins?" Goth eyeshadow, barefoot in track pants and a White Zombie T-shirt, Dara told him her mom wasn't home. Boxes stood stacked behind her.

"Need you to get out of the house for awhile," Karl said, guessing how this would go.

She blinked her goth eyes, then looked up at the sky, the rain pattering down on Karl. "You for real?"

"Could be some bad people coming. Look, Dara, I need you to get out till I call you—Cam, too. Come on."

"What does that mean, 'bad people'?"

"Just trust me, okay?" He needed to get back in his car, race to his place, get to PJ.

"You can see I'm moving my shit, right?"

"It'll have to wait."

"You go from uncle to daddy without anybody sending me a memo?"

"What I'm doing is asking you nice, trying to do this the easy way. You going to call Cam or you want me to?" He tried to go around her.

"This a joke, right?" She pushed at him.

"Go down to Turks, get yourself something to eat—on me." Reaching for his roll, he peeled off a twenty, saying he'd come back later and help her load the truck.

"Suppose I'm not hungry?"

"Coffee then."

Cam the groper came up behind her, eyes bloodshot and glassy, hair sticking up like he just got out of bed. "What's he want?" He asked her like Karl wasn't there.

"Wants us out of the house."

"Yeah, he want more one-on-one time with your mom?"

More aggressive than their first meeting, Karl guessed Cam switched up his medication.

"Think you scare me, man?" Cam said, trying to pull Dara back inside.

"Not me you need to be scared of, but the guy coming." Karl looked back at his idling Roadster, saying, "He'll lay some welts and bruises on you, go with that nice purple hair."

"That right?" the groper said, taking a step, getting in his face, sticking a finger against Karl's chest, his nails painted black. "Maybe I'll tell him to fuck himself like I'm telling you." Cam stepped back, trying to close the door.

The flat of Karl's hand stopped the door. Reaching out, he caught a handful of purple hair and tugged Cam onto the stoop, pulling Dara out with him, all three of them getting wet, Dara and Cam barefoot.

Karl pulled the key from the lock, pocketed it and smiled at Cam's raised fist, ducked under it, sending the palm of his hand into the groper's belly, just hard enough to fold him in two. He caught Dara's fist, the big skull ring on her finger. Stuffing the twenty between her fingers, Karl patted her shoulder and went down the stairs, telling her, "Be a doll and wait at Turks for my call."

"You just locked my fucking phone inside," Dara screamed after him.

Karl hurried down the walk to the Roadster, calling back, "Sure they got one at Turks."

"How about shoes, they got those, too?"

Getting to the driver's side, he looked at their bare feet on the wet steps, toes curled up. "It's the Drive, babe. Nobody gives a shit about footwear down here, trust me." And he was gone, rubber squealing.

TOEING THE LINE

She was an older babe, nice strawberry hair, not stacked like Bruna or packed tight like Sunny, but good enough. Despite his mangled leg and getting zapped, he had thoughts of giving PJ a jump right after he put a bullet in Morgen.

She was standing inside the front door like she was waiting for somebody, feeling the flu settle into her bones. He guessed who she was and who she was waiting for when he walked up to the door with the fob he took from the Knox box around the side of the building, the box that held emergency keys for firefighters and cops. One crack from the pistol butt and the cheap plastic housing fell away like a walnut shell.

Swiping the fob, he stepped into the lobby, giving her a smile, PJ putting together who this guy was a second too late. Forcing her into the elevator, he showed her the Vaquero and holster inside the folded jacket under his arm, pressing the fourth floor button, digging through her pockets, finding Karl's door key. Inside the apartment, he bound her wrists with a scarf he found in the hall closet, looked around for something he could use as a gag, a cleaning rag he found under the sink doing the trick.

Sitting her on the beanbag in the living room, he strapped on the low-slung holster and leaned on the kitchen counter, taking the weight off his leg, letting her have a good look at the pearl handle. In spite of his chewed leg, he'd stand there, in line with the front hall. When Morgen walked in, he'd give him the surprise of his life.

"That's some racket, sounds like it's in the next room," he said, meaning the construction noise. Reaching in a pocket, he pulled out his Newports with two left in the pack, sure he put a fresh pack in his jacket this morning, asking, "Mind if I smoke?"

She couldn't help being scared, mumbling through the gag, sure it was the same rag she had used to clean up Chip's furball, trying to ask what he wanted.

Wishing he had more of the Oxy, he lit the cigarette and told her he just wanted a word with her boyfriend. "Only way to communicate with that fella." He took a drag and patted the handle, playing the gunfighter now.

So this was the guy Karl dragged to jail, served papers on, playing the FedEx man. He didn't look like much, kind of like that creep from *Fargo* on a bad day, eyes crazy and hair all wild.

"Gonna set things straight." He blew smoke, kept on talking, thinking he caught her smile under the gag. "You think it's funny what he did?"

She shook her head, trying to say through the gag, everybody thought it was funny.

He let it slide, saying, "We'll see who's laughing when him and me go *mano a mano*." He blew more smoke across the room.

"Karl doesn't carry a gun," she tried to say.

He stepped over and tugged the gag down, saying maybe they didn't need it, patting the pearl handle again as a warning.

"Said he doesn't carry one of those."

"Should have seen him going crazy with his little stun gun down on the nudie beach." Miro opened the top of his shirt and showed her the red bites where the electrodes hit him.

In spite of the fear, she couldn't help the grin, thinking what's that, three times now?

Miro practically fell on her. The slap rang hollow in the near-empty place, sending her sprawling on the floor. Then he had her by the throat, pressing his lips against hers, her trying to twist away, tasting the menthol tobacco. He let her go, grimacing, getting up and reaching for the counter, saying she was a lousy kisser.

"Sorry to disappoint," she said, seeing the blood soaking his pant leg.

"Hope that knocked the bitch out of you," he said, waiting for the pain to subside, tossing the broken cigarette in the sink. "Got plenty more if you need it."

She inched back onto the beanbag, her head reeling, tasting blood.

"You ought to think what happens to you after," Miro said and hobbled across the room, bending to go through Karl's CDs.

"The cops'll be here, give you all the shootout you can handle."

"Be long gone when the donut squad shows up." He tossed CDs into the corner, one by one. "Boyfriend's sure got shit taste for music."

"Tell me about it."

"Far as shootouts go, you know anything about speed shooting?" He stepped back to the counter, taking the weight off his leg.

She told him no, getting how crazy this guy was, guessing Karl's chef's knife was still in the sink where she left it, the blade smeared with Skippy. Right behind him.

"You ever hear the name Bob Munden?"

"Can't say so."

"Munden was the fastest man alive, that's all—saw him one time."

She wanted to ask if he ever heard the name Carole Lieberman, the psychiatrist on Talk Radio, tell him she was pretty fast, too. Instead she asked, "So, you as fast as this Bob guy?"

"Munden," he said, liking that she took an interest. "Hard to say. See, there's a difference between drawing on an armed man and drawing on a coin tossed in the air, but, yeah, I'm likely as fast, at least in a real situation I would be. Who knows, probably faster."

PJ sniffled to keep her nose from running, hoping she had passed on her flu bug when he forced his lips against hers.

"Of course, shooting's not all I'm about."

"No?"

He asked if she needed a tissue. She nodded, but he didn't move to get her one.

Looking at the blood-stained pants again, she said, "There's coffee. You want I can fix you one," putting on a little Florence Nightingale, wanting to get to the knife covered in Skippy. She tried working at the scarf binding her wrists. "You want, I can take a look at that for you."

"I'm a fast healer." Then he asked what she knew about honey oil.

"That a foodie thing?"

It got him laughing. "Yeah, a foodie thing. Dumb broad. Let's just say I'm as handy with the butane as I am with this." He tapped the pearl. "When I finish up here, I can go anywhere, set myself up anyplace I want—Toronto, Montreal, even New York. Write my own ticket."

She nodded like she knew what the hell he was talking about.

Glancing around the place, Miro asked, "So, what's our boy got against furniture?"

"It's a work in progress. Got a few things coming from IKEA," she said, wishing the delivery was scheduled for right now instead of tomorrow. "Sure you don't want me to look at the leg?"

"You go playing cute, I'll put one in you. Understand? Don't matter you're a girl." He limped his way around the counter. "How do I do it?"

She asked what, and he said make coffee. She told him to check beside the stove, said there was half a bag of Folgers.

"You got any instant?"

"Who drinks that?"

"I do." He pulled the fridge door open. Drinking from an open Frooti Cool, talking to take his mind off the pain, he told her about this book he had taking shape.

"Oh, yeah, what's the book?"

He offered her some of the Frooti Cool. "*Grow Right, Grow Rich*." He watched her nod, then said, "That's just my working title."

"This about you?" She hated doing it, but she let him put the Frooti container to her lips, and she took a swallow.

"Yeah, how I made my name, tell some of my tricks and growing secrets, some of the characters I've met along the way, shit I've seen, record shot I made."

"Guess people would read it."

"Damn right they will."

"I'll keep an eye out for it."

"I mapped out some of the chapters, wrote the intro," he said. "Probably need one of those ghost writers, guy knows where to put the commas and shit."

PJ thinking he really should write Carole Lieberman's name down, give her a call.

Stax took the Fern exit, easing the Caddy down the ramp, making the lights, the big Holiday Inn across the intersection.

KING OF HANDGUNS

"This ain't it," Wally said, everything inside going to high alert. "Got to go up to Taylor Way. You can turn here." He pointed left.

"Making a pit stop first," Stax said, driving up Lillooet, past trees and parked cars, a forest fire rating sign, not far from the construction site where Wolf Klinger ended up buried inside a chemical toilet. He told Wally to relax.

Wally said he was cool, feeling fear like never before.

Stax drove by a sign for Lynn Canyon Park, nobody around. Wally had his hand on the door handle, palm wet with sweat, forgetting Stax locked the doors.

"You want, grab another beer," Stax told him, aiming a thumb at the backseat.

"I'm good. Thanks."

Nothing but tall pines around them as the road narrowed. Stax pulled to the side of a turnaround, signs on a post marking the trails.

Wally kept his hand on the handle, getting set.

"Going to ask one more time: who shot Ike?" Stax took the Python from under the seat, Wally recognizing it, the same one he took from Jeffery Potts.

"Told you it was Popeye," he said, then he jerked the handle. Couldn't get out.

Stax smiled, liked seeing Wally panic, hitting a button, unlocking the doors. Wally was out the door, running for all he was worth across the road, heading for the trail.

Counting ten, Stax got out like he had all day, leveling the six-inch barrel across the roof, wishing he'd brought a shovel.

The first bullet put Wally down at the edge of the turnaround. Stax walked across the road, thinking the Python had a nice bark to it.

Wally rolled on his back, blood pouring from his side, putting up his hands. "It wasn't me."

"I know." Stax shot him again.

Grabbing Wally by the ankles, he heard a vehicle approaching. No time to drag him off into the woods.

He came in through the mud-room, the alarm still down, the house dark.

THE FINE LINE HOME

Going through the main floor with the Walther cocked, he checked for the safe, taking the Chivas from the trolley in the living room, hoping for liquid courage, keeping an eye out for Artie Poppa's giant dog. Finding nothing, he went to the basement. Again nothing.

Upstairs, he checked the bedrooms, the den, the laundry, then the master suite. He stripped off his wet clothes; with Artie dead and the wife in Korea, he considered taking his time. The broken glass was gone from the shower stall. Standing in there, getting the water as hot as he could stand, would give him time to think where the safe could be, but it would take too long. Even a quick shower was risky. Looking at Artie's bed, he resisted melting into the mattress, pulling the covers to his neck, the bed cleaner than his own at the double-wide: the yellowed sheets he never changed, the lumpy pillow with its funky smell. A twenty-minute catnap under the archangel and he'd be a new man.

Rubbing his palms over his face, what Tolley used to call a bachelor's wash, he drank down more Chivas, hoping to keep his stomach from bubbling. Feeling the alcohol buzz, he went looking through the closet for something to wear, everything far too small.

Thinking how Miro had called the archangel over the bed Jesus, he tried to settle his nerves by talking out loud to it, Mitch calling it Michael, telling it about some CNN report about the King Kong–sized Jesus that got struck by lightning someplace in Ohio; carved out of wood, the thing burned to a cinder. Wringing water from his pant legs, he was saying that the Jesus was asking for it, having his hands raised like that.

Tipping the bottle, the liquid fire rolling down his throat, he caught a glint of something on the wall behind Michael. Putting the bottle on the nightstand, standing on the mattress, he lifted the carving down, heavier than it looked. He laid it on the bed, and the Sentry safe stared him in the face. Digging the key from his pocket, he held his breath, heard it scrape as he pushed it in. It fit the lock.

"Jesus," he said, staring dumbfounded at the combination next to the key lock. A key lock and a combination. Giving the dial a spin, he tried to work through the Chivas fog. Artie must have jotted the numbers somewhere—a kid's birth date, an anniversary or something like that.

Going through all the drawers again, then knocking Michael to the floor, he flipped the mattress. Nothing. Hurrying to the den and the other bedrooms, he flipped the rest of the mattresses, rifled every drawer, checked behind every piece of furniture, under the Persian rug in the hall, felt along the top of shelves, the medicine cabinets. Nothing.

Downstairs, he tore through the front hall closet, then the kitchen drawers, pulling everything from the pantry, cereal boxes, cans of tomatoes and sauce, bags of rice and pasta—everything tossed on the floor, the room still smelling like gym socks. He walked down the hall, checking inside the grandfather clock, behind it. Following the plastic runner back into the living room, he flapped through the romance paperbacks above the fireplace, some in English, some in Korean. Then he rifled through a stack of CDs by some guy named Rain, the Wonder Girls and some chick called Navi, Korean type all over the covers. The last one was *Sweet Sweet* by Burton Cummings, an old favorite of Ginny's from his days in the Hat. He tossed all but the Burton into the fireplace and grabbed the poker.

Back upstairs, he put the CD with his Walther on the dresser. Then he dug at the drywall around the edges of the Sentry with the poker. Spiking it into the wall, he jimmied and pried from all sides, striking the steel-reinforced wall studs. He remembered Miro talking about the Mexican drug lord hiding millions in his walls. Tearing away the drywall, he hooked electrical wires and yanked them out, sending the room into darkness. He spun the dial to random combinations, begging Michael on the floor for a miracle. Just three fucking numbers.

Bashing at the steel with the poker, he knocked the dial off. No way he was getting in now. He wiped at the tears and sweat. The grandfather clock downstairs chimed the hour.

He picked up the bedroom phone and punched in Wally's number, the king of breaking into shit. A voice that wasn't Wally's answered. Mitch waited a second, then hung up, figured he dialed wrong and tried again.

"That you, Mitch?" the same voice asked.

Mitch stayed silent, the big clock chiming from downstairs. He disconnected, not sure how many times the clock had struck, guessing it was six or seven.

Throwing his jeans, shirt and jacket in the dryer in the

laundry room, he pressed the sensor-dry cycle, the metal snaps and zipper clanging around in the drum, Mitch forgetting the money he stole from Artie was in a pocket, going round and round.

In the ensuite, he opened the medicine cabinet. Thinking. Desperate. Taking a toothbrush, squeezing on paste, he ran it around his mouth. Throwing water on his face, dragging a ladies' Venus over his stubble, he watched himself in the mirrored shower door, the dim light showing pallid legs in dingy underwear, the elastic long-retired, his middle sagging. His plumbing was churning, the Chivas failing, the tsunami in his gut forcing him onto the Kohler. Flicking the empty toilet paper roll, he figured he could put a 9mm round through the dial, maybe blast it open.

After a while, he felt his gut begin to settle. It was the sound of brakes that got him up, checking out the bathroom window. A dark Cadillac was pulling in the driveway, the headlights washing the house. The driver's door opened and Stax stepped out. Mitch ran to the dryer and tugged his pants on, then the shirt and jacket, shoving the Walther in his belt, the CD in his pocket.

Stax was coming up the walk to the door, the Python in his hand, checking his new watch against the grandfather clock's toll coming from inside the house, the chime marking the half hour.

Mitch pulled himself out the same window that he had before, shimmied down the same tree, the rain making the branches slick. Feet hit the ground, he ducked low along the hedge, running over the lawn, jumping into the waiting Cadillac, looking at the house. The keys dangled from the ignition. Thank Christ for that. The engine sprang to life, and Mitch threw the stick into reverse. Stax charged through the door at a dead run, chasing him down the driveway, grabbing for the door handle, Mitch plunging the locks down.

"Who killed my dog, you fuck?"

At the end of the driveway, Mitch threw it into drive, slammed his foot down on the gas, and the Caddy shot onto Chartwell. Stax leaped onto the trunk, hanging on, fishing the pistol from behind his belt, yelling, "Who shot Ike?"

Mitch screamed it was Miro, swerved, trying to grab the Walther on the seat. He rocked the Caddy into the ditch, and Stax flew off. The back wheels slung mud and stones, Stax rolling, getting up, taking aim.

Mitch crashed the Caddy through a yew hedge, expecting a bullet. He swerved back and forth, then he was racing down the hill, his heart beating double time when he hit the on-ramp for the Number One. He was cold sober now.

In spite of the hour, the traffic was rush-hour heavy coming down the Cut and across the Second Narrows into Burnaby. At the Willingdon exit, he rolled down his window, crying and yelling out, "This is Mitch Reno leaving Shitstain."

The boiling in his stomach eased by the time he hit Port Kells. To the east, the night sky was clear, inviting him home. He guessed the Caddy would fetch about thirty Gs back home. That and the balance of the thousand would give him a fresh start.

He stuck Burton Cummings in the player, "You Saved My Soul" filling the Caddy with prairie music he hadn't heard since the days of Tolley's swoops in the old Bronco. Back around the time of eight tracks.

Sweet Sweet was playing the third time around by the time Mitch hit the Crowsnest Highway. Adjusting the volume, he noticed the black do-rag on the passenger floor. An eighteen wheeler's air horn made him jump, Mitch wrestling the Cadillac back into its own lane, the rig hauling by him, the rush of air rocking the car. Looking in the rearview, he was cursing the truck when he saw the shape under the beach blanket on the floor.

It took a while before he asked, "You under there?" The sorrow and tears turned to laughter, Mitch thinking it was the first time Wally had ever shut up.

Sometime later he wondered if there was anything in the trunk, maybe a jack handle, he could use to bury his friend. On a quiet stretch, he pulled off the highway; he popped the trunk, got out and stared at the twin suitcases with their flimsy luggage locks.

"Get yourself a real gun, and play it like a man. That's what I'll tell him." His eyes went from her phone on the counter to PJ, her cheek red from being slapped. Her phone kept ringing. Outside, Marine Drive had become a blur of rain and brake lights, the rain slanting hard, pattering off the asphalt, cars leaving tracks on the street. A patrol car sped to an accident scene somewhere, the gumballs flashing red and blue against the River's Edge building next door, its siren wailing. Miro looked out the window, anxious for Karl to show. PJ was watching him, twisting and working her wrists behind her back.

SOMETIMES A SHIT SANDWICH

"That zap gun sure did the trick on old Artie. Your boyfriend, that's who they'll be coming for." He looked at her. "Shot him right in the pacemaker." It got him laughing.

"Think I believe that?"

"Calling me a liar?"

"You going to hit me again?"

"I was standing right there, seen the old boy jerking like he was strapped to the chair." Miro shook his body like Artie did when he got hit, lolling his tongue for effect.

"You ever like anybody?"

"I like you fine enough." He groaned, a fresh stab of pain shooting up his leg. "At least when you're quiet."

The piss stain was dry on his pants. She tried not to look at it. If she laughed again, it would buy her another slap, or worse. This guy was right on the edge.

Chip poked his head around the corner, assessing Miro from the bedroom.

"That your cat or his?" Showing how quick he could do it, he had the revolver out, giving a careless aim in Chip's direction, asking what kind of cat doesn't have a tail.

PJ stamped her foot, and Miro whirled on her, the black hole of the barrel staring at her. She thought she might die. Then he tipped the barrel up and looked back. Chip was gone.

Easing the hammer down, he holstered the gun, then went at her.

Knowing what was coming, she shot out her shoe, hitting the bad leg, Miro crying out, dropping down. She was up and running for the door, yelling for Anton, the super, for anybody. Turning her back to the knob, she fumbled her tied hands at the door lever, desperate to get out of there.

Using his hands, he scrambled, catching her at the door and pulling himself up, one hand dragging her by the hair, the other on her neck, squeezing the words between his teeth. "Shut the fuck up, or I'll do you right now." Then he bent forward, throwing up bile, some getting on his shoes, some on her. He flung her at the beanbag. "Liking you a fuck of a lot less by the second."

Holding the counter, hearing her cry, he waited till the pain in his leg subsided. "What you got to say to me?"

"Carole Lieberman."

"What?"

Her phone rang again, and they both looked at it on the counter, both knowing it was him, Miro changing his game plan, saying it was time to go wait downstairs.

GRIDLOCK

Karl was caught in the wrong lane, and first chance he got he made an illegal turn off Victoria, ducking around a bus. The rain pelted down, making the street signs impossible to read. Why didn't she answer? He tried again, making sure he got the number right.

Red and blue lights flashed ahead of him, the scene of another fender bender, a PT Cruiser and a Tundra locking horns, blocking the eastbound lanes all the way to the Second Narrows Bridge. Karl's thumbs drummed the wheel. The Roadster nearly stalled going through a puddle, then became pinned behind a Coke truck, the truck-back advertising this as bike month. He hit speed dial and got PJ's voice mail again, then dialed the number Bruna gave him.

She picked up on the first ring, Karl telling her to get someone over to his place. Bruna asking who made him chief.

"How about you start acting like a cop?"

"When I find you—"

Karl hung up, making up his mind, turning the car around, heading for the Lions Gate Bridge. Somebody honked, somebody else cursed out a window.

Beating a light and gunning it past a motorhome with a forest mural down the side got him brake lights as far as the eye could see. More gumballs flashing ahead. A work crew was setting up a detour on Broadway, the flagger waving drivers right to a single lane.

His phone rang—had to be PJ.

It was Marty starting with, "Hey buddy, how's it hanging?"

"Not now, Marty."

"One word, you serve the little shit?"

"And then some—looking to give him dessert."

"Everything alright?"

"Tell you later." Karl hung up and went left into oncoming traffic, rain drumming at the undercarriage. More horns honked, the workmen shouting at him to slow down. He hammered it through a puddle, soaking the flagger. Zigging through side streets over to Cambie, he tried PJ's number again.

SICK OF TELLING YOU TWICE

"My turn to pay a visit," Miro called as Karl stepped out in the turnaround in front of the building, the Porsche next to the Chev minivan. "Didn't need a FedEx get-up, girlfriend here just let me in." Pushing PJ out ahead of him.

The construction was over for today, the workmen gone home. Karl stood like a drowning rat by his open door, cars zipping by behind him on Marine. Somebody had to see the crazy with the six-shooter and call the cops. Miro gave PJ another shove, using the wall as shelter from the rain, getting set to do his *High Noon* thing, borrowing Wally's shit-eating grin, telling her, "Now's the time to say so long."

"Something I want to say to you first."

"Yeah?"

"Want to say they're still laughing at you. That's what, three times now he made you look stupid?"

Karl looked at her. How was this helping?

"Slapping her around doesn't do much good, huh?" Miro said to him. "Hey, where's your zapper?"

Karl pointed in the car. "Got to recharge it."

"This fucking weather, you'd just electrocute yourself," Miro said, thinking it wasn't sporting just gunning him down, preferring a real showdown, but what the hell, then to PJ, "Ready to see some Howard Darby moves?"

"Really into the spaghetti western thing, huh?" Karl said, stepping away from the car, wondering if Bruna got the address wrong, maybe stopped for Timbits.

"Yeah, I dig the old Sergio Leones, *Fistful of Dollars*, *Duck, You Sucker*, all that."

"You see that one about Tombstone?"

"*Tombstone*'s not one of his," Miro said. "But it's pretty decent. *Wyatt Earp*'s got them all beat."

"Haven't seen that one," Karl said, taking another step, wishing he had his old Smith, the one he gave Marty. "That the one with Costner?"

"Yeah, some of his best work." Miro hobbled a step, saying, "There's a scene goes something like this."

"Just gonna shoot me?"

"Got a better idea?"

"A wimp move, you ask me."

The cab flew around the corner—one of those hybrid ones, Karl sure it was Bruna. Stax climbed out, the driver calling after him for his fare.

"Keep it running." Stax pulled Jeffery's Python and walked into the turnaround, saying to Miro, "Found out who shot Ike." He stopped, Jeffery's gun down at his side. "The two stupid guys both swear it was you."

"Yeah, well, they're stupid, right?"

"Swore it on their lives."

Karl stepped wide, nicking his head, his eyes telling PJ to move away.

Stax was coming forward, saying to Karl without taking his eyes off Miro, "Clueless fuck. It's true what he said, getting you on tape taking Artie's deal. Ready to hand you to the cops for offing the two assholes."

"You know your girlfriend's a cop?" Karl asked Miro, buying time. "Yeah, told me after you went out the window."

Miro grinned at him.

"Told me she put saltpeter in your coffee, keep you from getting ideas in the bedroom. And the shit she was snorting was powdered milk."

"Funny guy," he said it to PJ.

"Ask her yourself in a minute."

Miro said to Stax, "Last chance, throw him the gun and we're square. Get back in your cab and split."

Anton the super stepped off the elevator, into the lobby, looking out at the armed standoff, crouching to the floor. The cabbie saw things getting ugly, forgot about the fare and backed up, nearly clipping the Taurus two-wheeling around the corner.

Screeching to a stop, Bruna jumped out with her .38 extended over the roof, delivering the routine cop lines, yelling for everybody to drop their weapons.

Miro wasn't seeing right. His topless shoeshine chick with a gun, her shield clipped to his shirt. "What the fuck you doing?"

Keeping a steady aim, she told them she wanted to see hands.

"Got to learn to control your women," Stax said to Miro, telling Bruna to take a number. Rushing it, he flipped the Python up and fired, the shot taking out the glass door, Anton the super crabbing for the elevator. Miro snapped off a shot, Stax staggering backward, falling with a bullet hole in his chest. Miro was turning and fanning the hammer, firing at Bruna behind the car. The first of the black-and-whites tore in from the underpass, Dom and Luca in the backseat, more backup coming like cavalry along Marine.

Bruna's passenger window exploded, Miro firing a third time, putting one in Karl, watching him fall. Three shots in two seconds. Grabbing PJ's arm before she could run to Karl, Miro was punched back. Mouth falling open to the rain, he stutter stepped, looking at Bruna behind the Taurus, like he didn't believe he'd missed. He worked at staying on his feet, the pistol heavy in his hand. Her pistol locked in both hands over the hood, she was yelling for him to throw it down.

Another squad car tore around the corner, sirens and gumballs going like a disco. Doors flew open and cops crouched, getting ringside for the O.K. Corral shootout. A dozen guns aiming at him, voices yelling. Losing hold of PJ, Miro felt his legs go to pudding. He brought the Vaquero up once more, wondering if Bruna was even her real name.

SOUNDS LIKE A WIFE TALKING

Karl's first thought was of PJ, that she was alright. Lying there staring up at the TV screen, the news running with the sound turned down, Lloyd Robertson's mouth moving with nothing coming out. Sun streamed through the slat blinds, a rainbow refracted through a pitcher of water, glowing on the wall. Taking in the disinfectant smells and the squawking of a paging system, he guessed he was in a hospital.

Putting together what had happened, he tried to feel where he'd been hit, but felt numb all over. The standoff, the shots fired, Karl knocked to the ground. That was it. All he cared about was that PJ was okay—praying to God she was.

Following the tube running from his arm to the IV bag, he focused on the valve dripping clear liquid. Something in the drip caused the fog inside his head, interfering with him replaying the scene: Bruna shouting, Miro gunning Stax down, then feeling the bullet like a punch. Then nothing.

Watching Lloyd's mouth moving, he fought it, the drifting dark coming. In the dream, Miro was coming for him, Karl lying in the hospital bed, hooked to IV, Miro prowling the halls with his six-shooter.

Next time he woke, the TV was off, and there she was sitting in the chair next to the bed, red roses on her lap, those eyes, that strawberry hair, that smile lighting the room.

She came to him, put a hand on his arm. Leaning in, she kissed his cheek, asking him how he was, calling him cowboy, her voice a whisper.

He felt her hair brush his face, his mouth dry. He smiled and said, "I'm a little pissed."

She asked if it was the food, and he said he hadn't eaten yet, told her he'd been counting on slapping the cuffs on Miro one more time.

She shook her head. "That isn't going to happen."

"He make a play for the whole precinct?"

"The lady cop put him down."

"Bruna, no kidding?"

"Hard to tell with all the other cops shooting, but she hit him first." She set the flowers in a vase by the bed, saying, "I wouldn't have minded taking a shot at him myself, and I only knew the guy for what, an hour?"

"Had a knack for rubbing people the wrong way."

"Speaking of which, she wants to see you when you're up for it—Bruna, I mean."

He frowned, guessing he was in the deep end.

"And your buddy's been calling from Seattle."

"Marty?"

She said yeah. "Day and night. He's been worried."

"You got to meet Marty." He caught an image of Marty standing in a tux next to him, handing him a ring. He watched her arrange the roses in the vase, asking her, "Red, you know what that means?"

"I'm the one who told you, cowboy. But before we head down that road, there's one thing . . ."

"Yeah?"

"You're going to find another job."

"Got one. Okay, I mean the pay could be better."

"Funny—lying there with a hole in you, hooked to tubes. I'll tell you this much, if this thing's going anywhere, this you-and-me thing, I can't be wondering every time you're late for supper."

"You can cook?"

"Lot of things you don't know. But if I'm going to fuss over my broiled pork loin with sage, I need to know you're going to show up and eat it."

"Pork with sage, huh?"

"Get yourself a job—one that won't get you shot."

"Serving papers in Canada's like child's play."

"You're the one who got wheeled in here."

It wasn't the time to argue. "What else can I do?"

"I had Dara browse the net, jotted down a couple of numbers—enough to get you started."

"Oh shit. Dara." Karl tried to sit. "I told her I'd pick her up at Turks."

PJ patted his wrist, smiling at him, asking if he had any idea what day it was.

"You sure make that look like work," he called out the passenger side, shifting to neutral, looking over his shades,  past the curb, putting on the Clooney. He tucked the Nikon under his jacket on the seat.

Helen Jackson stood bowed over, looking every bit as good as that time he walked in to serve her boss, Melnick. Doing justice to the hip-huggers, she flipped a mossy rock with a spade. Karl's words brought her up with a smile. Flipping her hair back, now a different shade of blonde, she clapped muck from her work gloves, looking at the guy with the shades sitting in the old-time sports car with the top down. Sizing him up, she guessed a slick realtor, any kind of renovation bringing them round like wolves. Starting to say somebody's got to do it, she blocked the sun with her hand and recognized him. "Hey, if it isn't Karl with a K, right?"

"That's right, Helen." He didn't say "with the double Ds," waiting as she stabbed the spade into the ground, coming toward him. What he did say was "That's some memory you got."

She took off the gloves, no ring or acrylic nails this time, and leaned on the passenger door, checking out his ride. "Can't forget a guy who brought me flowers. Yellow's for friendship; you told me that."

"That's right, I did," Karl said, keeping his eyes on hers. Not looking below her chin felt like not looking at the elephant in the room. "So tell me, how are things over at Marv Melnick's?"

"Not so hot since Marv's wife filed for divorce."

"Caught him having lunch with the redhead?"

"You remembered?

"Sinnamon with an S, right?

"Hey, you're good. But I think it was more because he's a jerk. In fact, I was hoping you'd be by to serve the papers."

"Sorry I missed it," he said.

"Yeah, the missus is going for the throat, the business, the kids, the whole nine yards."

"Where's that leave you?"

"Right now, I'm on leave—hurt my back lifting file boxes." She touched the small of her back, told him when Marv took the extra space after Rogers closed next door, he had her packing and moving boxes. "Felt like a piano wire snapping, you know. Next thing, I can barely stand."

"Better now?"

"I'm fine, really." She waved it off. "Waiting to settle with the insurance, you know?"

"Funny, running into you.

"Small world."

"Yeah, 'cause I've been thinking of booking a trip."

"Oh yeah, where to?"

"I'm thinking Costa Rica."

"Oh, great place. I can get you a deal on a suite at the

Red Palms. You want, I can do it right from my laptop." She flicked her head to the house. "Just let me wash my hands." Those blue eyes talking to him. She remembered giving him her number, guessing he might be after more than booking a trip.

"On the fly right now, Helen," he said. "Funny, I was just cutting across when I saw you working. The Drive's a parking lot—some Car-Free Day thing going on."

"Part of the Drive vibe. You come by tonight, they'll have cooking with music playing in the street—Italian, Chinese, you name it. You show up, I'll save you a dance," she said, those blue eyes working.

"Well—"

"You got a we-thing going, don't you?" she asked.

He nodded.

"My Ed's at some sales conference, always on the road when there's work to be done. Convenient, don't you think?" The smile was pure magic.

"You should be watching that back."

"Yeah, you wouldn't know we've got a crew of guys—came highly recommended—supposed to be here right now," she said. "Guess I'll have to sic Ed on them again."

The file said this Ed was easily agitated, weighed in at two-fifty and tossed the last adjuster from the porch two weeks ago.

Helen ran her hand along the door. "This we-situation a red flower kind of thing?"

"Yeah, but try being romantic when your girl's got her teenage kid in the basement suite," he said, shifting the jacket on the seat, picking up the Nikon, the Diversified Risk folder under it.

The smile was gone, her eyes on the camera and the folder.

"Not that we keep her prisoner down there. Kid's just going through that teenage hell stage, you know?"

Helen nodded like her head was made of wood. "You're not serving papers anymore, are you, Karl?"

He spun the Nikon around, saying, "PJ, that's my girl, figured it was getting too dangerous for a fellow my age—likes to know if she cooks it, I'll be there to eat it."

"Sounds like she cares." Her face went pale.

"Yeah, I'm a lucky guy. Guess that's why I took the gig with Diversified Risk. Work mainly fraud cases, Workers' Comp, you know? Get to play with the toys: night-vision this, wireless that, you name it. They send me to catch folks in the act, you know, cheating the company. You wouldn't believe some of the claims, back and neck stuff mostly. I take the pics, appear in court, put up my hand and swear an oath, that kind of thing."

Her eyes turned teary.

"Truth is I'm bored with it. Soon as five o'clock rolls around, I can't wait to get home." He drew up his sleeve and checked his watch. Ten past. He turned the camera so she could see the preview. He looked at her and hit erase. "Bastards don't pay overtime. You believe that?"

Blinking and sniffling, Helen looked at him, then the camera, getting his meaning.

"Better push on. PJ gets crazy when I'm late." He tucked the camera in the glovebox, no Taser in there now.

"So," she said, "will I be seeing you again?"

"Only if you invite us for a swim."

Her smile was slowly returning. "Soon as the concrete sets, you and your PJ are our first guests. We can barbecue something."

"Sounds real nice," he said, told her he'd call about the trip and shifted the stick. "Really good to see you again, Helen. Careful with the back, okay?" He winked and was rolling, thinking he still had time to stop at Berry Brothers for a bottle of Cru. A quiet evening in front of the fire, lay the Costa Rico trip on PJ, get a little romantic.

Helen was still waving when he checked the rearview at the end of the block, thinking he'd fill out the report in the morning, send the folder along with the medical reports and X-rays back upstairs. Helen Jackson's claim would get rubber stamped and processed.

His cell rang, PJ asking where he was, telling him Dara and Cam were joining them, asking how he felt about whipping up one of his curries, asking him to stop by Drive Organics, get what he needed, saying Dara and Cam were on a vegetarian kick now, adding Chip tossed up another furball, his turn to clean it up.

His quiet evening evaporated, turning into another night of Air Miles or cup sizes or whatever Dara was dishing up. It got him grinning, thinking what the hell, it would keep until tomorrow.